SLIPPERY
AS SIN

BEING THE SEVENTH OF THE SERIES OF THE
FANTÔMAS DETECTIVE TALES

BY PIERRE SOUVESTRE & MARCEL ALLAIN

Bibliographical Note
This Antipodes edition, first published in 2016, is a republication of
the work first published by Stanley Paul & Co., London, in 1920. The
original translation has been slightly altered to reflect modern spelling
and usage.

ISBN 978-0-9966599-2-5

Contents

SLIPPERY

AS SIN

1. Dead Jack

"Unbelievable! Dear old Juve! Your news has jolly well pleased me! You can plume yourself on that, old man."

Jerome Fandor was dancing with joy in his little room, a modest apartment in London he had occupied for the last few months.

Jerome Fandor was talking aloud. There was no one to see, no one to listen.

Every line of his face expressed satisfaction.

The cause of Jerome Fandor's exuberant gaiety was a telegram in cipher:

> Hurrah, Fandor, Victory, I have just found Lady Beltham again. Fantômas cannot be far off.

"By Jove!" monologued Fandor. "Juve and I have been so long on the trail of these two sinister bandits that his announcement does not come a day too soon!"

Fantômas had marvelously escaped from Juve and Fandor two years ago, while the French police had let Lady Beltham go free: they lacked proof of identity. Juve and Fandor had lost trace of the terrible bandit who, more than ever, merited the title of "elusive." They also missed the trail of the great lady, who had been the obvious and the hidden accomplice of Fantômas.

Reduced to despair by the death of Elizabeth Dollon, his ill-fated love, worn out by the Fantômas pursuit, Jerome Fandor went traveling, always keeping in touch with his friend, Inspector Juve of Paris. This celebrated detective had resumed his functions at La Sûreté, where he was glued to the spot for the moment, owing to the accumulation of criminal business requiring his presence.

So Juve had found Lady Beltham again! And Fandor had

been on the point of sending a telegram, a most interesting telegram, to his old Paris friend. But second thoughts had caused Fandor to put down his pen.

"No. What I have to tell him is of such importance that not the slightest doubt must remain. Before dispatching my wire I must turn conjecture into certitude."

Fandor carefully enclosed his translation of Juve's telegram in his pocketbook, took hat and stick, and stepped out into the sunshine of a radiant April day.

"Another cigarette?"

"Faith, I won't say no!"

"A tot of whisky? That's of course."

"I can't say no."

It was about five o'clock in the afternoon of this same April day. Two men were talking amicably in a luxurious room on the first floor of a sumptuous house overlooking Hyde Park. One was Lord Duncan, owner of the house, a tall, fair, distinguished looking man of thirty. His companion, probably some ten years older, had an intelligent face, rather weather-beaten, the face of a man who lives much in the open, goes in for sports, braving sun and rain and all the winds that blow. While Lord Duncan could boast a vigorous growth of thick fair hair, inclined to curl, his companion's locks were thinning to baldness, and were threaded with grey at the temples.

Lifting his glass, the older man bowed to his host: "My dear Lord Duncan, allow me to congratulate you on your Court appointment."

Lord Duncan's reply was a forced smile.

In flattering accents his companion continued:

"The Court is showering honors on you, the worthiest of recipients, my lord, and—"

With a gesture of negation, Lord Duncan interrupted:

"I count as nothing! If Their Majesties consider me it is because of my late father, and in memory of my unfortunate elder brother. Before his death you will remember I was known as Ascott, and it was a great grief to me when I became

Duncan."*

"It was Fate, my dear fellow., and you were powerless to prevent it," declared his companion.

Lord Duncan shook his head:

"No. That motor accident which cost my father and brother their lives, was not the result of chance. They were the victims of a crime, and I believe the odious companions of my abominable wife had some hand in it."

There was a weighty silence. It was broken by the older man's decisive words:

"My dear Duncan you are wrong. I assure you I made the most detailed inquiries, and I found nothing abnormal about the accident, quite the contrary. Your father and brother died victims of a fortuitous accident. That I declare on the faith of Tom Bob."

Lord Duncan uttered a sigh of satisfaction: "Is that so? Who could suspect a crime when Tom Bob, the subtle, the king of detectives, could not discover anything suspicious?"

Duncan turned to his companion with a smile:

"You are the acknowledged king of detectives, Tom Bob, there is no denying that!"

"That is not everybody's opinion, my dear Duncan. The contrary has been declared of me in the past."

Tom Bob alluded to rumors whispered by the French police, Inspector Juve among them, some two years before, alleging that Tom Bob, an American detective come to Paris in quest of Fantômas, was none other than Fantômas himself.

This rumor was discredited, and thanks to the protection of his friend, Ascott, Tom Bob entered the English police force, where his influence soon became predominant.

Tom Bob stopped short. Lord Duncan's glance was on the clock:

"You are expecting someone?"

Lord Duncan reddened:

"I expect my wife, Nini Guinon."

***

* See *The Long Arm of Fantômas* (Fantômas Series, Vol. 6)

"Your wife! She dares—"

"I ordered her to come—to bring her son, our little Jack. I have only seen him twice, and he is eighteen months old today. Ah, if only I were not the father of this child! If—"

There was a discreet knock at the door. It half opened. The head of John, the old servant, appeared:

"Excuse me, my lord," he muttered. "She is here."

The detective rose.

Lord Duncan looked at Tom Bob:

"Do not go," he begged. "I should like you to be present at this interview."

Tom Bob considered a moment:

"Very well. I will be present, but your wife must not be aware of it."

Tom Bob passed behind a heavy curtain leading to an adjoining apartment.

A minute later a young woman marched into the room. She looked little more than a child. An immense gaudy hat was perched on her untidy black hair. She wore neither veil nor gloves. Her eyes were big and bold and mocking, her lips thick and red, her teeth white, her expression sensual: a flashy beauty, unmistakably French—a Parisienne.

At sight of her Lord Duncan shivered. Scandalized, astonished, he snapped an interrogation at her:

"You have come alone?"

In tones contemptuous and arrogant, her eyes staring defiance, she answered:

"Yes, alone."

Lord Duncan walked up to her:

"You have disobeyed my orders," he said harshly. "You must have some serious reason for coming here alone, in spite of my orders. What is that reason?"

The young woman frowned. She put on a sneering look:

"A serious reason? Yes. It would have to be that when I permit myself to come alone to the house of the man who has given me the right to live at his side," she replied. Her tone was ironical.

"Do not revive these odious memories!" Lord Duncan's look and voice breathed disgust.

The girl sniggered. She snarled at him:

"Don't I know well enough that you want to forget that two years ago, you, Ascott the young Englishman who later became Lord Duncan—married me—me, Nini Guinon, a daughter of the people, a little work girl he seduced after an evening's orgy, and was forced to marry her for fear of reprisals and the police!"

Lord Duncan bent his head. He did not contradict her. The young woman had planted herself near the door. She moved forward:

"Very well. So be it! Forget your wife, but I tell you to forget not only your wife, I tell you to forget all that concerns her." Her tone threatened.

Lord Duncan feared to grasp her meaning. He questioned with a look this whirlwind in petticoats, now pacing up and down the elegant room. She was panting, bursting with suppressed rage. She stopped, turned, marched up to Lord Duncan.

This wife forced her husband to step back. He recoiled before the insistent menace of her wicked eyes as she confronted him:

"You wanted to take my child from me, you meant to steal my Jack from me! . . . Don't attempt to deny it!" she shouted, as Lord Duncan made a gesture of denial. "Don't dare deny it! Because you and your like are rich and powerful you think everything is allowed you. Whatever it may be in your country, I very well know that in France if they tear a child from its mother she lets all the world know it—and I swear to you, Ascott, that I'll make some music for you, if you—"

"Hold your tongue!" cried Lord Duncan beside himself with anger and disgust. His attitude was so imperious, so formidable that the enraged woman calmed down. "Enough of this play-acting, Nini. Drop your mask. I know you too well. I am not deceived as to the real feelings of what serves you for a heart. Yes, I have wanted to get back your child, my child. I want to save Jack from the horrible existence you are preparing for him. Cursed chance has willed that you should be a mother, but you are not worthy of such a privilege."

Nini Guinon, crimson with passion, shrieked at Lord Duncan: "You dare! You—"

"Be quiet!" commanded the unfortunate father. His voice softened:

"Alas, Nini, black and bitter with remorse is the day I met you! When I married you to legitimize the child you were to bear me I was a younger son, and did not anticipate my succession to the title and the responsibilities it brought with it. Thus I was obliged to keep our marriage secret. You must admit, madame, that I bought your silence at a high price. I did not intend to forget that I was the husband of my child's mother. That mother owed it to me to conduct herself with propriety. Your behavior has been the reverse.

"Not only have you blackmailed me perpetually in the most odious manner, but you have led an infamous life. If I insist on taking possession of my child you have only yourself to blame."

Nini Guinon drew back, glaring savagely at her husband:

"You will not begin this sort of thing again, Lord Duncan," she snarled at him, "and for this good reason, this very good reason—your son is dead."

"Jack!" Lord Duncan's cry was full of anguish. "Jack, my little Jack, dead!" He fell back in his chair.

Nini stared at him, cold, indifferent. She had shot her bolt.

Duncan started up: "Tell me, Nini, how this dreadful thing happened?" His voice was supplicating.

"Jack took cold. A window was open all night. He died next day."

Duncan walked up to Nini, looked her straight in the eye:

"Is that true?"

His wife did not flinch.

"It is true."

"Why did you not let me know he was ill?"

"Not I. Bet your life on that!" cried Nini. Duncan rushed at her as though he would strangle her.

Nini jerked out: "He died suddenly!"

A tense silence fell. Duncan strode up and down the room

with clenched fists and frowning brow.

Sneering, triumphant, Nini watched him: she had shaken her adversary, dominated him.

Lord Duncan pulled himself together. He faced this detestable woman with the dignity of a peer of the realm:

"Nini Guinon, there was a reason for my indulgence towards you, one only. In spite of your vileness you were a mother, and mother of my son." Duncan paused. Then gravely, in a low troubled voice, he continued:

"God has taken the child, perhaps for the best. It is the punishment imposed on me for my sin."

A burst of cynical laughter was Nini Guinon's reply.

Lord Duncan stiffened:

"Now there remains only husband and wife, between whom yawns an impassable gulf. You, madame, have again and again merited imprisonment. You have been the accomplice of the most degraded creatures in London. Again and again I have intervened to save you from the consequences of your actions. Nini Guinon you are a criminal. I tell you that you shall leave here only to enter a jail. An inquiry shall be opened to discover how my son died. This inquiry will, no doubt, lay bare many things."

At these words Nini Guinon paled:

"You are going to have me arrested!" she cried. "Don't forget that you will let all the world know of your marriage!"

"Well I know it, madame. I shall put up with the scandal."

Nini Guinon trembled. If her husband was prepared to face the scandal of their marriage, she would no longer be able to threaten and blackmail him—she was done for . . .

Lord Duncan walked up and down, a prey to the most sinister reflections.

Nini Guinon moved off to the far end of the room. She was desperately alarmed. What should she do? As she stood near the velvet curtain she heard a voice behind her murmur: "Imbecile!"

She smothered a cry.

The voice continued: "Fool of a Nini, listen. Keep quiet!"

Though startled, astounded, Nini managed to preserve an impassive face and a still body.

"Imbecile to say Jack is dead—Jack dead you are lost beyond hope—but there is still time to retrieve the blunder—invent no matter what—swear that he he is living, swear it—if you want to live, Nini, do not hesitate."

Nini's ears were a-stretch. She watched her husband out of the corner of her eye, terrified lest he should catch a sound. Lord Duncan was so absorbed in bitter reflections that he noticed nothing.

Nini was herself again and ready to play her part:

"Lord Duncan!" she murmured.

"What is it?"

Nini Guinon's attitude was now one of humble repentance. She was kneeling with clasped hands. Sobs punctuated her words:

"Forgive me, Lord Duncan! I have lied to you. My mother's heart inspired the untruth. When you wanted to take my little Jack from me, the one being left me to cherish, I was mortally frightened. Hoping you would then leave me in peace with him, I told you he was dead. But I see that grieves you too much, and I myself will not continue such a dreadful deception. Jack lives, Lord Duncan! My little Jack, and yours!"

Astonished, suspicious, Lord Duncan asked himself if this was not some frightful comedy, but Nini Guinon knew how to lend sincerity to her tones. It was only too easy to touch the heart of this father so willing to believe in the existence of his little son.

"You swear to me that Jack, my Jack is living?"

"I swear it," cried Nini Guinon. Tears were running down her cheeks.

In spite of instinct and reason, Lord Duncan was softened by his wife's emotion, degraded though she might be. Was he not the primary cause of her fall? he asked himself. While he had risen to a high place in the world had not this wretched woman sunk lower and lower?

"Poor unfortunate," murmured Lord Duncan.

Nini Guinon saw at a glance that she had regained her hold on this man.

"Promise me," she implored, "not to take my child from me, and I will try to behave better!"

"Is that possible Nini?"

"I will truly try."

The simple young peer was favorably impressed. Nini grew bolder:

"Misery is a bad counselor, my lord. I must nourish my child and myself, and I am not rich. . . ."

Lord Duncan drew a bundle of notes from his pocketbook, saying with a bitter smile:

"When I received your letter this morning announcing your visit, I had this money in readiness. Take it!"

Nini Guinon put out her hand.

"A moment," said Lord Duncan.

Nini's countenance fell.

"Oh, the condition I impose is not painful. I wish to see my child. I am determined to see him—absolutely. Four days from this, at nine o'clock in the morning precisely, you must be in Hyde Park with little Jack. That is agreed, is it not?"

Nini Guinon looked at her husband with open face and frank eye:

"It's give and take," she smiled. "Very well, I accept the bargain. You can hand over the money. Till Wednesday then, my lord."

Nini Guinon had barely left the room when the heavy curtain between it and the room adjoining, moved. Tom Bob appeared.

Lord Duncan went over to him. He seized the detective's hands and pressed them:

"Well, my dear Tom Bob, have you heard the conversation?"

"I heard everything."

"What do you think of it? Can one believe this woman? She lies so well that it seems impossible to distinguish her lies from the truth. Is my little Jack dead or alive?"

Tom Bob smiled:

"The question is easily answered."

"You will look into the matter for me?"

"I was about to suggest it, my lord. In forty-eight hours you will be satisfied."

"God grant it."

"I am convinced your child lives."

Tom Bob seemed in a hurry to leave. He wrung Lord Duncan's hand warmly, and as he left the room repeated:

"Count on me."

2. Jack Alive

The little birds!
The little birds!

"What a stupid refrain! You must know how to sing to make things like that go down! Sing? Ah, when shall I sing again? My engagement at the Empire finished yesterday evening, and *he* does not wish me to sign another till next winter!—

The little birds—tra-la-la!
The little birds—tra-la-la!

The charming cicada repeated the meaningless words, accompanying herself on the piano with the soft pedal down.

Françoise Lemercier was a music-hall artiste favorably known in London. She was living in Jewin Street in the West Central district, comfortably installed in rooms with her little boy. Her Canadian husband could, not tolerate her music-hall life. They had quarreled and separated some months ago. Each parent wanted sole possession of little Daniel.

Françoise was pretty, admired, flattered—a coquette. Her husband was loutish and brutal, but she had her adored little Daniel. Also she had a discreet love affair with a faithful and generous lover, who had a particular reason for not showing himself in her company.

On this Sunday afternoon, little Daniel was playing on the carpet, amusing her with his baby chatter.

Françoise glanced at the clock on the wall above the piano:

"Ten minutes to one! The shops shut at one, and no lunch bought!"

She jumped up and hurried into the next room, putting her hat hastily on the mass of her copper-blonde hair.

"Oh this English Sunday!" she grumbled. "Can't get a servant to come in, hardly a shop or restaurant open!"

She examined the contents of her purse and counted some shillings.

"It is sufficient to get Daniel and me enough food now," she murmured.

She was about to take little Daniel with her, but he objected to leaving his playthings. Françoise had no time to spare:

"Daniel will stay where he is," she reflected, "and I shall be gone only a few minutes."

She kissed her darling baby, saying tenderly:

"Be a good boy! Mama will be back quickly."

She looked round the room to assure herself there was nothing Daniel could hurt himself with. Doors and windows would safely shut him in.

"Be good, darling," repeated Françoise. She blew her little treasure a kiss as she hurried away. Noticing that he was absorbed in building a castle with his bricks, she departed with an easy mind.

About half an hour later a man walked along Jewin Street. It was deserted.

The man was Jerome Fandor.

He walked slowly along, examining the houses, searching for a certain number. After two or three fruitless attempts, he discovered the right one—that of Françoise Lemercier.

He entered the passage and addressing the first person he met, an old woman, he asked:

"Is Madame Françoise Lemercier here?"

The old woman seemed frightened. She stuttered unintelligible words.

Fandor repeated his question. The woman threw up her hands:

"Yes, sir, this is where she lives. Oh the poor lady! Do you know anything, sir? Have you any news?"

"What! Has she had an accident?" Fandor was nonplussed.

"Little Daniel? Do you know where little Daniel is?"

Fandor was at a loss. He did not even know that Françoise Lemercier had a child, a boy called Daniel. He knew the artiste slightly. He had met her only once or twice, and if he had a purpose in visiting her it was not to inquire about her offspring.

The old woman, seeing he did not understand, began to explain excitedly:

"I daresay, sir, you don't know about it—in fact you can't know—it's so sudden, and it's just happened. The poor lady is nearly off her head, and not without reason I can tell you."

"Will you be more explicit, my good woman? What has happened to Madame Françoise Lemercier?"

Fandor had to listen to interminable lamentations, but at last he understood that half an hour ago, Madame Lemercier had come downstairs and gone off to buy provisions. She had left her little boy, Daniel, in her rooms alone, playing with his toys. Ten minutes after, she returned to find her rooms empty. Daniel was gone. Where? How? No one knew. No one could imagine. Who had carried off the child? No one could say.

"You will go up and see her, sir?" concluded the old woman, the tears streaming down her wrinkled face. "Perhaps you can help her?"

Fandor hesitated.

It was hardly the moment to put Françoise Lemercier through a catechism on certain delicate subjects, as he had intended doing. But the journalist's curiosity was aroused. Perhaps, considering what he knew with regard to certain people, and certain occurrences, an investigation at Françoise Lemercier's would be most opportune.

Jerome Fandor therefore went up to her rooms. He found the artiste prostrate with grief, surrounded by neighbors chattering sympathy. He could get nothing out of the unhappy woman. Having ascertained that her boy had really vanished, he left the premises.

Up and down the pavement of Jewin Street marched Fandor, going over the "how and why" of little Daniel's disappearance.

"Ah!" he cried at last. "Perhaps I can answer that *why!* I hold the solution of the problem: I am convinced of it! Juve, my old friend, it will not be long before you have news from me! To your wire announcing your discovery of Lady Beltham, I shall reply with a wire informing you I have discovered. . . ."

Fandor, elated, rapidly regained his rooms.

Nini Guinon occupied a den in an old house of ill repute in 14a Belmont Street, Whitechapel. All the floors of this building were tenanted by a miserable population of evildoers. Not one of them suspected that she had a legal right to the title of Lady Duncan, two or three French hooligans excepted, who had thought it necessary to put between themselves and the Paris police, the reassuring barrier of the Channel and the North Sea.

Among the most notorious of these individuals was the Beadle, a bully from Ménilmontant, who had known Nini since her childhood; Beaumône, an expert pickpocket, and one or two others.

These bad characters had chosen Nini Guinon as their queen. In spite of all his efforts in the early days of their union, Lord Duncan had been unable to tear her away from her nefarious companions.

Nini Guinon blackmailed her husband, and had lived extravagantly on the money extorted from the young peer.

Now her future looked black. The talisman to conjure Lord Duncan's money out of his pocket and into her gaping one, had gone beyond recall.

Their son, little Jack, was dead.

One evening Nini had come home drunk, to find the window wide open and the dead body of her child in the cradle.

Nini was overwhelmed. She remembered that Jack had been unwell that morning. Forsaking him to run the streets, she had left him unfed and exposed to the inclement weather.

"He is a bad egg, and as like his mother as two peas," she had assured herself. "He's a hardy plant, like myself."

Nevertheless this vice-hardy plant had faded and withered in a few hours.

Nini Guinon was terror-stricken. Maternal grief did not trouble this horrible vixen; her one thought was that Jack dead and buried, her husband would not hesitate to obtain a divorce and be quit of her.

Uncontrolled spite had led her to confess the truth to Lord Duncan. Such news would make him suffer. Too late she saw the danger of such an avowal. Then the mysterious voice had ordered her to deny little Jack's death.

She had visited her husband on the Saturday afternoon. It was now Sunday evening. Full of perplexity Nini was waiting in her lodging, alone with her dead child. All her hooligan friends had gone off on the spree. They thought she was gadding on her own account, for Nini, cunning, suspicious, had not told a single soul of the child's death.

When she heard ten o'clock strike, Nini shivered:

"*He* should be here," she muttered.

That morning she had received a note by an unknown hand: "*Be at home with Jack this evening before ten o'clock.*"

A strange note, for within a couple of hours, the words, apparently written in ink, had quite disappeared. Nini held in her hands a blank sheet of paper.

Was it a ghastly joke? Or a threat?

Nini had not forgotten that this note had been signed, *Fantômas*. She knew that Fantômas had arranged her marriage with young Ascott, now Lord Duncan.

There was a light knock on the door.

Her heart thudded violently at the sound.

Who was it? Whom should she see?

Nini Guinon had been wrung with anxious fears during the past forty-eight hours. The least indiscretion, the slightest blunder might reveal the truth to those about her. Let it be known that her child had died suddenly, and natural though the death might be, the police would suspect foul play when they learned she had concealed her little son's death.

Shaking like a leaf, Nini Guinon forced herself to go to the door:

"Who is it? What do you want?"

A voice outside murmured:

"Fantômas. Open, Nini Guinon."

She obeyed. She drew back, startled. This Fantômas was a Fantômas she had never before set eyes on. It was the Fantômas of the legend now become for her the Fantômas of reality.

This mysterious being was enveloped in a big black cloak. A black slouch hat half covered a black hooded mask which hid his features.

This was Fantômas, beyond doubt!

Why had he come to see Nini Guinon in this garb of anonymity?

Fantômas closed the door at once.

The same voice that had called her "Fool," in Lord Duncan's house, now addressed her behind the hooded mask:

"You fool! To confess that Jack was dead, was that a thing to do? To tell Duncan, when your only hold on him was through his feelings for his son, and his sense of duty as a father towards this child he believes his! Fortunately I was there. Jack is dead—well here is a living Jack!"

The stupefied Nini watched her visitor take from underneath his voluminous cloak a big bundle. She guessed what it contained.

Fantômas unrolled linen wrappings, and from them emerged a pretty rosy child, robust, well-formed, smiling, gazing up at Nini Guinon with questioning eyes.

Nini Guinon was, after all, a mother. Tears rose to her eyes. Seeing this child, so pretty, so full of life and health, she thought, that only a few steps away in the next room, hidden by the coverings of the cradle, reposed the corpse of another child—her child, little Jack! Sobs rose in her throat. She mastered them. She dare not display sentimental emotion in the presence of Fantômas; besides he was issuing his commands:

"Nini, from now on this brat, whose name is Daniel, is to be called Jack, and is your son. Understand?" His tone was abrupt, harsh:

"Next Monday you will show Lord Duncan the son of his loins, little Jack. Understand?"

"Agreed," murmured Nini Guinon. "But I ask myself—"

Fantômas interrupted her brutally:

"Fool! Do not demand anything—obey. There is your son—
that is the one thing you are to keep in mind. Remember that
without me you would be lost. Recollect that thanks to me you
are saved. Where is the other?"

"The other?" stammered Nini Guinon, wondering what
more the sinister bandit demanded of her.

"The other one, I tell you!"

Moving like an automaton, Nini Guinon passed into the
next room. She uncovered the cradle, exposing the death-cold
body of poor little Jack.

Tears filled her eyes at the sight.

Fantômas seized the corpse, and wrapping it in the linen
that had enfolded little Daniel, tucked it under his cloak.

Motionless, terror-stricken, the miserable mother watched
the dark and threatening figure:

"Well! What now?"

Nini was about to explain. She stopped short, listening.

Fantômas listened.

Little Daniel was crying: "Mama! Mama! Mama!"

Nini had fallen on her knees beside the empty cradle.

Fantômas clutched the back of her neck:

"Well, what are you waiting for?" he growled.

He chuckled sardonically:

"Don't you hear him calling you? Go, attend to your son,
Nini, your son Jack!"

Half beside herself, the wretched woman heard the door
bang. Fantômas, the terrible, the mysterious, had disappeared,
and with him the body of her own child—gone from her
forever!

She heard the voice of little Daniel plaintive, entreating:

"Mama! . . . Mama! . . ."

3. The Hostage

"It will be a relief to sit down!"

Jerome Fandor lit his lamp, placed it on the table in the middle of the room, flung himself on his bed, transformed into a divan. Fandor was exhausted, yet restless from over-fatigue and excitement. His body rested, but his tongue clacked:

"A wakeful night is nothing out of the way, but to spend such a night as this last, following up improbable trails, discovering incredible, bewildering things! Such a devilish thousand-and-one of a night has earned me a rest at least! . . . And the day I have just lived through, running here, trotting there, inquiring everywhere! . . ."

Fandor jumped up, opened his window and stared out at the foggy darkening street lined with its monotonous rows of houses, their uniform ugliness stretching into the distance as far as eye could reach.

Fandor soon closed the window and paced the room smiling:

"How will old Juve look," he thought, "when he gets my telegram, just saying that I have found Fantômas again? That's something for him to swallow! He will rejoin me in London at once, I am certain! Ah, we shall start anew our good old life of struggle and danger. It's a declaration of war. . . . And I have promised to send Juve explanations—I must not keep him on tenterhooks! I've been hard at it all day. I am sure now I am not deceived. I can write with certainty.

All eager activity again, Fandor seated himself at his bureau, and started covering sheet after sheet of paper with his almost undecipherable handwriting:

> My Good Juve,
>   You must have jumped for joy when you got my wire, but, if I know you, on second thought you must have doubted that

I had really encountered Fantômas. Well, here are the facts.

I purposely came to England to find out certain things about Lord Duncan, whom we used to know as Ascott. Had he really married the infamous Nini Guinon? Was he still blackmailed by Fantômas, who bled him so successfully in Paris under the guise of Father Moche? I found Nini Guinon in a den of thieves, leading a lamentable existence. She had had a child by Ascott, a boy called Jack. I found Nini just at the moment when the child had died. Do not ask me whether he died a natural death, or was the victim of criminal action! All I do know is that his death is fraught with dire consequences for Nini, if not for Fantômas. Her one hold on Lord Duncan was through the child, and the child was necessary to Fantômas as an instrument to extract Lord Duncan's money. But what of Fantômas?

Did we not, dear Juve, some two years ago, and with great difficulty, identify Fantômas with Tom Bob, the detective? We and Monsieur Havard, with one or two La Sûreté men, were the only ones who knew of this identity. The personality of Tom Bob has never been laid bare officially. How I have admired the superb audacity of this monster when I realized that Fantômas, profiting by this official secrecy, has remained Tom Bob! At this moment, there is at Scotland Yard a member of the Supreme Council, a detective in high repute. I have seen, recognized that detective. He is Tom Bob-Fantômas! Having thus run to earth Fantômas on one side, and Ascott, now Lord Duncan, and Nini Guinon, on the other side, I was going to announce this news to you when events took a disquieting turn. Now follow me closely:

Jerome Fandor raised his head and looked about him, exclaiming:

"Nobody! Well, I must have pushed it to the very verge myself, when filling my fountain pen from the ink bottle!"

Fandor generally used his knife-dagger as a paper cutter. Seemingly he had just pushed this over the table. He must have moved it unwittingly, for when he saw it tip over he started. He was surprised, uttered his exclamation, but attached no importance to the incident. He went on with his letter:

Knowing my personages I am tracking them and I have made this discovery: Fantômas steals a child from a French artiste

named Françoise Lemercier, and he carries the child to Nini to
replace little Jack and deceive Lord Duncan. Organized blackmail of course, and it will succeed there is small doubt. Tom
Bob of Scotland Yard is above suspicion. Tom Bob is difficult
to attack. Yet he thinks he can act with impunity because he
believes Fantômas lost sight of and forgotten. It is this very
state of mind that may give us our best chance of arr—

Jerome Fandor stopped. What was happening? How explain
it? He was not dreaming!

A few minutes ago Fandor had placed his heavy pair of journalist's scissors on his paper and envelopes, as a paper weight.
Glancing mechanically in that direction, he saw the scissors
had disappeared:

"By Saint Anthony, what's the meaning of it? I am certain I
placed the scissors on the paper!"

With feverish haste he scattered and turned over all the
papers on his table:

"Where are my scissors? It is black magic!"

As Fandor displaced a pile of manuscript, he caught sight
of his revolver. Since living in London it had been his habit to
place it fully loaded on the table within reach. He picked it up,
examined it:

"In the name of Heaven, what does this mean? I left my revolver fully loaded, now it is empty!"

Fandor pushed back his chair, meaning to rush to his ward-
robe and load the weapon afresh.

As our journalist attempted to stand up he found that his
legs had been tied to the chair. He endeavored to free himself,
overbalanced, rolled over on the carpet, dragging the heavy
chair with him. Wild with rage he began to swear and shout.
A gag was clapped in his mouth, his arms tightly bound. He
could not move.

An ironical joking voice spoke at his ear:

"Ah, Monsieur Fandor, don't look for your scissors, your
paper knife, your cartridges! They are dangerous weapons in
the hands of so quarrelsome a person!"

Fandor could now see his assailant. It was Tom

Bob-Fantômas!

"I can say goodbye to life," thought Fandor. "If Tom Bob knows that I have recognized him as that accursed bandit, it is all up with me!"

Tom Bob-Fantômas spoke:

"Monsieur Fandor, I do not think I need introduce myself to you! You and I are old acquaintances. For ten years you have hunted me, sought my death, I, Fantômas! Yet I wish you no harm."

The bandit paused, and with a casual air took a chair from a corner of the room, drew it near Fandor, and seated himself:

"I do not wish to harm you, and you would do well to believe it. Once before, you will remember, we found ourselves face to face in a situation somewhat similar to the present. It was in the loft of Father Moche!"

Fandor could not believe his ears. Fantômas did not want his life? What then was he after? Meanwhile the bandit continued in a quiet conversational manner:

"Monsieur Fandor allow me to sincerely congratulate you. A while ago, when you were writing to Juve, to my old adversary Juve, I conjured away your dagger, scissors and revolver. Ah, how absorbed you were, Monsieur Fandor! I allowed myself to read over your shoulder. Your letter is a masterpiece! You explained to Juve a number of excellent things which would interest him greatly. Unfortunately . . ."

Tom Bob-Fantômas rose, took Fandor's letter, tore it into tiny bits, and stuffed them in his pocket:

"Unfortunately, Monsieur Fandor, this letter will not reach its intended destination." The bandit smiled, continued: "Monsieur Fandor, I have not the slightest intention of doing you any violence, but I mean to prevent you playing me mischievous tricks. Would you like a pledge of my good intentions? I will remove your gag. But I will warn you that I have taken the precaution to hire all the rooms in this house, therefore you will call or cry for help in vain. There is none to hear."

Tom Bob-Fantômas knelt near the journalist and unfastened the knots of the gag:

"There! You feel better now! You can answer me! . . ."

Fandor, quite self-possessed, interrupted the bandit:

"I am in your power, Fantômas. What do you want with me? What are you aiming at? My death, no doubt? Very well, kill me! But be quick about it! It would be a coward's act to torture me."

Fantômas smiled, kept an enigmatic silence, then spoke at last:

"Will you do me the pleasure to call me Tom Bob? It is as Tom Bob I am here now. . . . And, Monsieur Fandor, who told you I wished to torture you? What a villainous word to use! Do I look like a torturer? Come now! It seems to me I have not treated you so badly since I have removed the scarf that reduced you to silence." Tom Bob-Fantômas was still smiling. An ironic smile twisted Fandor's lips:

"Yes, you have removed my gag, but you have taken care not to loose my bonds."

Fantômas rose quickly.

"Oh, pardon me, my dear fellow. I see no objection to freeing your movements. You are unarmed. I am not."

While speaking the bandit unbound Fandor, and helped him to his feet, deftly slipping handcuffs on the journalist's wrists.

"I shall not remove these handcuffs. . . . You are so madly foolhardy that you might try to attack me, unarmed though you are!"

"You are right," said Fandor with calm approval.

"As always," retorted Fantômas. "You ask what I am going to do with you, Monsieur Fandor? . . . You are a hostage—just that. You must consider yourself the prisoner of Tom Bob—a prisoner of war until further notice. I wish to lead a quiet life for the present, and your friend Juve could seriously annoy me. It seemed to me that the best way to secure my being left in peace by him, was to hold you at my mercy. When Juve knows that if he attacks me, you will be first to suffer the consequences, he should leave me alone—is not that so?"

Fandor shook his head:

"No," he declared.

"No?" questioned Fantômas.

"No," repeated our journalist. "Juve and I, Fantômas, will pursue you without a pause, without mercy, because you are the enemy of Society, the appalling criminal who knows no pity. It is not a mere personal vengeance we mean to draw down on you. No, we are the avengers of all your victims. Juve will not stop on account of my safety, as you seem to think. He knows I hold my life cheap. Even though I am in your hands, your hostage, he will hunt you down, arrest you! It is his duty."

Fantômas and Fandor faced each other.

"Monsieur," said Fantômas abruptly, "you brave me! I admire your energy. You are worthy of being my enemy." The tones were harsh, the manner dignified.

Fandor considered this extraordinary bandit. Certainly this individual before him was an assassin, but this assassin was great in his evil way, his crimes wore the glamor of audacity. Fandor could not now despise this arch criminal—he had a dark dignity.

"What do you want to do with me?"

Fantômas placed his hand on Fandor's shoulder:

"I have told you. You are a hostage. You are going to help me to frighten Juve. No! Do not protest. Do not tell me that he will condemn you to death to obey his duty! Such devotion to the cause of Good, as that, would be criminal. I hold you, and through that I hold Juve. I know it! Do not deny it!"

Fandor did not reply to this. Though he would not openly admit that Fantômas had judged Juve aright, yet at the bottom of his heart he was not so sure. He knew well the deep affection Juve felt for him. He also knew only too well to what atrocities Fantômas would have recourse, and he feared the monster would find means to force Juve to leave him in peace to continue his horrible crimes.

A tense silence ensued. Fandor broke it:

"Where are you going to take me? You were able to rent this house to prevent my cries for help being answered, but—"

"Come!" commanded the bandit. Without further ado he drove his handcuffed victim before him.

They descended to the ground floor of the house.

"Halt!" ordered Fantômas.

An adroit twist of the scarf and Fandor's eyes were bandaged. Fantômas chuckled.

"Useless to shout for help, Monsieur Fandor. You cannot make the men employed by the carpenter-packer in the adjoining shop hear you."

Fandor heard bolts withdrawn, the scrape of unlocking keys.

"Here is your prison! I have made it as comfortable as possible. Enter!"

Our journalist entered a strange little room. It was like a small ship's cabin, and just high enough to stand upright in. Shelves filled with books hung on the walls, and one or two engravings; a bunk in one corner, a hinged, one-leaf toilet table in the other.

"Here is your retreat," said Fantômas. "It is not large, but you will be barely a month here. It is nicely furnished, and I add, Monsieur Fandor, that it is so perfectly soundproof that your most piercing cries cannot be heard. Look! I have put a violin on your bed. You are free to draw the most strident sounds from it. No one will hear you."

"You are pleased to be ironical," protested Fandor.

"Why?"

"I am handcuffed. How do you suppose I can play the violin?"

Fantômas shrugged:

"Because to leave you with chained hands for a whole. month is not my intention. See, against this wall I have had this little file fastened. You can use it to file through the rings of your handcuffs it will take some time to bite through the steel, but I know you are persevering. . . . You will manage it."

Fandor nodded:

"I have only to bow to your decision, Fantômas. But how long will you force me to live in this restricted space? It is a cell, this room. . . . To keep me here is to doom me to madness."

"Condemn you to madness? I shall be very careful not to do that, Monsieur Fandor! You will remain in this room about a month. I shall visit you every day and try to satisfy your needs, books, tobacco, and so on. The thirty days past, I promise you that your condition will be considerably ameliorated. In any case, do not be anxious. The room is perfectly ventilated, though it seems hermetically sealed; but that is my secret. As to food, I will contrive to take your orders. As I might have to travel unexpectedly, I have taken the precaution to provide you with wholesome nourishing tinned food. They are in that cupboard to the right. Do not fear then that you will die either from asphyxiation or starvation. Is there anything else you wish to ask me?"

Fandor drew himself up:

"I ask nothing from Fantômas."

The bandit ignored this defiance.

"Ah! Then there is nothing but to take my leave of you, Monsieur Fandor. Do not be anxious. You are in perfect security here. Be tranquil, l shall look well after my hostage. Your fate depends on Juve."

Fandor, pale and with trembling lips, bridled his anger:

"So be it. You are the stronger."

Fantômas smiled that eternal enigmatic smile of his:

"I certainly think so. Monsieur Fandor, I bid you adieu—until tomorrow."

Tom Bob-Fantômas made a little bow, the essence of irony, and left the room.

Fandor heard the complicated play of many bolts.

Jerome Fandor had been forty-eight hours a prisoner in the cell provided by Tom Bob-Fantômas.

Our journalist had been in the depths of despair, but the crisis was over. He was once more alert, indomitable.

He examined this black hole of his, minutely. He would search for any loophole of escape. The extraordinary little room was marvelously sealed up.

How to escape? He was on the ground floor, therefore not far from the street. Had not Fantômas said there was a carpenter-packer's workshop adjoining his prison?

What of it?

Behind a door of many locks, enclosed in a windowless room lighted by electricity, a soundproof cell, he was the hostage of the Master Terrorizer!

Fandor argued:

"I am the hostage of Fantômas. If Fantômas requires a hostage, it is because he needs to come to terms with Juve. If he needs to make terms with Juve, it is because Juve threatens to be stronger than he! Buck up, Fandor, my lad! Juve will come to the rescue."

Fandor began to file off his handcuffs with concentrated energy. Interminable hours passed consecrated to this work of liberation.

"Fantômas told me he would visit me today. He has not come. Why?"

Our journalist had to ask himself this question with wearisome iteration.

Day after day dragged by, but no Fantômas.

"He abandons me. If I had not food I should think he meant to starve me to death. But I have enough tinned provisions to last me over a month. Perhaps he means to prolong the agony! . . . Has Fantômas' absence to do with Juve? Possibly!"

Then in the middle of a monotonous day—the very day Fandor had finally freed himself from his manacles—he had a fresh surprise.

It seemed to him his room moved!

There was no seeming about it! Little by little his room moved, slid, shook. Soon it jerked, jolted, turned upside down, round and round!

Fandor was dazed, dizzy.

"Am I in a cylinder or a rolling motor van? What's happening to me? Juve! Juve! If you don't come I am lost!"

4. An Inquest at Putney

A policeman was supervising the fourth island in Elsted Street, a long, straight street of superior villas.

For some minutes he had had his eye on a ragged man leaning against the railings of a house opposite.

The policeman crossed the road:

"What are you doing there? That's not a place to sleep! Move on!"

The ragged man looked at the policeman. His air was quiet, respectful:

"I am doing nothing, officer. I am not sleeping. I am waiting."

"What of that?"

The ragged man smiled:

"I am waiting for someone I know to pass this way. I am expecting him, but the young fool must have swallowed too much whiskey and slept late. I shall have to be getting along."

The man moved off.

The policeman followed him with his eyes.

The ragged man vanished in the distance.

The policeman resumed his beat.

It was Monday morning. The Spring sun shone brightly. Smart servants were opening windows, airing rooms. Eight o'clock struck. The attractive odor of cooking breakfasts stole out on the fresh air. Bustle, preparations within comfortable houses; outside, pedestrians were hastening along the hitherto deserted street.

Putney was awake. Putney was making its toilette. At nine o'clock the policeman was standing on the edge of the pavement, exchanging words and smiles with some of the servants out on errands.

"Good morning, Mary!"

"Good morning, policeman!"

Presently the policeman resumed his beat. Frowning, he crossed the road quickly. The ragged man had returned:

"Look here! Haven't I told you to move off! What are you after?"

The ragged man nodded:

"Yes, policeman, you have. But I am waiting for that fool of a boy and I cannot tell—"

The ragged man was smiling. Feeling in his pocket, and with his eye meeting that of the policeman, he handed him a card, concealed in his hand, a small red card, saying:

"Excuse me, policeman, but it is necessary I should stay here; also that you should not attract attention to me."

"I beg your pardon, sir! I had no idea . . ."

The crestfallen cop was beating a retreat.

"Hey!" called the ragged man.

"Sir!"

"Doctor Garrick lives at 33, does he not?"

"Yes, sir," replied the startled policeman. "Is there anything?—"

He stopped. The ragged man had frowned.

"What were you going to say, my man?"

"I was going to ask you, sir, if it was with reference to Dr. Garrick you were here."

"Would that astonish you?"

"I don't say that, sir."

The ragged man reflected:

"You have heard the inhabitants of 33 spoken of?"

The ragged man pointed to an ornate villa whose blinds remained obstinately down.

"Is no one there?"

"I don't know, sir. I have heard Doctor Garrick spoken about."

"You know him?"

"I have often seen him."

"His description?"

"A man about forty-five or fifty, very dark. Whiskers and a mustache. Longish hair, inclined to curl."

"Good rich?"

"He is a dentist, as well as a doctor."

"Many patients?"

"No, sir. He practices at his pleasure. He's a bit of an amateur in that."

"Good."

The beggar man had risen:

"We have talked enough. When do you go off duty?"

"Till mid-day, sir."

"In that case, I shall no doubt see you again. As I may have to get you to take a note you had better know my name—Detective Shephard."

The policeman was taken aback.

This ragged man was the celebrated Detective Shephard!

"Yes, and I am on an interesting trail. . . . Tell me, who is the biggest grocer about here?"

"Over there, at the corner."

"Right! I shall see you again presently. Good day."

The spurious ragamuffin entered the grocer's shop, and drawing some loose change from his pocket to inspire confidence, asked for quite a number of spices which he wished ground to powder. This process would take some time. There was quite a collection of gossiping servants, men and women, awaiting their turn at the counters.

A cook entered, and the gossip ceased with common accord. There was a movement of lively curiosity.

"You, Miss Edith! Well I never!"

"It's me, John."

"And what news?"

"No news, John."

There was a terrified silence among the servants crowding round the newcomer.

"He has killed her as sure as day!" cried a plump housemaid.

"Yes! Yes? He has done for her!" cried some.

"Sure as faith, he's killed her!" cried others.

The ragged man, who had been sitting apparently indifferent to the babble, now approached:

"Why do you think he has killed her?"

John took it upon himself to reply, while the others stared at this ragged fellow:

"My good fellow, you evidently don't belong to the neighborhood or you wouldn't ask such a question. Why has Doctor Garrick killed Mrs. Garrick? Why to live in peace with his dear friend!"

"He has a mistress then?"

There was a general laugh.

"It's evident you don't belong hereabouts," repeated John.

"No, but I heard talk of the affair—and what they told me seemed so extraordinary!"

The others stared at this queer fish who doubted what all Putney was sure of.

A tall youth entered. He grinned amiably.

"Hullo Sam!" cried John. "Here's a strange gentleman who doesn't believe Doctor Garrick has killed his wife!"

Sam grinned broadly, staring at the man he took to be a tramp. The apparent tramp smiled genially:

"I say it's doubtful. Where are your proofs?"

"I'll tell you what we about here think," said Sam as spokesman: "We think this Garrick's a downright bad egg—a sulky, surly, miserly specimen, who hardly does a stroke of his own sort of work, is never at home, and no one knows where he comes from—"

"Yes, but that does not prove he has killed his wife!"

"Is it true, Miss Edith?"

"It's true as true, Sam."

"Now you see! This brute is the rightful husband of the prettiest woman in Putney!"

"Is Mrs. Garrick so pretty?"

"Better than pretty! Tall, fair, lively, generous, charming! It's a regular dove-and-bear marriage!"

There was a titter of appreciation. Sam continued: "So it's not astonishing that one day the bear kills the dove. They weren't a united couple. You've often said that, Miss Edith."

"That's true—it was a sad marriage. Mrs. Garrick had a miserable life of it, poor thing!"

"That still does not prove that Doctor Garrick has killed his wife," declared the ragged man anew.

"Well," said Sam. "What do you suppose has become of her?"

"She has completely disappeared for over a week!"

"Perhaps she is paying a visit?"

"No, Miss Edith hasn't done any packing for her."

"She may have taken only a suitcase."

"But she never told anyone she was going away! The day after she disappeared, several ladies were expected to tea. She had invited them for that afternoon. She never sent notes putting them off. They were all surprised. Isn't that significant?"

"Hmm! I fancy Mrs. Garrick went off unexpectedly," declared the ragged man, shrugging his shoulders.

"So we all thought, but in that case she would have written to the doctor—sent some news of herself!"

"And you are sure she has not written?"

"I am certain," declared Edith. "I read the doctor's letters every day, therefore—"

The ragged man hesitated:

"Well," said he, "there's nothing very serious in all this. If Doctor Garrick had murdered her, he would not have remained in Putney. He would have bolted, and—"

"But that is just what he has done!" cried cook Edith. "The doctor is no longer there, or at least, hardly ever. He is out all the time. I haven't set eyes on him for three days. He may be with his mistress and child! I swear he is a downright bad lot! I'll bet you what you like he has killed his wife—poor soul!"

The cook's audience was of her opinion. They nodded agreement: Dr. Garrick was a bad lot! He had killed his wife!

The ragged man slipped out of the shop. He had got what he wanted.

"Hey! Policeman!"

"Sir?"

"You know the gossip about Doctor Garrick?"

"Yes, sir."

"And you put faith in it?"

The policeman nodded. He looked scared. Detective Shephard seemed in a very bad temper.

"They declare Dr. Garrick has killed his wife!"

"Yes, sir, they do say so, and I am not far from thinking that Dr. Garrick has . . . has . . ."

"Has killed his wife," finished Detective Shephard.

"Yes!"

"You know that Garrick had a mistress?"

"I have heard say so, sir."

"You know where this woman lives?"

"No. I don't know, sir."

"Thank you, policeman."

Shephard went briskly down Elsted Street. He stopped by an antiquated four-wheeler drawn up beside the pavement. He whistled. The driver awoke, handled the reins, ready to start.

"Take me to the nearest District Messengers' station."

"Very good, sir."

No sooner in the cab, Shephard lowered the blinds, took off coat and trousers, drew others from a valise, and put them on. He was transformed into a respectable well-to-do Londoner. He was barely ready when the cab drew up before the District Messengers' office.

Shephard crossed the room, and whispering a word or two in the ear of the attendant, was at once shown into the superintendent's private office.

The detective made himself known:

"Detective Shephard of Scotland Yard. It is Mr. Wooland to whom I have the honor of speaking, is it not?"

"It is."

"You have among your clients a certain Doctor Garrick?"

"Yes."

"Kindly give me the full address of his mistress. I understand that he frequently sent her letters and parcels by your messengers."

Mr. Wooland bent his head.

"The name of this person?" demanded Shephard.

"Françoise Lemercier."

"Kindly wait a moment."

Mr. Wooland left the room. He quickly returned.

"Miss Frances Lemercier lives at No. 7 Jewin Street."

"Near the Bank?"

"In that neighborhood. Yes."

"Thank you."

Miss Françoise Lemercier?

Shephard drove to the Bank, left the cab, and went to make inquiries at various shops.

He found the house, and questioned a slovenly person who apparently acted as caretaker.

Shephard asked for Mademoiselle Françoise Lemercier. A young woman who has a little boy called Daniel."

The caretaker nodded.

"Oh I know her. But you have come too late, sir. She left yesterday."

"Gone? Where?"

"I don't know. She left without warning and after a queer thing had happened."

"To what do you allude?"

As the caretaker seemed unwilling to answer this, the detective showed her his card.

"You can speak. I belong to the police."

The caretaker became loquacious:

"Well, sir, Miss Lemercier, who is a singer, as you may know, went off in a hurry to try and find her little boy. She declared he had been stolen from her."

"Little Daniel?"

"Yes, sir."

Shephard pondered this startling development: "Had this young woman a friend, a gentleman who comes to see her pretty often? And has he called here since she left?"

"She had a friend, sir, a queer sort of a man, snappish, and surly, and always in a hurry. He used to sneak upstairs as if he wanted to hide himself. He had keys to get into the rooms.

He did come just after Miss Lemercier left. He went up, but he soon came down again, and he was in a dreadful rage."

"Has he been since?"

"No, sir."

An hour later, Detective Shephard drove up to Dr. Garrick's house, 33 Elsted Street, Putney.

He rang the front door bell, peal after peal. No answer. It might have been a house of the dead. He returned to the cab. Jumping in, he ordered: "Scotland Yard!"

5. The Departure of The Victoria

On the morning of April 26th, at flood tide, the immense gates of the Princess Dock, Liverpool, ground slowly open on their gigantic hinges, giving passage to a tug of the White Star Line, vomiting torrents of smoke, and pushing through the water at top speed. A taut cable connected the tug with a superb steamer, *The Victoria*, of the Liverpool-Montreal line, moving majestically out of the Dock, crowded with passengers waving handkerchiefs of farewell, and laden with merchandise.

Leaning against the netting on the starboard side of the second class deck was a young woman. Her look was troubled as she watched the bustle of departure. She wore a long black cloak. Were it not for the white feather in her hat, she might have been in mourning. She was carefully dressed and very pretty. From time to time she shivered as from hardly suppressed emotion, an emotion not caused by heartbreaking farewells, for she viewed the crowd massed at the end of the quay with indifferent eyes. As the steamer made its way towards the sea, the young traveler's eyes were raised to the gray cloudy sky, and with her delicate white hand she brushed away the teardrops from her long lashes.

The Victoria was about to lose all contact with land and port, when the sad-faced girl uttered a cry as though terrified by some apparition, and fell half fainting into one of the wicker armchairs on the deck behind her. She was unnoticed. The passengers nearby were rushing along the vessel excitedly.

A man was breaking through the crowd on the jetty, pushing his way in frantic haste, until he was level with the lock gate.

The sides of The Victoria were so huge that, despite the size of the lock, they were almost touching the walls of the basin. As usual, to protect the ship's bulwarks, balls of cordage were hung over the side.

The running man, profiting by the crowd's amazement, flung himself against the vessel's side, using one of the cordage fenders as a pedestal. With monkey-like agility he climbed up the rope to the top of the ship's rail.

The passengers stared stupefied at this unexpected performance.

He was a man of about forty, robust, muscular, with a face full of energy framed in black curly hair. His mustache was large and black, and thick whiskers almost covered his cheeks.

When his perilous enterprise terminated successfully there were bursts of applause from passengers and crowd.

No doubt it was a traveler behind time for some reason or other, who had not hesitated to jump on board *The Victoria* as though it were a moving tram.

It was a bit of luck for him! Touch and go!

A few seconds later, and the steamer would have been out of reach.

The passengers stared at him curiously.

The newcomer looked about him, and made for the stairs leading to the second-class cabins. He hurried along between decks, uttered an exclamation answered by a joyful cry. He had come face to face with the young woman who had been so overcome on deck.

"Françoise!"

"Garrick!"

They rushed into each other's arms.

Leaning on his shoulder Françoise Lemercier burst into tears.

"Françoise, my darling, what are you doing here? Explain!"

Françoise put her head in her hands, trying to collect her thoughts.

"I am distracted. Since yesterday I have been off my head. Oh, it is dreadful beyond words! Isn't it, Garrick?"

Garrick looked all tenderness and sympathy.

"I got your letter, and hastened to you directly, my love. But you had gone. Fortunately, you explained your intention. By great good luck I caught a train leaving for Liverpool, and it brought me in time to rejoin you. That is how I learned . . ."

"Daniel! Daniel! My poor little Daniel, what has become of you?" cried the distracted mother, bursting into floods of tears.

Garrick clenched his fists.

"Who is it? Who has been allowed to trouble us in the full tide of our happiness? Who? Who?" cried Garrick, threatening an invisible enemy:

"Ah, if only I had suspected! Yes, it must be *he* who was determined to get back his child—and yours."

Françoise, sobbing bitterly, paid no heed to the words just uttered by Garrick.

"But, Françoise, how is it you are on this steamer? Why do you want to go to Canada?"

"To search for Daniel. I shall not rest till I have got him into my own hands again."

Françoise was calmer. She had the support of her dear Garrick. Her courage was rising.

"I will help you," said he briskly. "Now tell me why you are going to Canada?"

Françoise was about to give her reasons when Garrick whispered:

"Let us go to your cabin! We can talk more freely there!"

He pointed to the passengers who, one by one were approaching, agape with curiosity.

Françoise and Garrick slipped away. Safely ensconced in her cabin, Françoise went into details not contained in her letter, as to why she was on a steamer bound for Montreal.

When the distracted Françoise could find no trace of her child, and was about to call in her neighbors to question them, she spied a newspaper on the table. Mechanically she read its title: *The Herald*. It was a Canadian publication. Françoise was not a subscriber. It must have been brought in during her unfortunate absence. Was it not the ravisher of her child who had left this revealing, document?

Who was interested in stealing her son from her? Her husband, and the father of little Daniel. Her husband was Canadian. The presence of this paper explained everything.

It was a consolation, for certainly little Daniel's father adored the child, and would do him no harm.

What should she do?

Her reflections were interrupted by the arrival of neighbors who had heard her agonizing cries. Françoise had left her door ajar. They came in to inquire and condole.

She questioned them, but said no word of the conclusion she had come to. Why should she reveal to these curious and indifferent neighbors her domestic troubles? When left to herself, the mother of little Daniel decided to sail for Canada by the first boat bound for Montreal. She was determined to find her child.

She started for Liverpool that evening. She wrote a letter to Garrick, giving a confused account of what had happened, and what she meant to do.

Her story ended, Garrick asked:

"Is that all?"

"Yes, all."

"It is mad, absolutely mad, my poor child!" he cried. "That paper was a trap, and you have fallen into it! Whoever put it there intended to turn your thoughts in the direction of Canada. It is only too successful. For my part, I am convinced your little son, far from having been taken to Canada, has been hidden in England, probably in London itself—possibly a few yards from your own home! . . . They wanted to get rid of you, and have succeeded. Oh, what a tragedy of errors!"

As Garrick declared his opinion, it seemed to the young mother, that a veil was torn from before her eyes and the light of truth appeared.

Françoise flung her arms round her lover's neck:

"Yes, I understand. I was misled. Daniel in England, and I on this odious ship! I am going further away from my little Daniel every minute! It is unbearable!"

Garrick sat silent, anxious, absorbed.

Abruptly he put Françoise from him, rose, hurried from the

cabin on deck. He saw one of the crew.

"The pilot-boat?"

"Left a quarter of an hour, sir."

"Too late!"

Far away he saw the rapidly disappearing boat—their one hope of getting back to England quickly!

There was nothing to be done.

With a smothered oath, Garrick descended to the cabin.

His depressed air told Françoise Lemercier that all hope of leaving the now hated steamer, was lost.

The miserable mother threw up her hands and fell back fainting.

6. A Drinking Den in the Docks

"Ralph, my lad, a glass of gin?"

"Whiskey, Bob, if it's all the same to you!"

"Whiskey it is! Now for a place where we shall not be disturbed, where the counter is a comfortable height for our elbows, and the glasses are not too small!"

"This detestable fog!"

"You never grow accustomed to London?"

"Give me Madrid!"

"You should have remained there, Ralph!"

"The *alguazils* bothered me too much."

"You get on better with our bobbies in blue?"

"For the present."

Bob and Ralph were threading their way among the tortuous streets in the sinister quarter of the London Docks.

"Where are we bound for, Bob?"

"I know a place, not so bad! . . ."

"With two doors?"

"Of course!"

"Is it far?"

"So-so. In Bell Street."

"Don't know it."

"You don't know London."

"That's true."

Onwards marched the pair past shabby folk thronging mean streets. Bob turned a corner and slipped down a dirty alley.

"You will see if the whiskey they give you isn't like imprisoned sunshine!"

"Sun! I've never seen what you might call a sun in this fog-ridden ant-heap of London!"

"Now and again, Ralph!"

They advanced a few steps. Bob pointed to a house whose

windows were effectually veiled by unclean muslin curtains.

"Here we are, Ralph!"

On the threshold, Bob drew his companion back.

"A word of warning, my lad. . . ."

"What's that?" interrupted Ralph.

"Don't get shirty, Ralph! I've only known you since we met on the Embankment of Father Thames! Just a friendly caution! . . ."

Ralph snapped his fingers.

"Police?"

"You never can tell! You've knocked about the world enough to know that the English police are the most terrible of all, the quickest to pounce. So, mum's the word! Come inside."

Bob pushed open the door and ushered in his companion.

In the crude glare of the brilliantly lighted bar, Ralph was seen to be wearing a jockey cap, the torn peak of it falling half across his face. He was rigged out in a clumsily big overcoat, greenish and threadbare. His frayed trousers hung over boots buttonless and cracked.

Bob looked as much of a ragamuffin. He wore a short coat and no waistcoat. Buttons were replaced by safety-pins. Like Ralph he lacked linen. His coat collar was turned up to his ears. A laced boot covered his right foot. His left had room and to spare in a boot with elastic sides. His trousers flapped inches above his ankles. His felt hat, battered, ribbonless, flopped over his forehead.

The *Old Fellow* bar was low ceilinged and blackened by pipe smoke. The room was cut in half by a horseshoe shaped counter of wood, edged by a narrow band of zinc. Dozens of glasses were ranged on it, piles of hard-boiled eggs, heaps of bananas, and a number of dice boxes.

Opposite the immense counter a low door opened on a dark passage, and through the bluish smoke-laden atmosphere a further room could be glimpsed. The odor of hot whiskey and rank tobacco was insupportable. Ralph coughed violently, but Bob, very much at his ease, approached the counter, pushed the glasses aside with his elbow, threw money down, and called the landlord:

"Ishmael! Two whiskies hot! And try for once to give us glasses bigger than thimbles!"

Inside the counter, a big, ferocious looking man, smart, spruce, swept up the coins in a flash.

"Ishmael's glasses, my boy, hold just as much as all the other glasses. Those who don't like them, or find them too small, have only to go and drink elsewhere!"

Bob shrugged and turned to Ralph:

"Our good Ishmael is always amiable! Have you never been here before?"

"Never, Bob."

"Well, you will come back again! It's liberty hall, so long as one has friends here."

Ralph nodded approval.

In this crowded den no one seemingly paid attention to the comings and goings; each individual, each group was immersed in its own affairs. Some better clad customers were eating and drinking at the counter, perched on high stools; a more ragged contingent leaned against the grimy walls, dipping bread in tea laced with gin.

"Best whiskey in the kingdom, Ralph!"

Bob emptied his glass slowly. Ralph swallowed his quickly, and called for another. He knew Bob was in funds.

"What do you say to a sausage, Ralph?"

"Famous! A sausage never harmed an honest die-of-hunger devil like me!"

"Two hot sausages, Ishmael!" shouted Bob. "Long ones! And we will have them in the end room!"

"Not in the end room!" protested Ishmael. "There's folks in there!"

"What of it, good Ishmael?"

"There's only one vacant table, Bob, and it's tuppence extra for the use of it."

"All right!" Bob flung two pennies on the counter, and taking Ralph by the shoulders, pushed him forward, through the dark entry and into the supper room, which was nothing but a covered courtyard roughly paved. As they entered, the eaters stared through the smoke-thickened atmosphere. Silence fell as suspicious eyes examined them. It was a cold reception.

"Good evening!" said Bob.

"Good evening!" echoed Ralph.

Vague "Good evenings" were heard as Bob seated himself with Ralph at a small table. A larger one was surrounded by men and women.

Already Ishmael had arrived with two fat sausages. "What'll you have to drink?"

"Ah," said Bob. "I want a mixture—my own particular. Bring us two of your biggest glasses, Ishmael, and fill them with ginger-beer, gin, and port in equal parts. A full pint each! That's a drink if you like!"

"Very well, gentleman."

Ralph did such honor to this frightful mixture that, elbows on table, head on hands, he was soon fast asleep.

Bob, his cutty pipe at full blast, head leaning against the wall, crosswise on his chair, was staring in front of him, absorbed in meditation.

Those at the next table were keeping an eye on the newcomers. Before them stood glasses and a regiment of empty bottles. A jet black negro, with shirt sleeves turned up to the shoulders, arms spread out on the table, sat motionless.

"My little pensioners won't die of hunger today!" he remarked. "What a pity they are all so sick!"

The pensioners were fleas which he placed on his arm to suck a savory meal.

"Job, old fellow, you feed your pensioners too well!" protested a pale, old-looking young man. "S'truth you treat the little comrades like bourgeoises!"

A tall, evil-faced fellow leaned over Job's arm.

"How many left, Job?"

"Seven."

"Seven tame fleas! As there are only four of us, you, me, the Beadle and Nini, what about supper? We'll whistle Father

Ishmael and tell him to put your pensioners on the spit straight away!"

The speaker pretended to sweep the fleas off the negro's arm. Job leapt back.

"You shall not touch my pensioners!" he shouted. "They're the girls that earn my bread for me!"

Job drew a matchbox from his opened shirt, put his fleas into it, and shut them in their prison.

Returning to the table, he poured himself a brimming measure of gin.

"Monsieur Beadle," said he, "you don't know how to count."

"A bit off your nut, Job! Not know how to count? Why not?"

"Because you say we are four, when we are five!"

"Where is the fifth?"

"Nini's son."

"True. Nini, give us a sight of your brat!"

The Beadle got up.

Strange reunion of these Parisian hooligans, in this London den! Beaumôme, the cruel ex-convict, the brutal Beadle, Nini, bad daughter of good Madame Guinon, and negro Job, were keeping company here! Nini, well known and popular, had introduced her friends. Evening after evening found them at the *Old Fellow,* drinking glasses of brandy. Job came now and again. He was stupid, said Nini, but he had fine fists to settle disputes with, and pence to pay for their drinks.

"Show your brat!" demanded the Beadle again.

Beaumôme jumped up—Beaumôme the hideous, the vicious, despiser of petticoats, who, placing his value high, had never put himself out for a woman!

Beaumôme was sweet on Nini.

Nini disdained him.

Beaumôme courted her assiduously, obstinately, tirelessly, and vainly. Beaumôme's courtship was food for mirth. The comrades made fun of him.

"Don't budge, Nini! I'll fetch the little beggar!"

"Look at him, playing nurse at this time of day!" rallied the Beadle.

Little cared Beaumôme. He made for a corner of the room, and cautiously unrolled a big bundle—his own overcoat—placed on the floor.

A child was exposed, sound asleep.

Beaumôme lifted it carefully, for Nini was watching him out of the corner of her eye. He seated the baby on the table, in the middle of the glasses.

"There he is, Beadle! Behold the heir of my woman!"

Nini snatched up the child and rocked it in her arms.

"Ha, you men, he's a little beauty, isn't he? He'll make a fine fellow—my Jack!"

"Whose son?" demanded the Beadle, in a sly and sneering tone.

"Hold your jaw! My son. That's enough!"

"Let's see if he's like you. . . ." The Beadle laughed.

"He resembles me, that's sure!" exclaimed Nini.

The Beadle bent over the child.

"Don't get angry, Nini. He's not a bad-looking little chap—that's so, Job?"

The negro, who had been steadily drinking, nodded:

"A pretty baby, but he's not the same!"

Nini vehemently protested:

"What! You don't recognize my son?"

Job, still nodding his head, declared:

"He is a pretty boy, but he is not your son."

The Beadle was amused. He wanted to take a rise out of the indignant Nini:

"It's true, Nini, the boy isn't at all like you!"

"He isn't like me! Possible. He's a boy!"

Job obstinately repeated:

"I have already seen him, I have, and I don't recognize him!"

The Beadle sniggered:

"Perhaps you've changed him at nurse, Nini?"

Nini was wrapping up the child:

"If my boy, Jack, doesn't please you, a lot I care," cried Nini. "He will grow a fine lad; he takes after his mother!"

"He will be a Hercules, your little brat ! Here's to his health!"

laughed the Beadle, raising his glass.

A drink all round sealed the reconciliation, while the child slumbered, unawakened.

"Who has read the papers today?" asked Beaumôme.

"I," replied Nini. "Why?"

"Anything new about the Putney affair?"

"What Putney affair?"

"Don't be such an imbecile, Nini! Why that doctor-dentist, who's supposed to have done for his wife! I heard them talking about it yesterday. They say there's going to be a regular dust up about it!"

"What's it to do with you?"

Now the Beadle protested:

"Good Lord! You know well enough, Nini, when there are affairs of that sort, the police always come down on fellows like us. It's not being copped, I'm set on! Two years hard labor! Running round like a squirrel in a cage! Not if I know it!"

Nini turned suspiciously to the Beadle:

"You aren't in this Putney business?"

"No. Neither is Beaumôme. When the police spread their nets there's always the chance of being pinched. That's why Beaumôme asked if you had any news."

Nini, between mouthfuls of gin, said sneeringly: "No need to worry. The police won't get busy in London. It seems the two turtledoves are on the way to Canada."

Beaumôme opened eyes of astonishment:

"How do you know that, Nini?"

"Oh, it was the talk of the neighborhood. I couldn't make head or tail of the story. It seems that Garrick's mistress is persuaded that her little boy has been stolen from her by her husband—an old fellow living in Canada. So away she's trotted to Canada."

"And her lover?"

"They say the doctor's nearly off his head about it, and has gone after her."

Suddenly the negro jumped on the table, and danced a cakewalk to the accompaniment of jingling glass and yells of laughter.

Ishmael appeared:

"Out you go, gentlemen! Closing time! We don't want the police in here!"

Nini hurried off at once. Job, supported by Beaumôme and the Beadle, turned down towards the Docks. The other customers hastened away and were lost in the darkness.

The last to leave were Bob and Ralph. Bob was master of himself. Ralph was as drunk as a lord.

Bob led his companion down a dark alley, tripped him up, slipped him along the pavement, and settled him in a door corner:

"Sleep, my boy!" Bob murmured, and hurried off towards the Bank. He picked up a cab there.

Bob's order to cabby was brief: "Scotland Yard!"

For Bob, none other than detective Shephard, considered he had not wasted his evening.

7. The Arrest

All that morning the White Star liner had gone ahead at top speed, and was well out in mid ocean.

Lunch was in progress on *The Victoria*.

Captain Hill, at the head of his table, looked unusually serious: The passenger on his left, a Mr. Higgins, suddenly laid down his fork, exclaiming: "Hullo, Captain! *The Victoria* is slowing down! Why is that?"

"I cannot tell you."

"Is it a secret, Captain?"

"It is."

"Secret! That's an important word, Captain! Is it a case of machinery broken down?"

"Oh, no. Nothing's wrong with the ship."

Mr. Higgins glanced at his vis-à-vis, a lady on the Captain's right:

"We can be trusted, can we not, Lady Prout? You had better let us into the know, Captain! Besides, how can we betray you in mid-ocean? If it's serious, we might be able to help you!"

Mr. Higgins and Lady Prout gazed expectantly at the Captain.

Glancing circumspectly about him, the Captain said in a low voice:

"It might be wise to take you into my confidence. Not now. After lunch."

Luncheon came to an end. Captain Hill mounted to his bridge with Mr. Higgins and Lady Prout.

"It is an abominable story," said the Captain, "and it will have its denouement on *The Victoria*, in a very short time. I learned it by wireless this morning—from Scotland Yard. There is a murderer and his accomplice on board!"

Exclamations from Lady Prout and Mr. Higgins. "This morning I received a wireless asking if I had a Mr. and Mrs.

Norman on board."

"That tall man and his pretty young wife?" questioned Lady Prout.

"That is the couple. I replied in the affirmative. Scotland Yard replies that they are criminals and must be arrested."

"But they are still at liberty!" protested Lady Prout.

"Scotland Yard's orders were to go at half speed and await the arrival of the Yard's detectives. They are coming on the *Majestic.*"

Captain Hill pointed with his cigar to a couple leaning over the side of *The Victoria:*

"There they are! An unsuspecting pair!"

That evening the *Majestic* got into touch with *The Victoria.*

The wireless crackled.

Captain Hill sent a message to the huge ocean greyhound speeding towards his ship:

"Going half speed. All's well. Normans suspect nothing."

The *Majestic* replied:

"Will join you at noon tomorrow. See that the two individuals do not suspect and commit suicide."

At noon of the following day, the *Majestic* drew alongside *The Victoria* lying-to in mid Atlantic.

Passengers crowded the decks. Intense excitement prevailed.

A boat was lowered from the *Majestic.* A portmanteau followed, then a man. Eight oars rhythmically rose and fell as this cockleshell moved towards the waiting *Victoria.*

The man in the boat was Detective Shephard. He came briskly aboard, and saluted an officer: "Can I speak to Captain Hill at once?"

"Captain Hill awaits you in his cabin, sir."

He passed rapidly by the passengers staring and whispering.

He was nearing the Captain's cabin.

Someone slapped his shoulder.

Shephard turned sharply:

"Good Heavens! Tom Bob! Am I dreaming?" cried the startled detective.

Tom Bob looked as startled:

"You in the flesh, Shephard! What the devil does it mean?"

"Don't you know?"

"Not in the least."

"You are not here for his arrest then?"

"Whose arrest?"

"Why Garrick's."

"What! Garrick's?"

"I say Garrick, Tom Bob. Doctor Garrick!"

Tom Bob recoiled. He had an air of bewilderment:

"You intend to arrest Garrick? But do you know who Garrick is?"

"I know he is one of the passengers, that he calls himself Norman, and is accompanied by his mistress, who poses as his wife."

Tom Bob pulled Shephard aside while the ship's officer marched on ahead.

"Ye gods!" exclaimed Tom Bob. "Am I the sport of a nightmare? Shephard, for the love of Heaven, what is happening? . . . Don't you understand that Garrick—Norman—is? . . ."

"Is who?" gasped Shephard.

"I! Me!"

"You?"

"I, myself!"

Shephard stood dumb. Could he believe his ears? He found tongue at last.

"You, Tom Bob? You, my chief and the most celebrated detective in England! And my friend? You dare to stand there and tell me you are Doctor Garrick? That you are Norman? Oh! I must be going mad! Mad!"

Tom Bob looked distracted. He seized Shephard by the arm:

"We are the victims of something extraordinary, incomprehensible! Shephard, come into my cabin! We must talk this over!"

The two men disappeared in the passageway leading to the first class cabins.

No sooner alone together than Tom Bob began: "Shephard, it is really Garrick, who has fled under the name of Norman, whom you are here to arrest?"

"That is so. And is it really you, Tom Bob, who as Dr. Garrick lived at Putney, and pass as Mr. Norman here?"

"Quite true. Now, Shephard, why do you wish to arrest me?"

"Because, as Doctor Garrick, you are accused of having made away with your wife—of having murdered her . . ."

"Murdered my wife?"

"Yes."

"Why?"

"She has disappeared."

"Don't I know it! But that does not prove I have murdered her!"

"Why have you fled, Tom?"

"Fled? But I haven't fled! I had no idea such an accusation was hanging over me!"

Shephard was plainly puzzled.

"Look here, my friend," said Tom Bob, "I will tell you exactly who I am, so as to clear up matters. Tom Bob, the name you know me by, is my official name. In private life I am Doctor Garrick. I am married. I have a wife who—"

"Yes, Tom, a wife whom you are held to have murdered."

"Not so fast, Shephard! I am married, but I do not love my wife. I have a mistress, Françoise Lemercier, whom I adore. She has come with me. I will call her in here presently."

Shephard was about to speak.

"No! No!" cried Tom Bob. "Listen to me! About a fortnight ago my wife left me. I can tell you the exact date by looking it up in my notebook. I swear my wife left me of her own free will. She was madly jealous of my mistress. Where my wife has gone I do not know. Up to the present I have not taken the trouble to trace her. I don't care if I never set eyes on her again! Besides, four days after my wife's departure I went to see Françoise Lemercier. She was not there. But she had left a letter for me, a terrible letter! Shephard, my mistress was a married woman separated from her husband who lives in Canada. Françoise had a son by him, little Daniel, the prettiest little fellow imaginable. I loved him. Françoise adored him. Well, Shephard, the child had been stolen from her! Stolen by her husband!"

"How did you know that, Tom?"

"Françoise told me in her letter! Told me she was off to Liverpool, and was going to sail for Canada on *The Victoria,* to get her son back!"

"And then?" queried Shephard, his eyes glued to Tom Bob's face.

"Why I went after her post haste. I meant to implore her to stay with me. I wanted her to wait till I could get official leave to go to Canada with her and search for little Daniel. Alas, Shephard! Fate was against me! While arguing with Françoise on *The Victoria,* the steamer sailed. I tried to get ashore by pilot boat! No go! I was forced to go on to Canada by this steamer. And now you are here to arrest me!"

Shephard was speechless. What a terrible blunder he had made! But, had he?

"Good Lord, Tom! Why the deuce did you behave as though you were in flight? Why take the name of Norman?"

"Why, not to give warning to Daniel's abductor! Suppose he kept an eye on the passenger lists of steamers bound for Canada, and saw the name, Doctor Garrick, among the *Victoria* passengers?"

Shephard bent his head in silence.

"The worst of it is, Tom," he said at last, "you know I must do my duty! Actually I hold a warrant for the arrest of Doctor Garrick, accused of having murdered his wife, and—"

Tom Bob nodded acquiescence.

"Yes, Shephard, and even when you know that Doctor Garrick is your colleague, Tom Bob, it is certainly your duty—I don't dispute it. . . ."

Strongly moved Shephard and Tom Bob gripped hands.

"Poor old fellow!" Shephard's lips trembled.

"It's Fate! That such a thing should happen to me, Shephard!"

"Tom, old man, you needn't worry about it! Since your wife is alive we shall easily find her, and you will soon be free!"

"That's sure!" replied Tom Bob. "It's Daniel I am thinking of. Who can look for him as I can?"

"Listen, Tom! I shall have to arrest you, but I need not arrest Françoise Lemercier as your accomplice unless I choose. I shall therefore leave your mistress free to search for her child, while you and I will return to England by the first home sailing vessel we meet."

There was a knock at the cabin door.

Tom Bob opened it on a sailor:

"A message for Mr. Shephard from Captain Hill, sir."

The sailor, brimming with curiosity, stared at the two men. Shephard rose.

"Captain Hill's compliments and he would like to see Mr. Shephard in his cabin at once."

"Come, too, Tom," said Shephard. "The Captain had better know how things stand."

The detectives followed the sailor into Captain Hill's cabin.

Before Shephard could utter a word, the Captain handed him a cablegram. It ran as follows:

> We beg Captain Hill to warn Detective Shephard as soon as he is on board *The Victoria,* that human remains, fragments of flesh and bones belonging either to a woman or a child have been discovered in the course of a perquisition in the cellar of Doctor Garrick's house at Putney. In consequence of this discovery, Detective Shephard is ordered to arrest Doctor Garrick at once, also the mistress of the said doctor, who is thought to be his accomplice in what appears to be the murder of Mrs. Garrick or of her own child Daniel. The arrests must be carried through without fail.

Shephard read this. White to the lips, his voice trembling, he said:

"Tom Bob, I must arrest you both."

Tom Bob replied with stoic calm:

"It is your duty."

8. The Mysterious Stranger

Night was falling.

Round about Bonnières, on the banks of the smooth-flowing Seine, a warm mist had followed a sweltering Spring day.

An old peasant moved slowly, heavily, along the towing path. On his robust shoulders he bore a basket full of vegetables.

Presently he stopped in front of a neat little dwelling. Three stone steps led up to the garden above the level of the high road.

The old peasant knocked his shoes against the lowest step, ridding them of the lumps of clay brought from the fields and orchards. He opened the little wooden gate.

No sooner had he entered the garden than a fresh young voice saluted him joyously.

"Good evening, grandfather!"

"Good evening my little Berthe! I hope you have had a good day! It's not been a good one for me! Few peas to be found! Bad weather!"

"How can you say 'bad weather,' grandfather! It has been a lovely day: sunny, birds singing, a blue sky!"

"Ta! Ta! Young ones like you only think of something to amuse you in the country! I say it's bad weather because the earth is too dry and the peas don't grow!"

The old fellow flung his meager harvest disdainfully on the little square of grass before the house. He bent, and tenderly kissed the fair-haired young woman who had called him "grandfather":

"Really and truly, do you feel better, little girl?"

The young woman's reply was a kiss.

In this neat little house, surrounded by its well-kept garden, lived an excellent old couple, Father Yxier and his wife Catherine. Possessed of a modest competence, a little house, a bit of land, their existence was calm and carefree. Their pretty young granddaughter, Berthe, had been living with them for the past nearly four years. When her parents died, little Berthe was an infant. Father Yxier and Mother Catherine had brought up their grandchild with tenderest care, giving her an education above the average.

Later Berthe had gone to Paris, had followed various callings, coming home at long and longer intervals, as though gradually detaching herself from her grandparents.

On a certain day, nearly four years ago, Berthe had returned. She had been dangerously ill. Father Yxier and Mother Catherine had received her with open arms, had lavished care and affection on their cherished grandchild, and in the peace of the country she had slowly recovered.

A shrill voice called from the house:

"Come in to your soup! Come in to your soup! It's past seven!"

Mother Catherine appeared in the doorway, her face glistening from the heat of the stove. She did not mean to be kept waiting a minute.

Nimbly Berthe rose from the long wicker chair on which she had been resting.

Her grandfather unlaced his dirty boots on the threshold, put on a pair of woolen shoes and passed into the house, crossing the well-waxed floor to the living room.

"I have made a special milk soup for thee, my Berthe," said Mother Catherine, "since thy digestion is not yet strong enough for the stewed meat."

Dinner was over.

Night had descended. All was still.

Father Yxier, Mother Catherine, and Mademoiselle Berthe sat together in peaceable silence.

Out of the silence rose a sound.

Father Yxier was lighting his pipe. He paused: "A motorcar passes," he announced.

Mother Catherine listened.

"Fine weather on the way, that's plain—the route from Paris

to Rouen is in frequent use again—that's the tenth I have heard today."

Berthe smiled:

"All the better, grandmother! More movement in the neighborhood."

"Possible," grumbled Father Yxier, "but that puts dust on the fruit; and the noise those machines make turns my head upside down."

"Listen!" interrupted Berthe.

The noise of a little explosion sounded through the night.

"A tire burst!" declared Mother Catherine.

"Listen!" said Berthe. "I hear steps. Someone is coming along the road. I hear voices!"

The old people listened.

The intense stillness of night enveloped them once more.

Suddenly it was broken by hurried steps scraping on the gravel of the towing path beyond the high road. They came nearer, receded, again approached. Someone was wandering to and fro, lost in the night's obscurity.

Father Yxier rose abruptly.

It seemed to him that the little garden gate was being opened.

Mother Catherine whispered:

"Someone is passing along the side of the wall. I hear the creepers rustling."

Father Yxier stepped to the door, pulled it half open, listened:

"Who goes there?" he called.

Berthe crept up behind him. She started back, repressing a cry.

In the gleam of lamplight projected into the garden, a dark form showed.

The door opened wider.

The outline of a tall slender woman emerged.

A supplicating voice cried:

"Monsieur! Madame! Help me!"

Father Yxier flung wide the door, drawing back to let this late visitor enter.

The unknown woman moved forward like a frightened

fugitive.

She fell into the nearest chair, breathless, gasping, incapable of speech.

Berthe examined the newcomer curiously. She saw a tall fair-haired woman, with bright pale eyes, certainly beautiful. Her beauty shone through the gauze veil that covered her face. An elegant dress could be seen in the opening of the dust cloak half thrown back. She had in her hand a pair of motor goggles.

When she had recovered her breath, the visitor explained:

"I apologize for coming among you in this fashion—I was frightened—I knocked at the first door I came to—I was motoring to Le Havre—to Le Havre where I was to set sail—I am an American—my name is Mrs. . . . I am called Maud—just that! The chauffeur behaved like a madman—he went at an unheard of speed, and just now, when he had raced downhill, a tire burst—we nearly overturned! Oh, it was too much! I was frightened out of my wits! I paid the man and went off. I would not enter that car of his again, not for worlds!"

"Yes, one should not go so fast. It is dangerous," remarked Father Yxier.

Berthe and Mother Catherine stared at the newcomer in silence.

"But I must be putting you out," cried the unknown. "Do forgive me! But, surely, there must be a hotel somewhere near where I could pass the night?"

Mother Catherine laughed:

"An inn, my beautiful lady! Why you won't find one nearer than Bonnières!"

"Is that far?"

"Six or seven miles," replied Father Yxier.

"Good Heavens! I shall never do that on foot! Is there a carriage to be got? A carriage with a horse, I mean! I want no more motorcars!"

Father Yxier shook his head.

"You will not find anything till tomorrow morning. The butcher at Relleboise might have driven you, but his horse had a long journey this afternoon and is too tired."

"What's to become of me?" murmured the stranger. She removed her veil. Her beauty was startling.

Berthe solved the difficulty:

"Stay here, madame! Stay, with us!"

Berthe turned to her grandmother:

"I will give up my room to madame. I shall manage quite well."

The old couple nodded agreement.

The grandfather declared solemnly:

"Madame you are in the home of honest folk, Father and Mother Yxier! We are well known in these parts, believe me! The young one standing is our granddaughter Berthe. They call her Mademoiselle in Paris, for she is a Parisienne!"

The American beauty rose. With a grace and charm which proved her to be a great lady, she went up to her hosts and shook hands with Mother Catherine and Berthe, thanking Father Yxier with a look.

"How kind, how good you are!" she cried. "You cannot imagine the importance of the service you do me! You offer your hospitality so simply, so ungrudgingly, that I say thank you, dear people, with all my heart!"

The arrival of the stranger coincided with the exchange of telegrams between Fandor and Juve.

One must suppose that the hospitality of these country folk in the isolated house on the banks of the Seine suited the American, for a couple of weeks after her intrusion she was still the guest of the Yxier family. She had wished to leave early next morning, but seemed so worn out that Berthe would not let her go.

The Yxiers were not people the American could offer money to, but she accompanied Berthe on her marketing expeditions and ordered additional provisions, which more than covered Mother Catherine's extra outlay.

Berthe and the stranger were instinctively drawn to each other. Berthe would have felt really sorry if this lovely distraction in her dull life had vanished, and the American seemed to have forgotten that she was to embark at Le Havre. She was at times so gay, at other moments so depressed without apparent reason, that Berthe concluded there were mysteries and misfortunes in the life of her "friend Maud."

One afternoon the two were walking by the Seine. The American asked:

"What caused your long illness?"

Berthe blushed, did not at once reply, but leaned affectionately on her friend's arm:

"I wanted to die," she murmured. "I poisoned myself."

The stranger trembled, sighed deeply. She questioned Berthe further.

Berthe gave details:

"A long time ago I started as attendant-nurse in a private asylum in Paris—"

"You were with mad people?" interrupted Maud.

"Well, I had been in a hospital or two first. It was in this asylum I came across a certain woman, a patient, who was the involuntary cause of the dramas which clouded my early years. . . ."

"What was her name?" asked the American.

"It doesn't matter—it can have no interest for you—except that I feel sure she is the mother of a journalist who was mixed up in all sorts of complicated and queer affairs—a journalist known under the name of Jerome Fandor!"

The American was now intensely interested in her young friend's revelations.

"Tell me! Tell me, what were your relations with this young journalist?"

"I had none, Maud—or at least—but it's the most abominable thing that has happened in my life, and I can't bear to think of it!" Berthe shuddered.

"There are names, facts, the mere remembrance of which freezes me with horror, tortures me with remorse. . . ."

Berthe turned to the great lady she called friend. "Madame, I cannot hide it from you, for I respect and love you—the girl before you, led away by bad examples has committed what amounts to crime—a man died through my fault! It was four years ago. He was an officer with a promising future, a Captain Brocq. I was his mistress."

The American had grown white as a sheet.

"Berthe," she murmured, "Berthe, are you not she who was once called Bobinette?"

The girl was shaking, her lips trembled. Yes, it was Bobinette, now repentant, but wretched at the idea that her past, which she believed unknown, should be so familiar to others. She thought aloud. She thought of the Baron de Naarboveck, really the bandit Fantômas, who hid his odious personality under a respectable name: she thought of the amiable Therese Auvernois whose paid companion she had been, her comrade, her intimate friend.

The American interrupted these recollections. When Berthe mentioned the name of Therese Auvernois, the stranger added mechanically:

"Therese Auvernois, the wife of Lieutenant Henri de Loubersac."

Berthe stopped short. She asked herself suspiciously:

"Who is this woman I am confiding in? How is it she knows about these dramas in which I was involved?"

An idea flashed through Berthe's disturbed mind. She knew that a mysterious woman, seductive and sinister, was mixed up in the doings of the elusive Fantômas, that she appeared now as the bandit's determined adversary, now as his devoted collaborator. This woman had again and again presented herself to the imagination of Bobinette as the philanthropic Lady Beltham, a great lady employing her immense fortune in aiding every good work.

Such was the portrait presented by Therese Auvernois, and many a time had Berthe gone with Therese to pray at Lady Beltham's magnificent tomb in the cemetery of Montmartre. It was believed that this philanthropic lady had been assassinated by Fantômas, and Berthe had seen no reason to discredit the report.

Then had come the disastrous events which had led to Berthe's attempted suicide in order to escape the rigors of the law.

A man had intervened to doubly save her. He had prevented her death and proved her innocence.

This man was Juve.

Juve, whose existence was consecrated to the pursuit of the abominable bandit, the elusive Fantômas. Through Juve, Berthe had learned that Lady Beltham was not the saint she had thought her: that she was not dead, but still living.

While Berthe was recalling all this, the American appeared to grow more and more agitated. She stammered question on question about places and people known to the former hospital nurse.

The two women paused in the shade of some trees. Silently they looked into each other's eyes.

Berthe uttered a cry. A veil had fallen from before her mental vision. In this beautiful great lady, so stately, so charmingly gracious, with her golden hair and blue eyes, Berthe recognized from descriptions often repeated, the mysterious associate of Fantômas. Her name was on Berthe's lips.

The beautiful stranger did not give Berthe time to speak. Placing her hands affectionately on the girl's shoulders she confessed in her melodious voice:

"Yes, I am Lady Beltham!"

Berthe was struck dumb, motionless.

Certainly it was Lady Beltham. She was in the presence of the woman who had been, was perhaps still, the mistress of Fantômas!

Was this a saint or a monster standing before her? A criminal or a victim?

Instinctively Berthe inclined to a lenient judgment. Lady Beltham perceived the struggle. She pleaded in a tearful voice:

"Berthe! Berthe! Do not condemn me unheard! Do not try to understand what I cannot understand myself! We are all here on earth nothing but poor bits of wreckage floating hither and thither at the mercy of unsurmountable waves—the waves of

Destiny! Do not cast a stone without having heard the sinner's confession—do not pronounce judgment . . ."

Berthe threw herself into Lady Beltham's arms. She wept gently on the shoulder of the seductive great lady. The poor girl was overcome by recollections of her past.

Suddenly Lady Beltham withdrew her support, and ran to the edge of the little wood:

"Berthe!" she cried.

"What is it?"

Lady Beltham pointed to two individuals in the distance:

"Those two men on the road! Who are they?"

Ordinarily Berthe would have paid no attention to these passersby, but today she was nervous. She watched them, trembling:

"I do not know them! They seem strangers," she muttered.

The two men were now hidden by a rise in the ground. Apparently reassured, Lady Beltham seated herself on a mossy mound. Berthe sat down beside her. The two women exchanged some bitter reflections on life.

"Ah," cried Lady Beltham, "let us leave the odious past behind us—if only it could be annihilated! If one could simply start life again on other lines!"

"Madame," questioned Berthe in gentle tones, "who will you be after this? How am I to address you?"

Lady Beltham raised her eyes sadly:

"I am the wife of a man I abhor, who deceives me, a man I have fled from, am still flying from."

"Stay here, madame! Stay with us. Share our tranquil country life. I like you so much. You do not dislike me. Let us be good friends!"

Lady Beltham bent towards Berthe, gazing affectionately at her. Abruptly she sat bolt upright.

"Those men again! I am afraid!"

But Berthe, who had risen to her feet, could not catch a glimpse of them. Either Lady Beltham was deceived, or the men had concealed themselves.

"Let us go into the house, my dear girl! I am anxious!" cried

Lady Beltham, greatly agitated.

The two young women rapidly regained the shelter of the Yxiers' house.

That honest couple were far from suspecting the identity of their guest, just as they were completely ignorant of the dramas which had convulsed their granddaughter's existence.

As the two young women were hurrying to the house, Lady Beltham said to the girl clinging to her arm:

"Perhaps you have recently heard of a mysterious crime everyone in England is talking about? It relates to an English doctor-dentist, a Doctor Garrick, whose wife has suddenly disappeared. They accuse this man, who has a mistress, of having made away with his wife. He denies it, but his wife cannot be found."

"I read about it in the papers," said Berthe. Lady Beltham's glance was enigmatic.

"Perhaps you know something about this crime drama, madame?" ventured Berthe.

"Perhaps," murmured Lady Beltham.

"This wife of Doctor Garrick," continued the girl, "supposing she were—?"

"Well?"

Lady Beltham pulled her companion violently forward, crying:

"Quick! Those men again! Good Heavens! What have they got against me?"

9. The Innocence of Françoise

Lord Duncan was being driven through the streets of London in his magnificent motorcar.

It was a foggy morning, but his lordship was indifferent to the weather: his mind was centered on his private affairs.

The chauffeur drew up outside one of the gates of Hyde Park.

It was Wednesday, the day fixed by Lord Duncan for his appointment with Nini Guinon, when she was to bring their baby son for him to see.

Would this dreadful wife of his play him false again? No. There she was seated on a bench!

She was quietly dressed, and looked respectable. He paused to gaze at her, stifling a deep sigh. If only she were honest! If only Nini Guinon had remained pure he might have loved her, and lived happily with her in retirement until she had fitted herself to take her place beside him in the great world which was his own!

So thought this duped husband.

He was roused from his bitter reflections by the sight of a pretty boy, who had been hiding behind Nini Guinon's skirt.

"Assuredly my little Jack," concluded Lord Duncan, hastening his steps.

Nini perceived him and rose. Her flushed beauty and big bright eyes shining through long lashes, her modest manner, appealed afresh to her husband. Her charm was incontestable, he felt.

He smiled. A truce to reproaches and vulgar quarrels!

Nini pushed the boy towards him:

"Little Jack," she said.

Greatly moved, Lord Duncan stood speechless. His glance went from mother to child searching for a common resemblance. He stooped, lifted little Jack and held him tenderly in his arms:

"Jack, my little Jack!" he whispered.

The child stared at this unknown man with questioning eyes. He did not smile.

Lord Duncan put him down.

The little creature murmured plaintively:

"Mama! I want my mama!"

Nini caught the boy's hand:

"Be good," she said.

The three moved on together.

Nini Guinon played the humble hypocrite. Her voice was cajoling:

"You see I have obeyed you! But don't try to take my child from me! You will always get on better with me when you drop threats and treat me kindly."

"Ah, Nini, if only you had wished to be different, if—"

Frowning, Nini interrupted:

"There is nothing to be done. We are not suited to each other! All I ask of you is to leave me alone, and not take my child from me! I want peace!"

Lord Duncan did not answer. He might say too much. Ought he not to take his son, and at all costs, remove him from the sinister surroundings in which his wretched mother was bringing him up? Was not this a father's clear duty? He must think it well over, and come to a decision soon.

He said goodbye abruptly, and turned on his heel.

He was horrified at himself! This meeting with his son had left him cold, quite cold. What about the so much vaunted blood-tie which rouses a vibrating emotion between father and son? He had not experienced one thrill of it! While Lord Duncan was walking away in the direction of the Park Gate, Nini Guinon was staring furiously after her husband. Her smile was hideous, menacing:

"The mug! To think he hasn't forked out a farthing, not even to get clothes to cover the boy's back with!"

Grumbling, the bad-hearted Nini set off, dragging the child with her.

She saw a group of musicians playing on open ground near the Marble Arch. With all the curiosity of the true Parisian lounger, she stopped to see and hear.

The brass band blared, cymbals clashed, men and women in a strange garb sang at the top of their voices. It was the Salvation Army.

Nini recognized the uniform:

"That's the style! Here's a spree!" cried the Parisienne of the gutter.

She slipped with little Jack into the front row. One of the Salvation lassies offered Nini a paper. She refused it, fearing she might have to pay for it. The Salvationist caught sight of little Jack and bent quickly towards him, staring at him intently, persistently.

Nini, always on the look out for a possible meeting with the real mother of the stolen boy, became alarmed.

Then she felt sick with fright, for she heard the distributor of tracts murmur:

"Daniel!"

A movement of the crowd separated Nini from the Salvationist. She made off as fast as she could go. Catching little Daniel in her arms, she hailed a passing cab, jumped in, quickly giving the driver her address, and bidding him get a move on:

"That was a near shave! Oh how scared I was!" exclaimed Nini. "No more Salvation Army meetings for me!"

"Why it is the Coroner! Can I speak to you, sir? It is urgent!"

The personage thus addressed turned round sharply to find himself faced by a Salvation Army lassie who, with lowered eyes, was awaiting his reply.

He glared at the Salvationist.

In a calm firm voice she repeated:

"I must speak to you, sir."

The Coroner had recognized her:

"Mrs. Davis! And in this getup?"

"All costumes are suitable where detectives are concerned, sir. There is something I must tell you at once. In this crowd, a second or two ago, I saw—"

"Mrs. Davis," interrupted the irate Coroner, "the Park is not a proper place in which to make reports!"

"Time presses, sir. The child may escape me—the crowd is increasing!"

"What are you talking about?" interrupted the Coroner.

The Salvationist made a movement of vexation:

"It's too late!"

She pointed to the cab into which Nini Guinon was pushing with a little boy.

The Coroner, much on his dignity, paid no attention to the Salvationist's annoyed exclamation:

"If you must speak to me, you will find me at home after two o'clock this afternoon."

Mrs. Davis had scarcely heard these words. She was forcing her way through the crowd, making a desperate attempt to catch up the cab. It was in vain! She could not even read its number.

Mr. Tipling, magistrate and coroner, lived near Paddington Station. In his comfortable study he was smoking a cigar and expecting Mrs. Davis.

At two o'clock Mrs. Davis appeared before Mr. Tipling. A widow of forty, she had risen high in the detective service.

Knowing that time was money, she spoke to the point at once:

"Mr. Tipling, you know all about the Garrick-Lemercier affair, do you not?"

"I do. I have charge of it for the time being."

"Garrick is accused of having murdered his wife, is he not? And Françoise Lemercier is accused of murdering her son, little Daniel?"

"That is so."

"Françoise Lemercier is innocent."

"I hope you can prove your statement?"

"I can."

Mrs. Davis took a photograph from her handbag, and placed

it before the magistrate:

"Here is a portrait of Françoise Lemercier's child, little Daniel. This photograph was taken in the Sigissimons studios three days after the departure of Françoise Lemercier, and when she was on board *The Victoria*. The date on the copies of the photograph shows that."

"It is an important point for the defense," agreed the magistrate.

"I have a still more important statement to make, sir. I have seen the child alive!"

Mr. Tipling sat up:

"You have seen him? When was that?"

"This very morning."

"Where?"

"In Hyde Park, sir."

"You don't say so! Why, in Heaven's name did you not tell me that at once?"

"You refused to hear me, sir."

The magistrate was walking up and down the room excitedly:

"Refused to hear you? Well, it's no use going into that! We must trace this child without further delay. Do you know where he is likely to be found?"

Mrs. Davis shook her head:

"I shall soon. It is a question of days, perhaps hours. Anyhow the innocence of Françoise Lemercier is proved, I consider."

"My opinion also. It merely confirms my previous judgment. I shall soon set her at liberty—poor woman!"

"Mr. Tipling?"

"What is it?"

"When will you set at liberty another innocent? Our friend, our colleague, the detective, Tom Bob?"

The magistrate frowned:

"I do not understand you."

"Mr. Tipling, you know very well that Garrick and Tom Bob are one and the same—and that it is impossible to believe Tom Bob culpable!"

The magistrate looked grave. He did not reply at once. Then

he made his declaration with solemn emphasis:

"I am very far from thinking as you do. My opinion is entirely opposed to yours. Garrick, the doctor-dentist, is explicitly charged with the murder of his wife, and unless he can prove his innocence he will be kept in prison for the present to await further proceedings. I believe with you that Garrick and Tom Bob are one and the same, but Tom Bob or Garrick impresses me as being an audacious bandit, and I suppose him quite capable of taking advantage of his position and reputation as a detective to cast doubts on his guilt as a private individual. There have been criminal policemen, there will be such again."

Mrs. Davis shrugged her shoulders. Her look was contemptuous:

"Possibly, sir, but not as far as concerns Tom Bob! Imagine it! Our best, most trusted detective?"

"Mrs. Davis," objected the magistrate, "you know very well that one must be prepared for anything. Enjoying the privileges they do, it is open to Tom Bob or any other detective, to commit criminal actions for a long time without being even suspected by those in closest contact with them. They are not accountable to anyone up to a point, consequently . . ."

"Mr. Tipling, I assure you Garrick-Tom Bob is innocent—of your grace set him free!"

"Mrs. Davis, I maintain that Garrick-Tom Bob is guilty, and until I obtain indisputable proof to the contrary, I shall continue to maintain that Garrick-Tom Bob is the murderer of his wife!

"Mrs. Davis, I wish you good day."

10. The Supreme Council

"You might as well ask Nelson's column to hop from Trafalgar Square and dump itself down on the Tower of London as make this lock, and them bolts, shine, covered with rust as they are— regularly eaten in! What can you expect with this everlasting rain and fog? It's the devil of a climate!"

So grumbled Teddy, an Old Bailey warder, on this foggy drizzling May morning.

Silence reigned in this inner court of the famous prison.

Teddy sighed, relit his pipe, and resumed his polishing attempts.

A low heavy door, set in the wall, opened, and a small group of people passed through. Teddy counted three, two men and a woman: Mrs. Davis, Inspectors Shephard and French.

Teddy went to meet them:

"Why, Mr. Shephard, sir, how are you?"

Shephard shook hands with the old warder and gave him a paper containing the following order:

> Let the accused Garrick communicate with Detective Shephard and the two persons accompanying him. The conversation will take place in the parlor without witnesses. Two warders will guard the door outside.

Teddy saw the signature of Tipling, the magistrate, considered the document, looked at the three newcomers:

"The usual procedure in such cases will be followed, Mr. Shephard. I hope you will not have long to wait."

Shephard nodded and smiled.

He and his companions were ushered into a large bare room, the high windows strongly barred. There were four chairs in it.

Minutes passed in expectant silence.

The door opened. A man entered briskly, bright-eyed and smiling. He extended both hands to welcome his visitors.

The door closed.

The three were alone with Garrick-Tom Bob. They did not realize that they were also alone with Fantômas!

Garrick-Tom Bob's first words were:

"And Françoise Lemercier?"

"Released," replied Shephard.

Tom Bob uttered a sigh of relief.

Shephard explained the situation.

His mind easy about his mistress, Tom Bob asked anxiously about Daniel. He questioned Mrs. Davis:

"Have you some clue, my dear friend? Do you expect to recover the child soon?"

He added, with tears in his eyes:

"I would bear without a murmur the most monstrous accusations if I knew little Daniel had been restored to his poor mother, who adores him more than anyone in the world—more, alas, than even me!"

His hearers, accustomed as they were to human misery, were affected in spite of themselves.

Mrs. Davis swore to Tom Bob to do the impossible to recover the child, and Detective French promised to devote himself wholly to the search for Daniel. Shephard brusquely changed the subject. Putting his hand affectionately on the prisoner's shoulder, who seemed overwhelmed by paternal grief:

"Tom Bob," he said, "we must save you. We mean to!"

Tom Bob looked gratefully at his colleague, who continued:

"There is only one way of doing it, my dear Tom Bob—we must find your wife! Even if we have to go to the North Pole we must find her."

Tom Bob nodded acquiescence. He was reflecting. Presently he spoke:

"My dear friends, Mrs. Garrick will be more difficult to find than you think, and for the good reason that she has gone away with the intention of making people believe I am the author of her disappearance."

"Why?" demanded Detective French.

"You are indeed young," replied Tom Bob, looking at the Irishman. "So much the better for you. But your question shows me that I must explain our private life as husband and wife. Mrs. Garrick was jealous, very jealous of me. If she did not know, and does not know now that I am a detective, she did know I had a mistress, an adored mistress. Again and again Mrs. Garrick has tried to get me to herself and force me to break with Françoise Lemercier. Poor woman! I don't blame her for that! But you cannot force love. I no longer loved Mrs. Garrick, but I loved, and still love, Françoise passionately. To Mrs. Garrick's entreaties I always replied by contempt, by disdain, I admit it. Mrs. Garrick suffered when living with me. I recognize that. She swore to avenge herself. She is doing it, and with consummate adroitness, since, by the mere fact of her disappearance, she has succeeded in getting put in prison, under the accusation of having murdered her, the one man she should have been unable to trick—the detective, Tom Bob."

"Exactly so," agreed Shephard. "Mrs. Garrick is no clumsy plotter!"

"Women have an imagination to be reckoned with when their passions are involved," said Mrs. Davis.

"Alas, it is true," murmured Tom Bob.

As to Detective French, the young Irishman, he listened to the remarks of his colleagues in silence. But, though he pitied Mrs. Garrick for having been forsaken by a husband she loved, his sense of right revolted at the idea that a wife, betrayed though she were, should deliberately put a husband in such a terrible situation as that Tom Bob now found himself in. All felt it was time to take steps to clear, and obtain the release of Tom Bob. More than three weeks had passed. Mrs. Garrick had had time to go far, and conceal herself, perhaps in some chosen hiding place. She must have read of her husband's arrest in the papers. If she regretted her action, deplored the punishment threatening her husband, she had only to show herself, or write, and the terrible accusation would fall to the ground. Her silence, her non-appearance, must mean that she did not intend to save her husband:

"We shall find her! We must find her!" muttered French.

Tom Bob spoke:

"In my opinion there is but one thing to do. We detectives here, the English detectives in general, are capable enough; but for such a case as this we require more than capability—we need a detective genius—that genius is a Frenchman, Inspector Juve of La Sûreté, Paris. He, and he only, can solve the problem."

"Juve!" cried Shephard. "Is your opinion of him as high as that?"

"Yes," said Tom Bob.

"Juve! Why he has one obsession, the pursuit of Fantômas!" exclaimed the young Irishman.

A smile, bitter, enigmatic, curved the lips of Tom Bob:

"It is just that, French. What you say is true."

"But how can Juve know where to find Mrs. Garrick? What connecting link can there be between your wife and Juve?" queried Shephard.

Tom Bob smiled:

"Why, my good Shephard, we have to ask Juve to establish this link in order to find my wife!"

"That's true," replied Shephard. "Listen, Tom, my friend! About a fortnight ago—a day or so more—just when you had gone after Françoise Lemercier, I happened to be in a low drinking saloon near the Docks, where I was keeping an eye on a bunch of Frenchies of bad reputation. It was there I heard of the flight of your mistress aboard *The Victoria*. Among the bunch was an individual the Paris police had warned us was a hooligan of the worst sort. He answers to the name of 'Beadle.' Well, that very evening I caught sight of a person on the track of the Beadle—keeping a close watch on him. I could not identify the trailer. But one of my subordinates has since told me it was Juve!"

"Juve?" cried Tom Bob, surprised. "Truly, Shephard, you have seen Juve in London quite recently?"

"I am convinced of it."

Tom Bob sat silent, absorbed in reflections.

Shephard explained to French that he would have to leave for France that same evening, with orders to join Juve, and obtain from him all possible information and help.

This suited the impetuous young Irishman. He would help right to triumph by proving the truth, and so save a colleague, a friend, a master!

His face shone with enthusiasm:

"Shephard! I swear to you that, with God's help, I will find Mrs. Garrick, and willy-nilly, she shall appear before the judge to proclaim the innocence of our friend!"

"May Heaven hear you!" murmured Tom Bob with a slight smile at this ardent Benjamin among the detectives.

Mrs. Davis took the word:

"Are you not struck, dear colleagues, by the mysterious link which seems to connect this affair with other affairs, that at first sight seem to be in no way related?

"There, is Doctor Garrick, accused of causing his wife's disappearance, and behold in the cellars of Garrick's house human remains are found, which at first makes one think the accusation well founded. Then there is Françoise Lemercier, who complains that her child has been stolen from her. Here, again, it looks as though she had murdered her child, whose disappearance she pretends to deplore. The discovery that little Daniel lives proves her sincerity and clears her. That is not all!

"Among the light-fingered gentry of London, we have business with a woman known as Nini Guinon, who, suspected of causing the disappearance of her child, declares her innocence, and produces her child for all to see! She even exhibits it ostentatiously, I hear. And that is not all! Coincident with the departure of Mrs. Garrick, we learn that Inspector Juve of Paris is in London, and that the said Inspector Juve appears to be extremely interested in the activities of an individual known as the Beadle, who frequents the band of swindlers, and worse, whose ornament is this girl, Nini Guinon, who is continually escorted by her lover, or would-be lover, the vile creature called Beaumôme.

"Here is a series of facts curiously resembling one another.

There may be some secret link whereby they are interconnected and hang together."

"What conclusion do you draw from this?" questioned Tom Bob, who had grown pale. He had been listening with close attention to the exposition of Mrs. Davis.

"Dear friend, I have the impression that we are spectators arriving at the theater at the close of the first act of a comedy—rather, let us say, a drama. These spectators see on the stage certain personages, they witness certain facts, hear certain words, and understand part of the situation. But all this does not suffice to make the plot clear to them. It is only in the second act, when familiarized with the characters, that they can, by reasoning, logic, induction, reconstitute in their minds what must have occurred before their arrival."

"I think you are right," said Shephard. "We have reached the end of the first act. Let us be careful not to miss the opening of the second!"

Tom Bob looked himself again. Smiling, he said:

"And above all let us be careful to see that, in the third act, the truth is made manifest, that vice is punished and virtue rewarded!"

The detectives rose, and shook Tom Bob warmly by the hand:

"Yes," declared Shephard, "we swear, Tom Bob, that you shall make a triumphant exit from this prison."

"I shall find Mrs. Garrick!" cried French.

"And I," declared Mrs. Davis, "shall know peace only when little Daniel is restored to the arms of his mother!"

A few minutes later the three detectives had quitted the Old Bailey. Tom Bob had returned to his cell, and old Teddy, the warder, continued his rust-moving task.

11. An Examination at Scotland Yard

Juve was cogitating in his flat, rue Bonaparte, his home for many years.

Although but three o'clock in the afternoon, he had tightly closed the shutters of his windows, drawn down the blinds, making complete night.

Having protected himself as far as he could from outside distractions, Juve arranged an atmosphere within favorable to reverie.

He lit his lamp, put a thick shade on it, and stood it on the floor, in a corner of his office.

In his study there now reigned a vague peaceful glimmer, which permitted him to leisurely follow the bluish rings of his cigarette, while resting on his divan, his hands behind his head.

He was absorbed in reflections, anxious, questioning, disagreeable.

Said Juve to himself:

"Either he is off his head, or something has happened to him! Over a fortnight and not a word from him! . . . He told me he was writing, but no letter has come!"

Juve jumped up, crossed the room, and struck a gong hanging on the wall.

The door opened. His old faithful servant, Jean, entered:

"You called me, sir?"

"Jean, were there no letters for me this morning?"

"You know there were none, sir! This is the tenth time this morning you have asked me that."

"And this morning, you are quite certain you faithfully sent off the fresh telegram I gave you for London?"

"Yes, sir. You have also asked me that several times."

"Jean, that telegram was for Fandor, and I have not had an answer!"

The old servant, well accustomed to his master's ways, merely nodded gravely. But as Juve seemed once more absorbed in his reflections, Jean asked presently:

"Do you wish me, sir, to go?"

"To the devil, Jean to the devil!"

This was Juve's usual way of signifying that he did not need his old servant's services for the moment.

If Juve felt a cordial sympathy for Jean, Jean was devoted to his master.

"Very good, sir! But the lamp is smoking!"

Juve did not protest. The lamp was not smoking, but Jean could not bear to see the extraordinary way in which his master was passing the afternoon.

To light a lamp in broad daylight! Why it was wicked! As Juve made no remark, Jean calmly drew back the curtains, pulled up the blinds, threw back the shutters, blew out the lamp. Having thus reduced things to a sane everyday appearance he was preparing to leave his beloved master to his reflections. His master recalled him:

"Jean! Don't go to the devil!"

"Very good, sir!"

"Pack my valise!"

"Which, sir!"

"Number 6."

"Number 6! Then you will be away some time, sir?"

"I am going in search of work. Be quick now! I must be ready in an hour."

Vexed, old Jean silently withdrew. When his master asked for valise number 6, it meant to cram into the compartments of a specially made portmanteau, wigs, false beards, grease-paints, stains, dyes, a medley of costumes, an assortment of complete disguises used by Juve when pursuing secret investigations. He would so make himself up as to deceive the most trained inquisitive eye: he was a past-master. While old Jean was packing at top speed, Juve also was busy. He had watched with a smile his servant's doings in the now day-lit room:

"The old fellow forces me to a decision. I cannot remain any

longer in this uncertainty! Besides, the little one needs me, I'll
swear. Dear Fandor!"

He could not forget Fandor's last telegram for a minute:

> Have found Fantômas in Tom Bob. Fantômas is in London.
> Letter follows.
>
>   FANDOR.

Had Juve been free at the moment of its arrival he would
have packed forthwith and rushed to London.

Fandor's silence tortured Juve with anxiety. He must act.

"Suppose Fantômas has recognized Fandor?" asked Juve. "In
that case the lad is in danger and may need me! I am off to
London, tomorrow."

Juve was not a good sailor. He preferred dry land.

Nevertheless, as the *Dieppe* was steaming for the English
coast at record speed, Juve gaily walked the deck, smoking his
eternal cigarette. He was in excellent humor. Was he not free
to act as he would? Before leaving he had had a satisfactory
interview with Monsieur Havard, head of La Sûreté.

"What could have happened to Fandor?" he was thinking,
as he continued his monotonous promenade. "Fandor is in
London—but so is Fantômas! One day I shall catch that bandit.
I have sworn it!"

At the moment when he learned that the sinister figure of
Fantômas was once more looming on the horizon, that the
struggle was about to recommence, with its dangers, its risks,
he congratulated himself on having again to endanger his life
for a cause dear to him, the cause of Duty, the cause of Good.

"You have all handed in your papers? Yes? Your birth certificates? Your references? Very well. Now for the gymnasium.
Come this way!"

The speaker was Mr. Chapman, of Scotland Yard, about to
put through their paces four candidates for positions in the
London police force.

They descended to a large underground room furnished

with parallel bars, ladders, springboards, a trench filled with cork shavings, and targets against the far wall.

"The gymnasium, gentlemen." Mr. Chapman waved an official hand. "You know, do you not, why I distributed handcuffs just now? You are asked to slip them on one another at the word of command. That word will be given unexpectedly. Now the revolver test! Pass in turn before the target. You first! You are a Belgian?"

One of the candidates advanced:

"Yes, sir, that is, you know! . . ."

The man marched to the firing line, and discharged the six bullets of his revolver. He made two bullseyes, three inners, one miss.

"Not so bad," approved Mr. Chapman.

He handed a revolver to the second candidate:

"You are French, my man?"

"Yes, sir."

"Fire away!"

The aspirant walked up to the target. He turned the cardboard target back to front, so hiding the iron central disk.

"I cover the bullseye," he said, returning to the firing station. Then, hardly taking time to aim, he fired six times into the exact center of the target, making but one hole. There was a burst of applause.

"Bravo!" cried Mr. Chapman, himself a first-rate shot. "Now I understand the encomiums of your former chiefs, my friend. Can you repeat this legerdemain?"

"I will repeat it, sir."

"Do so, for curiosity's sake."

The candidate took from Mr. Chapman's hands a second revolver. There was a sharp click, but no discharge.

"Why, what's the matter?" exclaimed Mr. Chapman.

The candidate smiled:

"Excuse me, sir," he said quietly, opening his left hand, in which shone six bullets, "I amused myself uncharging this revolver whilst you handed it to me, just to prove to you my manual dexterity."

"What! You uncharged without my having time to perceive it?"

"It seems so!"

One of Mr. Chapman's colleagues shouted:

"Handcuffs!"

Before Mr. Chapman had time to speak, the French candidate went up to him, seized his right hand, and slipped a handcuff over it, while he imprisoned in two other manacles the hands of two other members of the jury of examiners.

"Forgive me, gentlemen?" cried the candidate, "but I carried handcuffs with me, and I wanted to show you how quickly I could use them effectively."

No protest came from the handcuffed jury.

"You are extraordinary!" began Mr. Chapman.

"Marvelous!" cried a colleague.

"Stupefying!" cried another.

The candidate unhandcuffed the three in a twinkling:

"It is occasionally useful to act rapidly," he modestly observed.

"And, gentlemen, if as a policeman I can claim to know my business, I admit that as far as gymnastics and fireman's routine are concerned, I must crave your indulgence. I have never had occasion to—"

"It suffices," interrupted Mr. Chapman. "Do not trouble yourself about that! You have won your admission."

Mr. Chapman rummaged in his portfolio, and while his two colleagues continued testing the other candidates, he turned to the unknown:

"You have proved your powers brilliantly. Your certificates give your name as Durand. As you know we cannot permit you to take service under your own name. Choose a pseudonym. I see you ask to be exclusively employed in London: you are no doubt married?"

"No, sir."

"You have a special reason for wishing to remain in London?"

"Yes, sir."

"Very well. To what part of London do you wish to be

drafted?"

Durand hesitated:

"I should like to join the movable brigade, sir."

"You know the police of that division often have a bad time of it? Get nasty knocks?"

"I am not afraid of them!"

"This is a difficult service?"

"I care little for that!"

"That the pay is not high?"

"It leaves me indifferent."

"You puzzle me," declared Mr. Chapman. "Highly recommended, of proven ability, and you ask for such a position! What's your ambition?"

"I desire, sir, to be incorporated in the moving brigade because I think I have a better chance of distinguishing myself there. If I could attract the attention of one of my superiors— Tom Bob for instance."

Mr. Chapman cut Durand short:

"Tom Bob has other things to do, my dear fellow, than to bother about policemen. But you will advance rapidly. According to custom your service will commence this day week."

On the very day Durand was accepted as a member of the London police force, Juve crossed to France in the *Sussex*.

Juve was in a bad temper.

"It amounts to very little," he grumbled. "True, I have run Nini Guinon to earth, seen the mystery-child, little Jack, found in Lord Duncan our old friend Ascott—all things Fantômas has no doubt discovered. Now I am tracking that corrupt blackguard the Beadle, returning to France, I don't know why—some fresh villainy one can be sure. Yet my investigations have failed. Tom Bob? Yes, I have ascertained that he is highly placed on the Scotland Yard staff—but I have not been able to see him. . . . It looks as though the Yard had agreed to keep him hidden! Why? Has he fled from me? And then Fandor? What, oh what has become of Fandor? Fandor has disappeared. At his rooms they told me he had left without paying his rent! Good Heavens!

What has happened to my dear lad?"

Juve's chief idea in trailing the Beadle was that he might gain information that would lead him to Fandor, and so relieve his torturing anxiety.

12. Detective and Policeman

Had those on the *Sussex* not been suffering from the rough crossing, they might have noticed that a passenger landed at Dieppe who had not embarked at Newhaven.

A stout young man, with a thick black mustache, clad in a long blue blouse, and having the air of a holiday-making butcher, disembarked at Dieppe. He was really a slim, clean-shaven young man, none other than Detective French.

He made for the tidal train drawn up alongside the pier, and seated himself in a second class compartment.

He had much to think over. How was he going to save Tom Bob, the highly placed colleague to whom he owed gratitude for past kindness? Mrs. Garrick must be found without delay. In a final interview Tom Bob had said:

"Find Juve. He knows me slightly. Tell him Tom Bob sends you. Impress on him that Lady Garrick is really Tom Bob's wife. Juve will then do all in his power to aid you to join my wife."

"But Tom Bob has not been able to tell me where I can find Juve," thought French. "I shall not find him at Police Headquarters. He will be pursuing his eternal quest—Fantômas. Fantômas, the monstrous genius of crime in whose existence skeptics do not believe."

French had learned at Scotland Yard that the Paris hooligan, the Beadle, had returned to France from his London visit. Scotland Yard had notified Paris Police Headquarters of the Beadle's return. Granting that the Beadle had been one of the Fantômas band, Juve might be on his track.

The conclusion French came to was:

"I have three persons to trail: the Beadle, who may lead me to Juve; Juve, who will conduct me to Lady Garrick; Lady Garrick shall do her part, I will see to that!"

When the express drew into Saint-Lazare station, French

meant to start his search for the Beadle forthwith.

The Irish detective knew that individuals like the Beadle pass half their life in low class wineshops and taverns, of which there are many in the suspect quarters of Paris.

French knew the Beadle had made the La Chapelle quarter too hot for himself, and that the police were on the alert to nab him should he show his nose there at present. No, the Beadle would not go there yet. He would not go near Les Halles either, for the same set of police supervised that neighborhood also. French fixed on the Vangirard quarter.

As his detective name indicated, French had lived much in France and spoke the language like a native. Lost in the crowd of travelers he left the Saint-Lazare station by the rue Amsterdam. Depositing his limited luggage in the cloakroom, he strolled along, hands in pockets, till he came to a little wine shop.

He ordered a simple dinner. It was quickly eaten. Now for the chase!

"It is just half-past nine," said French to himself, "no use visiting haunts of the underworld till after eleven o'clock. I have time to call at Juve's flat, rue Bonaparte, though the only use that will be is to satisfy my conscience.

When French asked for Monsieur Juve, the concierge laughed in his face:

Monsieur Juve was traveling, had been absent nearly five months said she. He had sent no news of himself, and his rent was paid in advance.

French did not think this absence and lack of news mattered in the least:

"Now for Vangirard!" he cried.

Those not in the know might pass a certain entry without suspecting that it led to a much frequented drinking saloon.

French was faced by a low door, half concealed by a projecting house. No signboard hung above this thick panel of wood covered with inscriptions and devices in picturesque disorder cut with a pen-knife: names, emblems, hearts transpierced with an arrow, swallows, outlines of pen-knives, clasp-knives, big knives.

This door opened on a short passage cut, some two yards down, by worn steps, slimy and green with moss. At the foot of the steps, French again was faced by a massive door, more solid than the first.

He had to grope for the iron latch-bar.

This was the entrance to the big saloon of the *Cutthroats' Tavern.*

It was not much used by the butchers employed in the municipal slaughter houses. Rather it served as a club for the numerous hooligans infesting the neighborhood, who were seldom disturbed by police raids.

Many tables were scattered about the big room, surrounded by high wooden stools. On a pedestal in the center reigned the god of the place, a giant gramophone, bellowing ceaselessly silly popular airs. When our Irishman was supervising the anarchists, he had been a constant frequenter of the *Cutthroats' Tavern.*

Now, in butchers' blue blouse, loaded revolver in pocket, he flung open the door, shouting the traditional greeting:

"Drinks many and merry, gentlemen, ladies!"

The traditional answer was roared back at him:

"Amen!"

Swaggering from the hips in correct hooligan style, puffing clouds of smoke from his short clay pipe, he made his way to a corner of the big room farthest from the door, where he could best keep a watchful eye on the comings and goings.

He banged an elbow on the table, shouting:

"Hi, boy! By thunder and Holy Moses! Two of the best—a coffee and pickled cabbage! Hop!"

He drank, he ate. He ordered more brandy and poured it under the table. Then he pretended to sleep. Seated askew on his chair, one leg on the table, the other on an overturned stool, he leaned against the filthy wall, pulling his jockey cap over his eyes as though to shelter them from the glaring incandescent gas jets.

Apparently sound asleep, he was very wide awake indeed, surveying the customers through a rent he had made in the peak of his cap.

He caught sight of the Beadle!

French had learned by heart the three police photographs of the Beadle he had in his pocket.

The hooligan, enthroned on a stool, was holding forth to a group of loose women and young blackguards. French was near enough to hear scraps of his talk:

"A deuce of a letdown I tell you! If ever I return of my own will to the Albions it'll be because the bobbies here are hot after me. What a miserable bit of all wrong that confounded country is! Why you can't get a crust without fighting for it. *Bread* they call the stuff. And the petticoat brigade! Not a good looker among them! Not one to get your soup for you! And the bobbies! They'd get a bulge on any of ours, I bet. Give me old Pantruche* every time! London's a pig of a place! I've got to foot it back there, more's the pity! I've some accounts to settle!"

One of the girls asked a question:

"You were alone there? Did you glimpse a pal of mine? Didn't Beaumôme accompany you? I had a fancy for him, I don't mind owning up to that!"

What the Beadle said was drowned in the clamor.

The owner of the *Cutthroats' Tavern* had just put the gramophone out of gear, and the customers had started the chorus of a popular sing-song:

"I have lost my sister who was a worker!"

French had fixed curious eyes on a stranger not far off: a stout man, wearing a short light blue blouse, soiled trousers, a bibbed apron, spotted with blood and dirt. His arms were crossed on the table before him, his head was bent. He seemed asleep.

Prolonged scrutiny convinced French that the stranger was awake and watching. He was staring at a large watch swinging over his stomach. Was its bright cover silver?

---

*   Pantruche = Paris

It was a mirror!

What did it reflect?

Why, the Beadle's table close by! It was at the right angle.

"If I am watching the Beadle," thought French, "this man is watching him also. Who is he? . . . Why, can luck have brought me into the presence of Inspector Juve? It is on the cards. I must find out."

Rising hastily, French paid the waiter the usual charge. He walked over to the table where the pretended butcher was seated, and put his hand on the sitting man's shoulder: "Hey, old fellow!" he cried, manner and tone of the slums. The sitting man stared up, dumb:

"What are you snoozing there for? Listen! I have a proposition to make to you. Come with me for a couple of minutes!"

The impulsive Irishman plunged:

"Quick!" he whispered. "Come out! I am Detective French of the English police. I have recognized you, Monsieur Juve. I need you. But not a word here!"

Then aloud in his best slum manner:

"What, old pal! Asleep still? A cow you might be, staring at an airplane!"

The stranger's face was all bewilderment. He did not seem to understand what French was saying to him:

"An affair to propose to me?" the stranger muttered at last. "What are you stuffing me with? Not talk here? Why? Nice manners you've got! Business is done with a glass in the hand, a glass of the best! What's exciting you? Sit if you like. We can talk if you want to. But what name do you go by?"

French had a moment's fright. Was this bewildered individual not Juve? Had he made the shocking blunder of addressing a real member of the pickpocket community?

If so, there would be a row, and he would have to defend his skin against the assembled hooligans, who hated the police worse than poison!

French stared hard at the man.

No, no! He was not deceived, not the victim of a resemblance. It was certainly Juve!

He would have to come to a decision. A remark reassured French. When he had said bluntly: "I belong to the police," this butcher had not flinched, had not recoiled. It must be Juve! . . . Was it?

French knew a moment of cruel indecision.

What should he do?

Be prudent.

French was the hooligan again:

"Don't get your dander up, old pal! I took you for someone else while you snoozed there! My mistake! I see you're not the fellow I'm after—pardon—excuse! . . ."

The butcher sprawled over the table, growling:

"There's a fool for you! Drunk! So!"

Leaning head on elbows the butcher pretended to go to sleep again.

French was saying to himself:

"It *is* Juve! I am certain! Perhaps he does not wish to be recognized! Confound it! I will know the rights of this!"

French, with an air of perfect ease, slowly made towards the door of the *Cutthroats' Tavern*:

"We shall soon see," he thought.

The Irishman had bethought him of a ruse, whereby he would learn the identity of this butcher he persisted in taking for Juve.

13. Dark Designs

Beaumôme walked up and down on a deserted bank of the Thames.

Beaumôme was in a murderous temper. He paused by a gas lamp whose flickering flame hardly pierced the foggy air. He reopened a letter and read it, stopping at each word to weigh the sense of it. The host of the *Old Fellow* had handed it to Beaumôme that morning, when he had turned in for his morning's nip of rum:

> Come this evening at eight o'clock to the place you know of on the banks of the Thames. I have serious things to say to you.
>
>   NINI.

The impatient hooligan stamped his ill-shod feet: "Serious things to say to me! And I've been waiting for her over an hour! What serious things? She can't have been arrested, because she has written this. As long as you aren't arrested there's nothing serious! Things settle themselves! Nini's a lovely girl, but she's a weathercock! You never know which way her wind will blow! One day it's wheedling and coaxing, the next it's cascades of abuse!"

Beaumôme shouted abuse at Nini, furious at her failure to keep her appointment. But he was angry with Lord Duncan's outrageous wife because she disdainfully rejected his courtship.

Beaumôme was "trapped," as he described it, and Nini would have no pity on him.

Up and down marched the exasperated hooligan, uneasy also. It was an uncertain world. The police so clever, always on the watch, so quick to pounce. Was that letter a police trick? If so, better be off! Yes, he would cut and run!

A tap on his shoulder! Beaumôme jumped. With a bound he

twisted about. His hand grasped the knife in his pocket, open, ready for action.

He smiled:

"It's you, then! That's not a misfortune!"

It was Nini.

"Here I am, Beaumôme. What's up? You look furious."

"I don't like waiting, Nini. What can I do for you ? I've not known what to think since this morning—been in a regular stew!"

"Whatever for? I have detained you, Beaumôme? For six months and more you have declared that I'm the one woman for you, that I please you, suit you to the ground, and when I decide to give you a rendezvous, behold you rampage, hair on end, and claws out!"

"Nini, I don't understand you!" protested Beaumôme.

Nini pretended to march off:

"All right! I don't insist. Plenty men about—too many!"

Beaumôme went after her:

"What? No need to hurry off like that! What's the matter with you? If you told me to meet you here, it's for some reason, I suppose?"

"It was to see you, Beaumôme."

Beaumôme thought this extraordinary. True he had been sure in his mind that Nini was really madly in love with him, but she had given so many proofs to the contrary up to now, that he hesitated to take her at her word:

"Nothing but to please me, you've come? Then you are going to agree to my terms, after all?"

Nini shrugged her shoulders:

"Your terms! Don't know. Shall have to see."

Suddenly Nini burst into speech:

"Look, Beaumôme, to tell the truth, I'm properly fed up with everything. Nothing's doing for the likes of us. If you want to eat and be jolly, you want someone with you you've a fancy for! Now there's the truth for you!"

Beaumôme was reassured. Did he not know the particular kind of melancholy these women of the underworld often suffered from: a gloomy loneliness which led them to pay for a lover to console them!

Perhaps Nini had been left in the lurch by her protector? For she must have one, surely?

Beaumôme's voice was oily:

"Ah, how I love you! Oh, Nini, if only you would—you and I, Nini, my little rabbit!"

But Nini, an accomplished flirt, who judged Beaumôme sufficiently worked up, avoided a direct answer, and drew back:

"Oh, you are like the others, all talk and no doing! As for the rest? Nib!"

"What rest, Nini?"

"Suppose one had a service to ask of you?"

"Well, Nini, one would render that service."

"Oh, yes! I'd like to see that! I don't believe a word of it, Beaumôme."

But Beaumôme was no fool:

"It's right enough. Don't beat about the bush! What do you want?"

"Nothing!"

"Listen, Nini. We're not here to pick straws. It's important. Yes or no! Do you wish to be my woman?"

While talking they had walked some way along the Thames bank. Nini stopped. Leaning against a huge pile of timber she faced Beaumôme, who had planted himself in front of her. He was staring at her with questioning eyes:

"I have no use for flighty weathercocks. I'm plainspoken, straightforward, frank. Say it's agreed? Your hand on it? Now then?"

Nini stood up. She kicked the remains of an old basket into the river, then caught hold of Beaumôme's arm, and suddenly said in a voice full of rancor:

"I have worries."

"Ah!" Beaumôme was not astonished.

Nini was silent.

"Worries?" he repeated. "What kind of worries? Come now! Spit it out, my girl. What is it?"

"Serious bothers."

"I suspected as much."

"Worries, Beaumôme. You might perhaps arrange things for me!"

"Go on."

"Will you do something for me?"

"And you, Nini? After?"

Without a moment's hesitation, Nini replied:

"If you will manage this for me, it will be we two for life and death. You can count on that!"

Beaumôme's reply was to whistle three verses of a popular song. Then he remarked:

"To put it in a nutshell: I'm to pay the piper for you!"

"What?"

"Well, it's something like that, your arrangement! You say to me: Get me out of my trouble and then it's we two together!"

Nini had nothing to say. Beaumôme was right, she had proposed a bargain.

"Good. I agree. It's not often I've paid the piper. Count on me to talk them over for you!"

"It's no case of talking over. It's no joke—nothing to laugh about, I can assure you! Look here, Beaumôme, you know the police about here?"

"Yes, one or two. I have friends among them—intimates—who invite me to their houses now and then."

"You know French?"

"I know him for sure. A tall Irishman who did me in once. At the Derby. I had seven purses. And another day, too. He's earned anything he gets, and richly too! The pig! What have you against him, Nini? It's French, isn't it?"

Nini nodded:

"Yes, it's French. He's a police spy. Understand, Beaumôme? He's a police spy who annoys me!"

Beaumôme understood well enough. He put his understanding into words:

"You want him done in properly, for good and all?"

Nini said nothing. She did not deny it.

"Ah, you want him smashed to smithereens! The devil! That's a tough bit to swallow! Must have a drink to help it down!"

Nini flung at him disdainfully:

"You're white livered!"

"Never on your life! To do a man in doesn't frighten me! And French and I have accounts to settle. Only . . ."

Nini disdainfully repeated:

"You're a smock-faced milksop!"

Beaumôme raging, burst out:

"Not on your life, my girl! An idea like that sprung on you, when making eyes, sitting quiet, going along peaceably, was all one was thinking about! Then she says, 'Smash up a police spy,' and she's astonished that one is taken aback! But anyone can do that! Only it's probable, if Nini came to find Beaumôme, that there's bad business, and maybe blabbing, mixed up with it! Then Nini doesn't give details. Beaumôme must have them. Where and how is the job to be done?

"Nini, why do you want French done in?"

"Oh, if you've got to be talked into it, whipped up to the mark?" cried Nini, and again seemed about to march off.

Fortunately for her, Beaumôme did not mean to let her think him an utter coward.

"Stay now!" Beaumôme caught her arm. "I must know. What I ask is natural enough."

"I'll tell you, all right, Beaumôme. But you'll get a move on—carry it through? You swear it?"

"I swear it."

"Well! Do you know where French is at this minute?"

"Not sure. He's here and there like a flea!"

"That's so. He's in France."

"Like the Beadle?"

"Yes. It's by the Beadle I know it."

"The Beadle's written you?"

"Yes. I had his scrawl this morning."

"Good. Well?"

"French is on the hop—he and his fleas—in France—poking his nose into a lot of things that don't concern him."

"What things?"

"They don't matter to you, Beaumôme. What's certain is, this brute is coming back soon. That's certain. Well it doesn't please me that French sees England again—you understand, Beaumôme?"

Beaumôme blinked his eyes in non-committal fashion:

"No. I don't understand. I'm waiting to hear more."

Nini was exasperated:

"More? There's no more! It's things to do with me I can't tell you about. I do not want French to return, that's all you need know! You understand that now, I suppose?"

Yes, Beaumôme understood:

"Then instructions are to settle his hash before he gets back?"

"Yes, old boy."

"You know when he's coming?"

"Tomorrow evening."

"Ah! Tomorrow evening!"

Beaumôme felt a little sick when he learned that the detective's return was so near.

"So that," he said after a silence, "he has just forty-eight hours to live!"

"Forty-eight hours to live, yes," repeated Nini in a muffled voice. "Beaumôme, in forty-eight hours you must have rid me of this fool brute. You wish to?"

Beaumôme shrugged:

"You know what you have promised?" was his reply.

"Go along, my man! Can I refuse you anything after? Besides, down at bottom, I shan't find it so disagreeable. If I've given you the back-push up to now, it was because I really didn't know if you could come up to the scratch—but when you shall have proved it to me! . . ."

Beaumôme was not satisfied with this disputing and contending. He knew what talk amounted to:

"All right. Enough! I don't lie about it! And you don't need to swear love eternal. We shall see!"

Returning to the pressing question Beaumôme said:

"Do you know which way French is coming?"

"By the Dieppe boat."

"Will he be by himself, do you know?"

"Yes."

"Does he cross by day or night?"

"Night."

Beaumôme looked more cheerful:

"That's the ticket. If he crosses at night it's a child's job! It's perfect, my pretty dear—only there's a question! . . ."

"A question? What question?"

"It's just that I haven't a sou—nothing to burn—and I shall have to go to Dieppe, as far as I can see. . . ."

Nini looked anxious:

"Ah, you want brass! You'll have to have that! But, I haven't any at this moment, not any more than you have! In my pocket it's threshed corn!"

"And your lovers?"

"All cleaned out."

Both were silent. Then Beaumôme played the magnanimous lover:

"The little birds shall provide it. We don't live in the Sahara, so there are ways of getting the dibs. If one hasn't the stuff, one takes it."

This time Nini looked at Beaumôme admiringly. "You know it's no nonsense this time: it's truth—if you clear him out of my way!"

Now that it was settled, Beaumôme did not wish to take advantage of the situation:

"All right, all right, pal! Your police spy'll be done in. It would be queer if I couldn't do you a trifle of service when I've spent six months in getting you up to the starting point!"

Beaumôme did not doubt that he would find it very easy to "do in" Detective French.

14. The Return of Madame Garrick

Detective French had just stepped out of the *Cutthroats' Tavern*
onto the muddy pavement. He walked up and down determined to wait for the man he believed to be Juve. An eternity
of time seemed to pass. The flickering flames of the gas lamps
grew yellower: dawn was breaking, cold, rainy, sinister. French
shivered in the blast. He took refuge at last in a corner of the
jutting house wall. From there he could watch all who left the
Cutthroats' Tavern.

Soon after this, French was overjoyed to see the man he took
for Juve.

No impulsive action this time! French was cool, his actions
calculated. He let the unknown man go forward a little in front,
and quietly followed him step for step.

The man had gone past French. With lowered head he
slouched along in the middle of the roadway, his hands in his
pockets. He looked like an idler going home; not at all like a
man who wishes to cover his traces.

"Where the deuce is he going?" French asked himself. "If
it really is Juve, it seems to me he would be going towards the
center of Paris, yet here we are in the rue des Morillons, and, if
I have not lost my sense of direction in Paris, we shall shortly
reach the wasteland close to the fortifications."

French was not mistaken. Soon he saw, at the corner of a
dismal street, the grassy rampart slopes surrounding Paris.

Just then the Irishman noticed that the man he was following had turned to face him. He cried in a controlled voice:

"Halt! What do you want with me? Who are you?"

French stood still.

This man who had spoken so imperatively, was pointing a
revolver at his pursuer.

French kept calm:

"Who am I? I told you just now. I am the English detective, French. What do I want? I come to see you, sent by Tom Bob, to speak to you about Mrs. Garrick."

When the man heard this he seemed excited:

"I must be the victim of a nightmare!" he cried. "You are a detective? And it is Tom Bob who sends you to me?"

French felt that he and the pursued were coming to an understanding. He made a proposition:

"Monsieur Juve, I declare I am telling you the truth, and I do not see why you should be so surprised. Look now! I am a colleague, and I come to ask a service of you. Let us have a talk? Will you put up your revolver and give me permission to approach you?"

The unknown hesitated, then quietly said:

"My faith, Monsieur French, possibly you are right. If you are really sent by Tom Bob, I have given you a queer reception."

Slipping his revolver into his hip pocket, he walked towards French with outstretched hand:

"You have really recognized me! I am Juve. But I must confess that I should like a proof of your identity."

"Here is my card of identification and introduction," said French, taking it from his pocketbook.

Juve glanced at it:

"You are French then, really! But that tells me nothing. What do you want of me?"

French was in no wise upset or offended. He had heard of Juve's peculiar ways.

The two men began to walk up and down. French informed Juve of all that had happened up to the present.

Juve was intensely interested.

"Then Tom Bob asks me to find Mrs. Garrick? Not knowing where she is himself he thinks I may be able to find her?"

"Exactly," affirmed French.

Juve was silent with stupefaction. This Tom Bob, whom French believed to be an honest detective, was certainly Fantômas! Juve knew it. Consequently, this wife of Tom Bob who had vanished, who must have seen from the papers that her non-appearance was equivalent to a sentence of death on her husband, this wife could be none other than Lady Beltham!

In a second Juve understood the dramatic history. Lady Beltham, the lover madly infatuated with Fantômas, must have got to know that Fantômas, under the guise of Garrick, had a mistress, Françoise Lemercier!

It was an extraordinary intrigue:

"If Tom Bob has sent French to me," argued Juve with himself, "it is because he is aware that I know he is Fantômas. He has divined that at the moment French asks me to help him to find Mrs. Garrick, I shall know that it is really Lady Beltham I have to look for. But it is almost a service asked me by Fantômas! Why has he not feared that I should let him hang? There is only one explanation possible. It is tit for tat! If I bring Lady Beltham back to England, if I prove Fantômas innocent of a crime which he has not committed, he has a means of repaying this service, and this means cannot be any other than restoring Fandor to me! For I no longer doubt that it is Fantômas who has caused the disquieting, inexplicable disappearance of my unfortunate friend."

Juve soon replied to French, veiling his burning anxiety under a quiet manner, a calm voice:

"No doubt whatever your chief has been well inspired. In fact I do know where Mrs. Garrick is . . . or at least I think I do! . . ."

In the train that was carrying Juve and French to Le Havre, they talked:

"What I am afraid of is that Mrs. Garrick will refuse to return to England with me!" said the Irishman.

"Bah!" declared Juve. "Don't worry about that! I have some reasons to think the contrary, that you will persuade her easily. Mrs. Garrick lives some way from Bonnières, in a little house—a quiet spot I will point out to you. You will appear before her, you will tell her that her husband is accused of having murdered her, though that will be no news to her! You will ask her very nicely to return to England with you to prove his innocence. And, my faith, if she refuses, I will intervene."

"You are not coming with me to find her, Monsieur Juve?"

"By no means!"

"But why?"

"Because . . ."

French dared not insist. He asked timidly:

"May I at least mention you? Tell her that you advise her to return?"

"Hum! No. Do not mention me to her. It must suffice you to know that I am behind the scenes, ready to back you up if necessary. If needed, I should act at once! But I would rather you managed without me! See her, persuade her to accompany you, and leave with her by the 11:15 train in the morning. This evening you take the boat at Dieppe, tomorrow you will be in London, and the business is settled. One word more. With Mrs. Garrick you will find a girl who will probably accompany you to Dieppe. This girl, I warn you, will seem to be your enemy, to make common cause with Mrs. Garrick, who will probably try to give you the slip. I guarantee that in her you will find an ally. You will see I am not mistaken. Everything will go as easily as could be."

Juve took down his valise from the netted rack, valise No. 6, he had gone to his flat for, before taking French to the Saint-Lazare station:

"We must be ready! Here is Bonnières!"

"Good Heavens! It is she! Certainly it is she!" exclaimed the excited detective. "Tom Bob is saved!"

French had separated from Juve some twenty minutes before. Now he was hiding in a thicket before the house Juve had pointed out to him, and at one of the windows French had just caught sight of a lady he recognized as Mrs. Garrick from the description given him.

"How can I make a woman such as she, go to England?" thought French. He was scared. He doubted Juve's ability to aid him. He watched Mrs. Garrick from his hiding place with palpitating anxiety.

She was quietly enjoying the pure morning air. French drew out his camera.

Click! Click! He had taken two snapshots of the unsuspecting lady.

"Whether she comes or no, I have now a proof of her existence!" said French. "But she must come with me!"

French ran out of the thicket, calling:

"Mrs. Garrick! Mrs. Garrick!"

The lady at the window started violently, grew pale, stared wildly at the detective. Scarcely able to articulate, she asked:

"Whom are you asking for, monsieur?"

"Mrs. Garrick! Grant me the favor of an interview, I beg!"

"You ask, monsieur?"

"I must speak to you! We have not a minute to lose. You understand me? I *must*."

Mrs. Garrick bowed. She was deathly pale.

"Very well. I will come down."

While French was meeting Tom Bob's wife, events of some importance were occurring.

At nine o'clock that morning, Bobinette had gone into the village, marketing. She was following a field path when someone called her:

"Mademoiselle Bobinette!"

Bobinette saw an old beggar making friendly signs to her:

"Mademoiselle Bobinette!" he called again.

As this old man with a white beard drew near, Bobinette clasped her hands in terror:

"You?"

"Yes. You are well, Bobinette?"

"You! Here!"

"That astonishes you so much?"

"What do you want, Monsieur Juve?" cried the terrified girl. "I am afraid, afraid!"

"You are beside yourself, my dear child. Why afraid? Why should you be so surprised to see me, when Lady Beltham is but a step or two from here?"

"Lady Beltham! You know, then?"

"Why, certainly," said Juve.

Making Bobinette sit beside him on the grass, he told her how he had tracked Lady Beltham:

"My dear child," concluded Juve, "while we are talking, French is persuading Lady Beltham, become Mrs. Garrick, to return to England. She will agree to go, for she will guess that I, Juve, have sent French to her. Also, she will try to escape going on board an English boat, which is English territory, for then French could arrest her. Bobinette, she must not escape. She must go to England. You must accompany her to Dieppe. You have become her friend. She will believe you will help her to escape. As a fact, you will prevent her from giving us the slip."

Bobinette shook her head:

"Monsieur Juve, I certainly have serious faults to expiate, but I cannot play the part you wish. I cannot betray Lady Beltham, give her up to justice, for she is now my friend."

"I promise you, Bobinette, that nothing unpleasant shall happen to Lady Beltham—it is a question of preventing Fantômas from doing harm. It is not betrayal I ask of you. I simply ask you to do your duty."

Bobinette was silent.

"You will return home at once," continued Juve. "You will go to Dieppe with Lady Beltham. You will prevent her escape, and after the departure of the steamer you will find me. There I will explain many things to you which you cannot understand."

Juve had risen. He was greatly moved. Bobinette was thoroughly upset.

"Good day, my man! I see someone over there waiting for me."

Juve, who had been talking with a custom-house officer, hurried off. In truth Juve had not seen anyone, but the great electric lights had been turned on, and he did not wish to be in the full glare of them:

"Confound this illumination! So long as she hasn't seen me!"

Since morning Juve, who with consummate art had changed

his disguise again and again, had trailed French, Bobinette, and the extraordinary Mrs. Garrick. Now he was watching the departure of French and Lady Beltham-Garrick. He caught sight of Bobinette, leaning on one of the great chains which barred the quay. She was waving goodbye to Mrs. Garrick.

Juve was on tenterhooks. Would anything happen to frustrate his plans?

Ah, the steamer was slowly leaving the shore and making for the storm-tossed water outside the harbor.

Juve was rubbing his hands with joy. Suddenly, he left his shadowy corner, he rushed towards the jetty:

"That young blackguard! I'm not mistaken! It's Beaumôme!"

Juve ran, breathless. Soon he could not recognize the individuals on board the fast receding steamer. Juve returned slowly, certain that he had seen the sinister hooligan among the passengers.

Juve went up to Bobinette:

"Ah, here you are!"

"Here I am," replied Juve, who was amused at Bobinette's stare, for he was now made up like a very fat bourgeois, rotund as a wine barrel.

"Nothing happened?"

"No, Monsieur Juve. She has gone."

"Easily?"

Bobinette shook her head:

"Oh, no! That's what has upset me. . . . Lady Beltham did all she could this morning, at Rolleboise, to get away from French. Once we had decided to go, she twice attempted to leave us."

"Naturally!" Juve smiled.

"Why 'naturally'? Why did Lady Beltham not wish to go to England? Does she desire Garrick's death?"

Juve walked with Bobinette into Dieppe, and along the deserted streets:

"Lady Beltham's position is a terrible one," he said. "She does not wish to prove Garrick's innocence by returning to England. She is madly jealous of him, of Garrick-Fantômas, who has for mistress Françoise Lemercier. Also she is afraid of him. Tomorrow Garrick will be freed, because her appearance will clear him. And Madame Garrick asks herself, terrified, if he will not take a dreadful vengeance for the danger she has made him run—for she is the cause of his accusation and condemnation."

Bobinette was overwhelmed:

"But, Juve, why did you not show yourself? Why allow Garrick-Fantômas to be at liberty? You should have joined forces with Lady Beltham! You ought to prove that Garrick is Fantômas!"

Juve chuckled:

"No. I could not act in that way. Had I shown myself I would have been obliged to prove that Mrs. Garrick is Lady Beltham, obliged to prove that Garrick is Fantômas . . . but . . . I have no proofs. Only one person in the world can unmask Fantômas, that person is Lady Beltham, and I cannot force Lady Beltham to bear witness against Fantômas!"

"Why not?"

"Because, my poor Bobinette, Lady Beltham is always legally reported dead. In order to subpoena her as a witness, I should have to institute legal proceedings, a terrible business, an endless lawsuit which would give Fantômas every chance of escaping in the meantime!"

"But what are you going to do?" asked Bobinette.

"Garrick will be freed. Well, Garrick is also Tom Bob. From tomorrow on I have only to stick to him, watch him, collect a series of proofs. It should not be difficult for, if he is not attackable as Garrick, as Tom Bob-Fantômas, a usurper, he is at my mercy. I take him when I choose."

Bobinette asked in a trembling voice:

"Why don't you go to London at once? I am afraid for Lady Beltham."

"Don't fear for her," replied Juve gently. "For some time at least Fantômas will not be able to touch her. It would be too risky. And, since the Beadle is in Paris, Bobinette, I want to know if this fellow is not up to some diabolical game, probably on behalf of Fantômas, for the Beadle was one of his most active lieutenants."

Juve added in a low tone:

"I really thought for a while that French, emissary of Tom Bob was in France to carry out the orders of Fantômas!"

Bobinette was too upset to speak.

15. The Supreme Sentence

Monsieur Mirat, the journalist, had been sent by *La Capitale*, a Parisian paper, to report on the remarkable trial of Garrick, to be opened that day before the Central Criminal Court at the Old Bailey. It was Monsieur Mirat's first experience of English law procedure, and he was obtaining all the information he could extract from a barrister named Kidney, briefed for the prosecution. He had ascertained that from the arrest of Garrick up to this day, barely seven weeks had passed:

"Justice acts expeditiously here?"

The barrister smiled:

"True. Our procedure is however somewhat complicated and must, in some ways, seem strange to you French."

"Will you kindly explain?" asked Mirat, notebook in hand.

"Willingly. What happened after the arrest of Garrick? First of all a jury of twenty-three members, presided over by the Coroner, had to decide by an impartial verdict whether or not it was a question of crime in the Garrick case. They pronounced in the affirmative, adding that to the best of their belief, Garrick had murdered his wife.

"Garrick was held prisoner pending his trial on a murder charge. The case then went before what we call the Grand Jury. This Jury declares whether or not there exist presumptions to justify sending the prisoner for further trial. If the Jury's finding is in the affirmative, the president of the Grand Jury writes on the indictment sheet: *True Bill,* and that determines the sending of the prisoner before the Central Criminal Court. This has occurred in Garrick's case. You will hear the last stage today."

The barrister hurried away.

A clock struck.

Mirat followed a crowd hurrying towards the room where

the Garrick case was to be tried.

Mirat was surprised at the small size of this room, and by the simplicity and paucity of the furniture. The audience sat quiet in a state of controlled excitement.

On a raised platform opposite the journalist the presiding judge, Lord Pilgrim, dominated the Court. His jolly face was clean-shaven, large and fat, his smiling lips thick, his nose broad and flat. Clothed in the robes of his high office, Lord Pilgrim's appearance was at once jovial and majestic. On his left was seated a barrister in a blue robe trimmed with dark fur. Before him, as before Lord Pilgrim, was a vase of artificial flowers.

Mirat learned he was the Attorney General.

The journalist's attention was then drawn to the benches on the left of the Court reserved for members of the Bar. A dozen barristers in black gowns and white wigs had come in to hear the proceedings. In the first row of these men of the law, looking through their documents, were Kidney for the prosecution, and Islingford for the defense.

A door in the wainscoting lining the Court opened. A man, accompanied by a policeman, entered the enclosed space in the center of the Court. Before seating himself on one of the two chairs placed there, the man bowed respectfully to the judge.

It was the accused.

Calm but pale, he faced the judge. After one rapid glance round the Court he concentrated his attention on Lord Pilgrim, who had roused himself from an apparent torpor, and proceeded to question the accused:

"What is your name?"

"Walther Garrick."

"Your age?"

"Thirty-nine."

"Your profession?"

"Doctor-dentist."

"You hold a diploma granted by an American Academy, although you are an Australian subject? You have been established in London two years?"

"Yes."

Lord Pilgrim was making his own notes in the course of this interrogation, in conformity with English law:

"Your papers are in order."

Then in a scarcely intelligible voice, he added: "You exercise in England another profession, but it is not necessary to mention it here?"

"It is not necessary," replied Garrick.

Mirat strained his ears:

"What did they mean by that?" he asked.

To his great surprise no one took any notice. He had counted on the intervention of the barrister for the defense, or for the prosecution.

Mirat questioned his neighbors in vain. They attached no importance to the question.

The Supreme Council at Scotland Yard had decided that only the Judge, the Attorney General, and a few of Tom Bob's colleagues should be let into the secret of Garrick-Tom Bob's detective activities. This in the public interest. The Clerk of the Court now read the indictment, amidst a religious attention.

The twelve good men and true of the jury had been sworn in, and had taken their seats.

Lord Pilgrim addressed Garrick:

"Do you plead guilty, or not guilty?"

"Not guilty, my lord."

The Counsel for the prosecution, Kidney, K.C., stated his case. He then called his witnesses.

The Clerk of the Court called:

"Shephard!"

Detective Shephard entered the witness box. He concisely narrated what had happened since he had been employed on the case, down to the moment when Garrick had entered the Old Bailey.

In answer to a question from Counsel for the defense, Shephard stated:

"One of our colleagues, Detective French, went to France some days ago, where Mrs. Garrick is believed to be. We have had no news of French for nearly a week. Yesterday he sent a telegram to the presiding judge, and a duplicate to Scotland Yard."

Counsel for the defense asked his colleague:

"I ask your permission to make the contents of the telegram known to the Jury.

"I see no objection to that," replied Kidney, K.C.

Islingford, K.C., then read as follows:

> Just made an important discovery. Returning to London in time for opening of Garrick trial.
>
> FRENCH.

Kidney, K.C., asked Counsel for the defense:

"Should we hear the evidence of Detective French at once?"

"It will be advisable."

Detective French was called for.

The Clerk of the Court announced:

"Detective French is not here yet."

Garrick grew pale at the news.

Garrick-Tom Bob glanced questioningly at Shephard, but Shephard made no sign.

Various witnesses were called whilst awaiting French. Among them was Miss Edith, servant of the Garrick couple, whose incriminating statements produced a marked impression.

The grocer and the coachman's testimony went to show their firm belief in Garrick's culpability. The doctor's evidence went to show that the human remains must have been placed in the cellar at the same date as the supposed departure of Mrs. Garrick.

A telegram arrived, addressed to Lord Pilgrim, stating that no detective of the name of French had been found on board any steamer which had arrived last night at Newhaven, nor that same morning, coming from the French coast.

The Counsel for the prosecution's comment was:

"I infer from the contents of this telegram, that Detective French did not embark at Dieppe yesterday as was stated in the first telegram of which you have cognizance, for had he embarked he would surely have arrived at Newhaven. The first telegram must therefore be the work of an impostor, and I will ask the Jury to take no notice of it, and to consider that Detective French has searched in vain. Add to this, if Mrs. Garrick still lives she would certainly have learned of the accusation resting on her husband. This apparently she has not done. She has made no sign."

The Counsel for the prosecution sat down. Garrick spoke:

"Your lordship, I have a declaration to make."

The prisoner entered the witness box.

Quietly, sincerely, Garrick said:

"I swear that I am innocent of the crime of which I am accused. My wife suddenly left me. She was jealous of my love for another woman. Appearances are against me since I was arrested at the moment when I seemed to be flying from justice. I was leaving for America. My only intention when I went on board *The Victoria* was to rejoin my mistress, who believed her child had been carried off by her husband, who lives in Canada. If my wife knew of the criminal accusation laid against me she would return. I cannot suppose that her anger against me would be so great that she would keep silence."

Garrick's declaration was received in icy silence. There was not the slightest demonstration as he regained his seat.

The Counsel for the prosecution made his speech; the Counsel for the defense likewise.

Lord Pilgrim's summing up, his address to the Jury, was lucid, dispassionate, weighty.

The Jury retired to consider their verdict. The Court room emptied instantly.

The Jury deliberated a bare twenty minutes. They solemnly filed into the Court room again.

During these fateful twenty minutes, Shephard obtained an interview with Garrick.

The two men shook hands:

"Well, Shephard!"

"Well, Tom Bob!"

"Shephard, what do you think of it?"

"This absence of French is a deuce of a business, Tom Bob! Those jurymen are fools if they refuse to believe in the authenticity of that telegram . . . but . . . what the devil has prevented his return?"

Tom Bob shrugged.

"The deuce and all, Tom! I am terribly anxious."

Tom Bob looked Shephard fixedly in the eye:

"Shephard, tell me truly. Do you think I am going to be condemned? You do, don't you?"

Shephard evaded an answer to this. He questioned in his turn:

"Tom, tell me the truth. Have you, yes or no, murdered your wife?"

"No, Shephard. I have not killed her." Shephard heaved a sigh of relief.

"We shall save you, Tom. Whatever happens we will save you. As to . . ."

Shephard stopped short. He had heard the bell which announced the return of the Jury. The policeman entered to lead Garrick back to the Court.

Shephard slipped away to mingle with the tensely expectant public.

Garrick was in the allotted space, facing the Jury. The verdict, the unanimous verdict, dropped into the dead silence:

"Guilty."

Garrick stood motionless.

He stood like the frozen similitude of a man while the Judge, more moved than the prisoner, placed the dreadful black cap on his head, and pronounced the sinister formula:

"Garrick, you are sentenced to be hanged by the neck till you are dead, and may God have mercy on your soul!"

16. A Hooligan's Crime

Nini had just left Beaumôme.

He watched her till her figure faded into the darkness. Beaumôme was irritated:

"She's astonishing, that woman! I have to pay for a ticket to Dieppe and back! First class too! Does she take me for a shareholder in the Company? I've got to lie low and get out of it as best I can."

Beaumôme did not object to knife French. That was a pleasant bit of revenge on the detective. The hand of every hooligan was against the police. But Beaumôme had not a stiver to bless himself with. And he knew not a soul in London from whom he could borrow the five pounds he needed.

Beaumôme was at his wits' end as he mounted the steps to London Bridge. Then he had an inspiration:

"The church rats! That's the ticket. Their collections won't be in vain, I'll lay!"

He hurried off through little winding streets, and arrived at one of the Catholic churches of Central London. Beaumôme removed his cap on entering the sacred building, took holy water and crossed himself. He did not wish to make himself noticeable.

Beaumôme's sacrilegious comedy was wasted. The great church was empty.

Beaumôme made a tour of the church.

Except an old woman in the Lady Chapel, who was changing the places of the candles for some reason of her own, and a young woman kneeling near the altar, absorbed in fervent prayer, Beaumôme saw no one. He remarked to himself:

"That's all right—no need to be scared. Thing's running on roller skates!"

Beaumôme had gone to the west end of the church. He had

spied the poor box of Saint Anthony, placed in a dark recess:

"Ah, ha! For once the pig will fast! I feed in his place! Monsieur Saint Antoine, you will make my apologies to your animal!"

Beaumôme, while talking to himself, was not losing his time.

He was evidently an expert at opening poor boxes. He inserted a tiny jimmy which he always carried in the lining of his jacket. Two turns of a wrist like steel, and the door of the poor box was open.

"Anyone about? No. Now for a bit of juggling!"

He raked out the money in the box, pushed up in its place the opened side, and slipped out of the church.

Sixty francs in small money were snug in his pocket.

Beaumôme made for a knife grinder known to the London thieves as trustworthy. The cutter put a razor edge on Beaumôme's superb clasp-knife. He made no comment.

Beaumôme hurried to a secondhand clothes dealer. He bought a complete change of garments. He was allowed to put them on in a little room behind the shop.

In high good temper Beaumôme presented himself at the Victoria Station ticket office:

"First class to Dieppe."

Arrived at Dieppe, Beaumôme bought cold ham, bread, and a bottle of brandy. He spent the day wandering about the country; the less he was seen in Dieppe the safer.

By eleven o'clock at night he was drunk enough to face the future with equanimity.

Re-entering Dieppe, he dawdled about the quay obtaining information useful for his murderous purpose.

The steamer sailing that evening was the *Scotsman*. Beaumôme examined the arrangement of the vessel. He noticed with pleasure that the portion reserved for first-class passengers—and French was sure to travel first-class—was simply surrounded by low bulwarks and netting openwork, for Beaumôme had decided that he would not knife French; he would tip him overboard into the Channel.

Taken by surprise, his victim would not have time to struggle. This appealed to Beaumôme, who was far from being a Hercules.

Beaumôme resumed his walk up and down the quay, reflecting:

"French will embark at midnight. I will go on board one of the last. I don't want to meet this excellent detective face to face."

When the boat train drew in, Beaumôme, standing in shadow, grew worried. Not a glimpse of French among the little crowd rushing to the steamer's gangways! Suddenly he caught sight of the detective, followed by a lady who did not seem to be with him, who was waving goodbye to a young woman on the quay.

"There you go, my fine fellow," laughed Beaumôme sarcastically. "I won't promise that the crossing will be undisturbed for you, but I guarantee you a diversion!"

When the gangways were being hauled in, Beaumôme leapt on board and made his way to the first class passengers' deck.

Beaumôme, in gay humor, chewed the stub of a cigarette. His quarry was under his hand. He watched the gray-green waves tipped with foam racing past under a gray cloudy sky. The wind blew in gusts from the northwest.

"Certain to ship a sea or two," thought Beaumôme. "Suppose French stays below! He may object to a douse of salt water!"

Beaumôme grew anxious. The cowardly, chicken-hearted hooligan meant to murder in the safest way. The sea would guard his crime. What if he had to knife French when landing at Newhaven!

Beaumôme went below. Entering the saloon, he spied French talking to a waiter, apparently giving him instructions.

Beaumôme, keeping his back to French, drew nearer.

"You do not wish to reserve a berth, sir?"

"No, no!"

"They will all be taken very soon, sir."

"I prefer a turn on deck."

"It's cold above, sir, and you'll be soaked. Wind and water in plenty, sir!"

"I am going up to have a look at it!"

French turned on his heel. Beaumôme followed at a discreet distance.

The *Scotsman,* now in open water, was buffeted by squally wind. She sped onwards, her nose buried in wave upon wave, her decks dripping with high-flung spray. The few passengers on deck soon went below. Beaumôme sought a sheltered spot and kept an eye on French.

The detective stood smoking a cigar, hands deep in pockets of his greatcoat, hat pressed down to his ears. He seemed to be enjoying the voyage.

A series of spray showers drove him to seek shelter. Like Beaumôme, French installed himself behind one of the lifeboats, leaning on the ship's rail, and, indifferent to the tossing of the steamer, continued to smoke. Beaumôme, lurking, ready to spring, eager to hurl his victim into the heaving waters, dared not move. Two passengers, young men enjoying the bad weather, were staggering up and down the deck to prove they had sea legs. Would they never go?

Beaumôme ground his teeth.

"The spoilsports!" he muttered. "But for them, I'd finish the job in a jiffy! To hell with them!"

He had not long to wait. Soaked, dripping with sea water, the two youths went below.

Only the hooligan and his victim remained on deck. The sailors had their hands full. Beaumôme's chance had come!

A wicked smile on his crooked lips, the hooligan, all devilish malice, crouched and staggered in jerks across the heaving deck.

Not a soul was in sight.

Taking advantage of a moment when the steamer danced a little less, Beaumôme leaned his elbows on the rail close to French.

There was no danger of being recognized in the darkness:

"Excuse me, sir, you smoke? I would like to do ditto, only I can't manage to light a match. Would you give me a light from your cigar?"

"At your service," replied the unsuspicious detective. Leaning his back against the rail, French held out his cigar to Beaumôme.

The hooligan threw aside his cigarette:

"Thank you, sir."

With these words the hooligan struck French a violent blow on the face, while with his right leg he caught the unfortunate detective under the knee.

Surprised, blinded, half-stunned by the savage attack, rendered helpless by this knee trick, French collapsed on the deck without a cry.

At this crucial moment the *Scotsman* heeled over and the deck sloped sharply downward on the side the murderous hooligan was bending over his half-stunned victim.

Straining every muscle, Beaumôme caught French by the shoulders, dragged him up, and hoisting him to the edge of the rail, toppled him into the heaving waters below.

Poor French sank at once in the foaming swirl of the screws.

It was over! How easily done!

Beaumôme stared at the waves that had engulfed his victim. The hooligan's relief was so great that he joked:

"Don't drink it all, old fellow! You'd leave the boat stranded, and that would not suit my book at all!"

Beaumôme jerked upright.

He was livid.

He trembled.

His forehead dropped sweat.

His coward heart was thumping to, suffocation point.

Through the whistling of the wind, the uproar of the waves, Beaumôme had heard a voice cry:

"Assassin! Help! Assassin!"

Beaumôme turned round. He understood:

While attacking French, someone had come on deck, had seen him commit the murder!

A moment of terrible emotion, and Beaumôme rushed towards a shadowy figure halfway up the staircase leading to the deck.

Beaumôme had drawn out his knife.

He saw red. The madness of crime went to his head.

He came close to the denouncing shadow.

The shadow was a woman.

Beaumôme recognized this woman.

He stammered her name in an amazed voice.

"Lady Beltham! Madame Garrick!"

Many a time had Beaumôme seen Lady Beltham. He had also seen her portrait in the papers, and had recognized her and Mrs. Garrick as being one and the same.

What was Lady Beltham doing on the steamer? Or, rather what was Mrs. Garrick, as she now was, doing? Mrs. Garrick a passenger on the same boat as French! Ah, he saw it! Madame Garrick must have been arrested by French, and French was bringing her back as a witness in the Garrick trial! And if Nini had made him kill the detective it was assuredly because this appearance at the trial did not please her!

Why was Nini interested to such a point in the mysterious drama of Putney?

Beaumôme did not know, nor did he lose time thinking about it.

The woman he had rushed towards was silent.

Beaumôme caught her by the arm and dragged her on deck. He hissed words at her in a low tone:

"You were with French?"

"Assassin!" retorted Lady Beltham.

"If you denounce me, you are lost!"

Lady Beltham stared at the hooligan with frightened eyes, ready to call for help should Beaumôme make the slightest suspicious movement:

"Lost!" she gasped. "Lost? I don't understand you!"

"Come now! You were with French, isn't that so? Yes? He was bringing you over to clear Garrick? Listen! If you tell what I've just done, they will think it was you gave me the order to kill. . . . You understand? Yes? . . . If you don't say a word—well I shan't have set eyes on you. You are free. Do what you like! . . . Are you going to denounce me?"

Lady Beltham remained mute. Beaumôme insisted:

"It's all to your own interest to hold your tongue. You are assured of my silence. Is it settled?"

White to the lips, Lady Beltham muttered:

"Leave me alone! I do not know what you are talking about! I have seen nothing! I do not wish to be your accomplice! I have seen nothing!"

Beaumôme was his callous devil-may-care self again:

"Oh," said he, with a snigger, "from the moment you have not seen anything! That's all I ask for! Till our next meeting, madame. All the same, you are not grateful, for I have done you a great service. The devil I did! And never suspected it!"

Beaumôme, pirouetting away on his heels, went below:

"It's a funny job, this of mine! I wish to do a job for Nini, and its Madame Garrick I especially do a good turn to. It's a muddled business. I snap my fingers at it. They must get out of their own mess!"

Ten minutes later, Beaumôme was sleeping the sleep of the innocent.

Twenty-four hours later, on the same spot where the murder of French had been decided, Beaumôme was waiting for Nini.

It would not do to let Nini into the know.

On the contrary, Nini must be deceived. Beaumôme had prepared a series of lies. This time Nini was not late. The hour fixed by the two accomplices for their meeting was six o'clock in the evening. Six had just struck when Nini appeared.

Lord Duncan's wife rushed up to Beaumôme:

"Well?"

"Well," retorted Beaumôme, "the job's done. French is done, dead and cold, unless he has been swimming as far as this!"

But Nini did not want jokes. She wanted precise details:

"You have pitched him into the water?"

"Yes."

"Easily?"

Beaumôme would not admit that. He wished to impress Nini.

"Easily? No. But he's in the soup for all that. You know, Nini,

I'm not the sort of fellow to be scared out of my wits, I—"

Nini had no use for this boasting.

"He cried out? Struggled? Do they suspect you?"

"When I down a bloke to zero, it's generally done in silence. No, Nini, you may trust your two ears when I say, not a soul will ever suspect not ever."

Beaumôme now wanted his promised reward:

"But you know what you promised me, eh? We two together now?"

Alas! Nini did seem to have made up her mind to that:

"Down with your paws!" she cried, breaking away from the amorous hooligan. "I have promised you what I have promised—it's true—but when I am easy in my mind—and I'm not that yet by a long chalk!"

"What about?" asked Beaumôme, frowning. "What's bothering you now?"

"Something."

"It is?"

"A woman."

"Who then?" Beaumôme was scared.

"A policewoman—Davis."

Beaumôme breathed again—it was not Lady Beltham. He played the braggart:

"Good. Look here, Nini. If you wish it! That one too? Eh? What do you say to it? Clear off the policewoman too?"

Beaumôme was surpassing himself!

17. The Amorous Negro

"You must be making excellent profits, Mr. Sigissimons?"

"Really? You surprise me, Miss Daisy!"

"Yes, your artistic photography combined with your photographic exchange, constitutes a lucrative business. If your ledgers are to be believed, the receipts have been considerably greater than the expenses, and by many pounds sterling."

"I admire you, Miss Daisy, for having discovered that in the space of a few hours, and I am asking myself why you will not take over the bookkeeping of this establishment on a sound business basis. Will you not definitely join our staff in that capacity?"

"It is very kind of you. I fear I might not be able to stay long with you."

"But it would suit you better to work quietly and comfortably in a superb office, than to spend your time in police investigation! It's the other way with me, I should adore being a detective."

"Mr. Sigissimons, who told you that I belonged to the police?"

"Yourself, Miss Daisy. When a lady like yourself comes to a place such as this, and asks to work for no pay, who has taken no end of trouble to learn the ins and outs of this business, who does four times as much important work as our best paid clerks—why, it is not natural. You must admit that! On the contrary, it is very suspicious. Come now, Miss Daisy! No more humbug. Though I am a photographer, I am not an imbecile. You have come to my place to make an investigation?"

"It is true. I am a detective. My real name is Davis—Mrs. Davis."

"What have you come to search for here?"

"I had to find out who the person was, who, some weeks ago,

brought a child here to be photographed—a child of about two years old. I have identified the person and the child. The child is a little boy called Daniel, his mother who brought him here is Françoise Lemercier, the mistress of poor Garrick."

"The Garrick condemned to death for murdering his wife? I know about that, Mrs. Davis."

"You must not call me Mrs. Davis."

"Why not? It is your name!"

"Precisely. Why I come here must be kept secret from your staff."

"Quite right, Miss Daisy! . . . But what is this?"

The office door opened and a negro entered. A big, broad-shouldered fellow, ebony-black, clad in a green ulster, trimmed with sparkling buttons and silver braid. Tags of gold ornamented his chest, and on his fuzzy locks was an immense cap with glazed peak. His feet were shod in large yellow shoes, while his hands were hidden in white gloves too large and too long.

This negro was the "footman"—factotum of Sigissimons' photographic establishment.

"Sir, I come tell you someone below wishes his portrait. Shall he come up to stand before the big machine that imitates figures?"

"Job," replied his employer, "it is not for you to come up with messages. You ought not to leave the hall. I pay you to be on view, to attract attention, and I'm hanged if you are worth your job!"

"Good sir! Don't be angry. I go to the pavement. I tell the good woman to wait in the salon."

Job withdrew.

"Where did you come across this negro?" asked Mrs. Davis.

"I don't know anything about him. I hired him a week ago, on account of his striking appearance, his fine color, and because of a little advertisement in the *Times*."

"It is not very prudent to take into your service no one knows who," remarked Mrs. Davis.

Sigissimons shrugged:

"If only because of your attitude of perpetual suspicion I would have guessed you belonged to the police! The least thing appears complicated to those of your profession, and you always scent mysteries where there are none."

"Oh!"

"Believe me you should not exaggerate things," admonished the photographer. "This good Job now is certainly an honest, well-meaning fellow, because he is completely imbecile. Besides, he is in love."

"In love?" repeated Mrs. Davis.

"By Jove, yes! And in love with you, Mrs. Davis. Though you are a detective you are nonetheless a woman. Surely you have noticed his lovesick glances whenever he meets you in his coming and going?"

Mrs. Davis smiled enigmatically:

"You are deluding yourself, my dear sir. I am past the age which inspires such passions."

Sigissimons was about to reply, but one of the staff, white this time, entered the office.

He carried a large bag. He placed it on the floor, opened it, and took out a number of photographic accessories:

"There, sir ! A few things I thought worth bidding for at an auction. They are in first-rate condition."

Sigissimons cast an appraising glance over them, examining some closely:

"You have done very well, Charley. Quality all right, but did you have to go to top prices to get them?"

"I got them for a mere song, sir."

Charley was about to expatiate on his bargains when Mrs. Davis gave Sigissimons a significant glance and pointed a finger at the door.

Sigissimons took the hint:

"Run along, Charley. I'm talking business with Miss Daisy. I'll hear all about your bargains presently."

Charley took himself off with his bag, leaving his purchases scattered on the floor.

"Well—" Sigissimons had turned to Mrs. Davis. He stopped

short, scarcely believing his eyes.

She had thrown herself on the floor, and was rapidly turning over the articles. She drew from among them a tiny kodak.

Adjusting her eyeglasses, she tried to decipher the initials on the corner of the kodak.

She failed.

She passed the kodak to Sigissimons:

"Please tell me what is written on it."

The photographer examined the letters:

"S.Y." he read out. "Wait—there is a number—it is 4. Certainly it is a 4."

Mrs. Davis was greatly excited:

"You said 'S.Y. 4?'"

"I did."

"For how much will you sell that kodak to me?"

"I will not sell it. I will lend it to you for as long as you like."

"Thank you," cried Mrs. Davis, seizing the kodak.

"Can you tell me if there is a film in it on which photographs have been taken?"

Sigissimons examined it:

"Yes," said he.

"I beg of you to let me have the use of your darkroom at once. I must develop these films. Do not bother! I can manage. I know how to do it."

Without questioning, the photographer pressed the bell.

Charley appeared:

"Make ready the red lantern in the darkroom."

"Yes, sir."

Sigissimons turned to the disturbed Mrs. Davis:

"The dark room will be at your service in a few minutes."

Why had Mrs. Davis been so moved at sight of this kodak? Because it was one of a special make used by Scotland Yard.

Mrs. Davis felt sure it had belonged to one of her colleagues. This astonished her, as detectives are not in the habit of selling their cameras.

S.Y. signified Scotland Yard. The number, 4, meant something definite to the detective: 4 was the registered number of her colleague and friend, Detective French, fourth member of the Supreme Council.

How was it, by what extraordinary chance, had this camera belonging to French come into the possession of Sigissimons, after having been sold by private or public auction? And that, a few days after the inexplicable disappearance of the detective, gone in search of Mrs. Garrick? Mrs. Davis scented a mystery.

The developed negatives would tell some tale.

What?

Mrs. Davis was in the dark room dimly lighted by a red lantern. The effect was sinister. She was absorbed in her work.

The first negative developed had evidently been taken at night by a magnesium light. It showed the deck of a ship leaving port.

Mrs. Davis examined it, and identified it as Dieppe. In the foreground was a lifebuoy with the word *Scotsman* on it.

Scotsman was the name of one of the Newhaven-Dieppe steamers.

"That's surprising," said Mrs. Davis to herself. "It seems by these photographs that French must have been on this ship."

She examined another developed film:

"Here also are persons whose appearance I seem to know. That blackguardly looking youth, that lady! . . ."

Mrs. Davis shivered. She had felt a warm breath on her neck. She seemed to hear breathing.

She looked round and saw nothing but darkness: "How silly of me!" she murmured.

She was thinking of her vanished colleague, who was dead, perhaps.

Mrs. Davis fancied she heard a deep sigh:

"Who is it?" she whispered.

There was no reply.

"I am an idiot! Nervous as no woman of my age has a right to be—above all a woman detective!"

Mrs. Davis became absorbed in the print just developed.

First she saw the outlines of a house, then more and more distinct, the figure of a tall woman standing at a window—a woman with fine features and a distinguished bearing.

"It looks like Mrs. Garrick," exclaimed the detective. She held the print at a certain angle.

Beyond a doubt, the woman leaning on the window balcony was Mrs. Garrick!

The portrait closely resembled that published in the papers.

"What a discovery!" cried Mrs. Davis. "It proves that our poor Tom Bob, so abominably condemned to death, is innocent of the crime imputed to him! These photographs, taken after Mrs. Garrick's disappearance, after her husband's arrest, will cause the reversal of his sentence. For proof I have the series number of the film roll—it is quite a recent number. I know that."

Highly delighted, Mrs. Davis was about to place the negative in a fixing bath, when she stopped, startled at what she saw in the rusty colored water at the bottom of the ebonite dish. A negroid face glared up at her with white globular eyes and a double row of ivory teeth.

Mrs. Davis restrained a cry, as she glanced over her shoulder. By the light of the red lantern she glimpsed the colossal figure of negro Job. What did he want?

A stout arm was round her waist. The negro was drawing her towards him.

Was this the embrace of an infatuated fool?

The arms tightened round her. A huge hand was fumbling, snatching!

Mrs. Davis kept her head. She slipped from the negro, ran to the door, kicked it open, letting in a flood of light.

Job rolled his eyes, made no further attempt to molest her, rushed out muttering unintelligible words.

Mrs. Davis closed the door of the dark room. She examined the film. The unfixed film was spoiled by the light let into the room—it was clouded. She could not distinguish the house balcony, or the woman leaning on it!

So much the worse!

However she had the first photograph unspoiled, that reproducing the deck of the steamer and a recognizable portrait of Mrs. Garrick standing among the passengers.

Mrs. Davis called Charley, who hurried in.

"Charley, here is a document of the highest importance! How long will you take to get this proof finished?"

"Four hours in all, Miss. Two to dry the films and two to finish them off."

"Good. Do it at once, please, Charley. It is most urgent."

A few minutes later she left the Sigissimons studios, passing by the negro, who was once more at his post. She called a cab and was driven off in the direction of Temple Court.

"You wanted to see me?"

The Coroner was in his office.

Mrs. Davis was standing before him:

"I have just made an important discovery about Tom Bob—I mean Garrick. He is innocent of the murder of his wife."

"Still this Garrick affair?" The Coroner frowned: "Garrick has been condemned to death without appeal."

"A revision of the sentence is a duty, sir! . . . There absolutely must be a revision! There is no question about it!"

Mrs. Davis then gave a detailed account of the sensational discoveries she had made.

The Coroner was roused from his attitude of apathetic indifference:

"Bring me those photographs and I will submit them in the proper quarter. Possibly it may lead to a new trial."

Mrs. Davis lost no time. She re-entered her taxi and was driven back to the Sigissimons studios.

No sooner had Mrs. Davis left the studios than the negro, Job, appeared greatly upset. He marched up and down in an agitated manner. He then left his post, slunk into the studios, and slipped into the darkroom.

Just as he was leaving the room Charley met him. Job's black face paled to a dirty gray.

"What are you doing there, Job?" asked Charley. "Nothing at all, Massa Charley! Not doin' any harm."

Charley did not notice Job's excited condition. The negro stammered out:

"Massa Charley!"

"What is it, Job?"

"Tell master, please, I can't stay here—very glad to earn these shillings, but not good work for negro—and Job is vexed for behaving silly to Miss Daisy! Wanted to hug her. Very bad. Job a bad black monkey!"

Charley stared at the negro in bewilderment, while he hastily got out of his great green ulster:

"I give back the cloak with gold on it!" declared Job, casting a regretful glance at the showy garment. Then, throwing his cap at Charley's feet, he tore out of the studios, went up the street at a smart pace, and was soon lost to sight.

Charley was in a state of amazement. The negro had bolted for some unexplained reason and had not even claimed the week's wages due to him!

Mrs. Davis appeared:

"Where are my photographs?" she asked Charley at once.

The lad raised his arms:

"I've forgotten all about them!" he cried. "But don't you trouble, Miss Daisy, I'll make up for lost time!"

"Oh, do be quick! It's very urgent!"

"I'm going directly now, Miss!" cried Charley, entering the dark room. . . .

Precious moments passed:

"Miss Daisy?"

"What is it?"

"Where have you put your negative? I can't find it!"

Mrs. Davis, filled with dismal apprehensions, ran into the dark room.

She and Charley looked in every hole and corner for the precious film, picturing Mrs. Garrick on the steamer deck.

The film was not to be found.

"Heavens above!" cried the distracted detective. "What fiendish ill-luck is pursuing us!"

She uttered an "Ah!" of astonishment as she caught sight of Job's showy ulster in a heap on the floor:

"What does that mean?" she cried.

Charley explained, adding:

"I thought that as Job had behaved disrespectfully to you he didn't like to let you set eyes on him again, and that was why he left in such a hurry, and without the wages due to him."

"Really!" was Mrs. Davis's enigmatic reply. She stood silent, absorbed in thought. The mystery deepened: Was the disappearance of the photographic document and the flight of the negro interconnected? Was it premeditated? Were the two occurrences coincidence?

She went to the telephone box:

"Hello! Hello! Scotland Yard?"

Connection made, she asked for Shephard, giving her pass number.

A few moments later Mrs. Davis recognized the voice of her colleague:

"What can I do for you?"

"Shephard, do you know a certain negro? Goes by the name of Job. Recently employed as porter at the Sigissimons studios?"

"I know Job quite well. African. Was employed on cargo boats. A bit of a drunkard and thief. Used to show trained fleas!"

"Shephard, do you think him capable of initiative? Could anyone trust him to carry out a delicate or an audacious plan? Is he intelligent or a crass idiot?"

"An imbecile," was Shephard's unhesitating reply. "Thanks! I will see you about this matter!"

Mrs. Davis hung up the receiver, but remained in the telephone box.

She had also considered Job little removed from an idiot. But—was he? she now wondered.

Either Charley's explanation of Job's flight was the true one, it was plausible enough—or, Job had played a part, in order to see the photographs she was developing, and seize the opportunity to destroy the most compromising.

If this were the true solution, Job had played his part to perfection.

In this case Job must have been acting for an interested party, who wished to destroy every trace of the journey of French to France, and also to make away with every document likely to prove Tom Bob's innocence. The revelation of his wife's existence through the film in French's camera was decisive.

"I must get at the rights of this!" said Mrs. Davis to herself.

She hastened to Scotland Yard to interview Shephard. On her way she summed up the matter in great vexation of spirit:

"It just comes to this: Two hours ago I held the documents which would prove Tom Bob's innocence. I have not got those documents now!

"Who wishes to injure him? Who is the adversary who is determined to destroy him?"

18. In a Whiskey Dream

Inspector Juve and his colleague, Inspector Michel, were deep in conversation as they walked up and down Victoria Station.

It was ten minutes to eleven in the morning. The station was full of bustle. The Dover boat-train would start in a few minutes.

Juve had returned to Paris after he had seen Lady Beltham with French on the steamer *Scotsman* at Dieppe. Then learning from his friend, Inspector Michel, that the Beadle had suddenly left for London, Juve returned to England, glad of the excuse, not only to track down the hooligan, but to realize the great project for which Monsieur Havard had given him an absolutely free hand, at his own risks and perils.

Juve had brought Michel to London for a short holiday. His leave was expiring today, and he had to present himself at the Quai des Orfèvres without delay. Juve, free, remained in London.

Michel had put his valise in the chosen corner of a compartment!

Now they were discussing the many sensational events which had occurred since their arrival in England. Though they understood certain happenings, too many of them remained mysterious.

For the fiftieth time Michel asked:

"My dear Juve, what do you really think about the disappearance of French? The fact that he has not returned to London, that he did not turn up at the Garrick trial, makes me think that this Irish detective was much more an agent of Fantômas than an authentic representative of our Supreme Council."

"My dear Michel," replied Juve, "your conclusion is detestable! French was assuredly not a messenger of our terrible adversary! I am more and more convinced that he has not brought his mission to a successful finish, that he has been forcibly prevented from doing so, that the power which has prevented his success is a power which cannot be gainsaid—death!"

"Juve! You believe French has been murdered?"

"I do not think it, I am sure of it!"

"But by whom? And why?"

"You go too fast, my friend! Let us ask: By whom has French been assassinated? When we have the answer to that we may solve the second riddle: Why was French murdered?

"Listen, Michel! We must eliminate Fantômas as the probable criminal.

"Fantômas is in prison: be sure he had the greatest possible incentive to leave French alive, since he was bringing with him the proof of the innocence of Fantômas.

"Remains—Lady Beltham.

"Has she assassinated French that she may not be dragged before the Central Criminal Court? Hardly. Besides, I do not think Lady Beltham could carry such a plan through, seeing she had to deal with French, a member of our Supreme Council."

"Who, then, is the murderer?"

"Probably an evil-looking blackguard I saw on the *Scotsman*. I am considering the pros and cons, Michel."

The porters were calling to the passengers: "Take your seats!"

Michel stepped into his empty compartment, closed the door, and leaned out of the window:

"Juve," he questioned in a discreetly lowered voice, "what do you really think about the condemnation of Garrick? Do you believe it final? Since Garrick is Fantômas, can Fantômas let himself be caught in such a trap? Why it would be childish, unworthy of him!"

Juve glanced about him whenever Fantômas was mentioned.

Were they being spied on?

Quite likely.

Juve smiled:

"Have you noticed, Michel, that in England for every six Englishmen you meet eight policemen? They are the most numerous of all officials in the United Kingdom. I like to think that the simplest way to pass unnoticed if you wish to hide yourself is to join the crowd of Scotland Yard officials."

Michel did not want irony; he wanted a direct answer. Juve complied:

"Like you, I think if Fantômas had committed the crime he would so have covered his tracks that the police would have had all their work cut out to catch him.

"Fantômas has been arrested with the greatest ease, because he is innocent of the crime of which he is accused.

"Nevertheless, since his imprisonment he must be repenting with fury, with anxiety, that he ever let himself be put in such a position. He knows how rigorous English prison rule is. He knows, too, that sentences once passed are very, very rarely annulled.

"You ask, Michel, what will become of him?

"One of two things will happen. Either Lady Beltham—Mrs. Garrick for the public and justice—will show herself, and they will have to declare her pseudo-husband not guilty, and will revise the trial, and Fantômas will be freed, or Lady Beltham-Garrick will not show up to save Garrick-Fantômas, and he will be hanged by the neck till he is dead, in conformity with the sentence passed on him."

"Is that the end you wish for Fantômas?" asked Michel quickly.

Juve shook his head:

"No, Michel, no. I prefer to see Garrick at liberty. I want to see Fantômas resume the personality of Tom Bob. I should prefer to unmask the monster before the eyes of all, then annihilate him for all time! But the end is not yet!"

"It is through women you hope to corner this elusive Evil Incarnate, at last, is it not, Juve?"

"By means of women? It well may be, my dear Michel," replied Juve.

"There is another affair, Michel, more closely connected with this Garrick case than the police seem to realize. They do wrong not to go thoroughly into it, because innocent victims and abominable criminals are implicated. You know Françoise

Lemercier mourns the loss of her little Daniel? You know that Nini Guinon ostentatiously exhibits a child which she declares is her boy Jack?

"Michel, my opinion is that little Jack is dead, that his death almost certainly lies at his mother's door, and that Nini for some purpose of her own, replaced her dead child by the living Daniel, stolen—heartlessly stolen—from his devoted mother, Françoise Lemercier! It is only a hypothesis, but I bet on it."

Michel was intensely interested:

"Dear Juve, keep me informed, I beg of you! What are you going to do?"

Juve's reply was a cordial handshake.

The train was moving out of the station. Juve ran along the platform for some yards beside Michel's compartment.

The train was moving faster. Juve shouted his last words:

"I told you that the best way to pass unnoticed in England is to become a policeman! Michel! I have an idea!"

*   *   *   *   *

"What is your name?"

"Daniel."

A resounding smack was the answer to this reply. The smack was succeeded by a child's heartrending sobs.

"Say what your name is!" commanded a shrill voice. "Say you are called Jack! Don't you understand! Daniel does not exist any more! You are Jack! Jack! Jack! Do you hear!"

It was just on midnight. Nini Guinon had come back to her dirty Whitechapel lodging at 14a Belmont Street. The four-story house was let out in furnished apartments, reached by a narrow hall passage, and a steep ill-lit staircase, going up like a corkscrew to the attic floor.

The house was a shelter for an ever shifting crowd of thieves, vagabonds, and cadging loafers.

In this unsavory den Lord Duncan's wife chose to live. Nini Guinon rented a flat on the fourth floor—two rooms and a kitchen.

On the same landing, opposite Nini's door, was a poverty-stricken room. Its sole furniture, two trundle beds and a rickety table.

This was the haunt, from time to time, of Nini's two chums, the Beadle and Beaumôme, when they had nothing worse to do, when they were not snoring off some drinking bout beneath a Thames bridge arch, or occupying a cell at the police station.

This evening, forty-eight hours after Michel's departure for France, Nini Guinon came in, excessively drunk, and in uproarious spirits.

To use her own expression, she had jolly well amused herself all that evening!

Those of the men who were flush with cash ordered a princely dinner, and they drank to the return of negro Job, who had refused to be slave to a bourgeois!

The rowdy crew had stuffed and guzzled their fill when Beaumôme, cheered on by his pals, tried to make Nini's child swallow a glass of whiskey. The poor baby had obediently tasted the burning liquor forced down his tender throat. Nearly choked to suffocation, the suffering boy struggled, black in the face. The laughing Nini had a moment's terror. She thought the adored child of Françoise Lemercier was going to die. All the same the kid had made such faces, she had to laugh. There was a chorus of laughter.

An orgy followed.

Beaumôme and the Beadle accompanied Nini to their den.

They had to help her upstairs. She dragged the wretched Daniel bumping after her.

Beaumôme meant to take advantage of Nini's intoxicated state, and clinch his amorous bargain. But Nini was in merry mood—she had no use for love. When Beaumôme was marching into her room with the swagger of a victor, Nini banged the door in his face, leaving him on the landing staggering and crestfallen, his sole companion, the Beadle, which was not at all the same thing!

Obsessed by one idea Nini undressed the pseudo little Jack

clumsily, trying to force the trembling child to call himself Jack. Each time the sickened boy declared his name was Daniel, the tipsy vixen playing the part of mother, cuffed his ears, thus informing him he would have to lie to escape hard blows.

The more Nini insisted, the more obstinate the terrified Daniel grew.

Fortunately Nini was too tipsy to continue her maltreatment. Her head was whizzing. She groped her unsteady way to her trundle bed, never made. She let herself fall like a lump of lead on the tumbled bedclothes, and soon was snoring.

Little Daniel, shivering with cold, moaning and whimpering with fright and suffering, crouched half-undressed on the dirty floor.

After a while, disturbed by strange dreams in which Beaumôme played a fantastic part, Nini half woke. There was a noise. It came from the direction of the window. Nini felt a stream of chill air blowing on her throat, cooling her burning lips. It was refreshing.

But with the draught, something, someone had entered the room. Nini wished to find out who it was, but the torpor of intoxication benumbed her.

Her half-shut eyes could see. They told her someone had entered the room by the window opening onto the roof.

A ray of moonlight outlines a mysterious form.

A human form, unknown to the watcher, tall, tragic, graceful—all black. It glides forward slowly, irresolutely. It approaches Nini's bed.

The prostrate woman has sense enough left in her fuddled brain to realize this is no nightmare. Someone is bending over her!

She tries to cry out. She mutters: "A drink! A drink!" She wants to say more.

She is incapable of further effort. Nini sees the form draw back, then bend over her anew. Nini perceives an unknown face, strangely beautiful, is gazing at her.

The low crying of little Daniel, crouching on the floor, pierces the silence.

It mingles piteously with the whistling noise of Nini's breathing in her drunken slumber.

Again she awakes, or dreams she does.

She seems to see a graceful form listening in the moonlight. She sees it approach the whimpering child, raise him, fold him tenderly in her arms, murmuring softly the while. Little Daniel's plaints died down as the low melody of a cradle song floated sweetly on the air of that squalid den. Nini's throat was swelling with emotion.

Had an angel of Paradise come to visit her in the glamorous moonbeams?

Nini, too, would sing, but only raucous sounds issued from her lips, far removed from harmonies of celestial music. So touched is she to see this gracious vision caring tenderly for little Daniel that she weeps for gratitude and joy. She sees in thought her little Jack, dead through her fault, and carried away by Fantômas. She shivers, trembles at the remembrance—but she rejoices:

"It is not Daniel who is there," she half dreams; "it is my little Jack come back to me!"

Nini utters a cry of joy, then weeps afresh, turning on her miserable bed. No! It cannot be little Jack! Jack is dead. Nini has replaced him by Daniel—Daniel, the child of Françoise Lemercier, that someone stole from her for Nini!

Oh, no one must know—must ever know!

Nini at this idea stiffens, revolts, clenches her fists—in a dream she beats little Daniel because he does not know the name he ought to bear, because he must forget he is called Daniel.

Why has she uttered a cry of alarm?

Because it seems to her the being who had entered the room has vanished through the window bearing the child with her! No. That cannot be true! She thinks it is so because she has not recovered her senses. But has she imagined it, deceived herself? Little by little, Nini opens her eyes, looks about her, sits up, and with moist hands presses her burning forehead. What has been happening? Is it a dream or no? Nini is wide awake now. She gets out of bed. Her feet touch the cold floor, also through the open window comes the chill damp air of morning, making Nini shiver.

"Jack? Where are you?" she calls in a low voice.

A poignant silence persists.

"Where has the little brat got to?" she mutters. She must speak more kindly, then he will answer: "Daniel! Daniel! Where are you?"

Nini remembers her dream vividly. She is scared. She manages to light a lamp. She takes it in her none too steady hand, searching every corner.

The yellow lamplight mingles with the moon's pale rays, with the pallid gleams of breaking day.

Nini's rooms are empty. Little Daniel has vanished. Nini Guinon has let the child be stolen!

The vixen calls on High Heaven in strident tones.

Nini's shrieks aroused her neighbors. Beaumôme and the Beadle jumped out of their lair, frowzy with sleep, disheveled, scared.

Nini screeched.

"They have stolen my Jack! I shall go to the police! He must be found!"

The two hooligans, who had been sleeping off their potations, did not understand at first what had happened.

When they had hunted over Nini's rooms, they grasped the fact—Jack had vanished. It was a nuisance of a business—but to call in the police! Only a mad or drunk woman could think of such a thing!

The huge Beadle whispered in Nini's ear:

"It will be daylight soon. We'll see about finding your kid then."

"You keep quiet, my woman," advised Beaumôme. "It'll be a deuce of a business if the bobbies get their noses into it."

In a lower tone he added:

"The brat they've taken from you, and your little Jack—well, it's not the same thing! You keep mum!"

Nini approved. She nodded to the pale-faced young rascal.

Yes, she must keep a still tongue.

Swallowing her rage, she went back to her den. Behind her stalked silently Beaumôme.

Nini was so absorbed she did not hear him enter. The pallid rascal thought his chance a good one. He clasped the form of his charmer, audaciously. Alas! It was not the right moment.

Nini turned round on him. A violent blow from her fist gave him a black eye. She thumped his nose black and blue.

Cursing and growling, Beaumôme beat a hasty retreat. Nini, left alone, sought for some trace of little Daniel.

In vain.

19. Policeman 416

"Hop! Policeman! What would you say, policeman, if you were asked to raise your eyes to the wall above you, and to give your opinion on the said wall?"

"I should say, gentleman, that the question is ridiculous, and that it is not necessary for me to examine it."

"What would you say, policeman, if it was pointed out to you that this immensely old wall is furnished, on its upper part, with cramp irons which form a veritable ladder, by which one could get onto the roof?"

"I should reply that is not the pathway of an honest man, and I should advise anyone who spoke of it, to go on his way."

"What would you say, policeman—"

"What would you say, gentleman, if I invited you to turn about quick and take yourself off quicker than you came?"

"What would you say, policeman, if I refused to go away?"

"What would you say, gentleman, if I arrested you?"

The joking tone of this odd dialogue was assuming a more and more acrimonious quality.

It was four o'clock in the morning, and a clear dawn was throwing the housetops into sharp relief, when this bandying of words occurred in Belmont Street, Whitechapel, between a stout policeman—Number 416—and a jovial fellow, also solidly built. Quietly dressed, he had the look of a respectable artisan.

The policeman and the wayfarer eyed each other from head to foot.

The policeman's threat had not made his confronter turn a hair. Evidently this ironic personage did not sufficiently respect authority expressed in uniform!

Number 416 concluded that this personage had been so often arrested that the threat of arrest left him cold, or that he was in a position to claim indulgent treatment from the police.

Was he some privileged person?

The civilian bent to Number 416 and whispered in a bantering tone:

"What would you say, policeman, if I told you I was Shephard, the detective, and member of our Supreme Council?"

Number 416 was stolid:

"I should tell you to show your card."

No sooner said than done.

The card was at once produced.

Instinctively the policeman rectified the position. He saluted.

The face of number 416 grew red. His question was ironic:

"What would you say in your turn, Inspector Shephard, if I myself . . . !"

The enigmatic Number 416 stopped short.

Had he pulled himself up because the moment for self-revelation was inopportune?

Inspector Shephard had moved away. He was off like an Indian on the trail.

He went to the corner of the street, hugging the walls, brushing past the houses, evidently a man accustomed to walk noiselessly and evade notice.

Number 416 watched him suddenly turn and hasten back:

"A sleuth-hound who has scented blood, he might be!" was the policeman's comment.

Shephard breathed: "I smell game hereabouts. You will lend me a hand?"

Number 416 scratched his chin:

"Well, Inspector Shephard, I'm not now on duty—it's not my beat! Still I will gladly lend a hand—but you will excuse if I am not as good a guide as I could wish. I repeat, it's not in my division."

Shephard had noted that the uniform of Number 416 lacked the significant blue and white armlet:

"I saw that," he said. "But what are you doing here, at this hour, in this out-of-the-way part?"

Number 416 smiled a meaning smile.

Shephard laughed:

"As for me," he said, "I am looking for an individual—a suspect—whose means of existence I must examine, whose domicile I must identify. This man lives in a house let out in furnished apartments. The door of that house is only fifty yards or so, down the street. There it is—on the right. Next to that tavern!"

"Yes, Inspector, I see it."

"This individual," continued Shephard, "is a Frenchman called the Beadle—I do not need to tell you more than that! It seemed to me that a short while ago the roof of his domicile was the scene of abnormal activity."

Number 416 interrupted:

"I thought I saw someone passing along the parapet of that house, about ten minutes ago, Inspector Shephard."

"It was a woman, wasn't it?" asked Shephard.

"No," replied Number 416, hesitating slightly, "I rather think it was a negro."

"Policeman, do not let us lose a moment! Follow me! Are you armed?"

"Not being of the regular service, I always carry my six-chambered revolver fully charged, but only for use in the last resort."

Shephard and Number 416 moved nimbly towards the wretched tenement house.

Vaulting on a six-foot wall, they made rapid use of the cramp irons for footholds. In no time they were on a level with the roof. They found themselves among a wilderness of chimneys, of sloping roofs of old tiles and slates, of dormer windows overlooking the street or inner courtyards.

Shephard passed with the dexterity of an acrobat from house to house, mounting pointed timber-work, hanging on to gutters as though to the manner trained.

Number 416 followed with agile care.

Shephard congratulated himself that he had a colleague equal to the occasion.

Shephard abruptly signaled: "Stop!"

He was crouching behind a dormer window, ready for the spring, if need be.

A sash window was flung up. A gallows-faced fellow pushed head and shoulders out. He gazed about him, staring suspiciously at the nearby roofs.

Uttering a cry, he drew back.

This vanishing trick was too late!

Quick as lightning, Shephard had seized him by the wrist, had leaped into the house with him, keeping a vigorous grip on the jailbird.

Number 416 was at his heels. They found themselves in a squalid garret, dismally lit by a smoky lamp. Two dirty trundle beds stood at the opposite side of this lair. A huge black trunk was planted in the middle of the floor. Its half-open cover showed a disorderly mass of objects. This species of dustbin contained old clothes, empty bottles, torn shoes, rags, and musty odds and ends.

Shephard, still clutching his prisoner, took his flashlight from his pocket and turned its ray full on this inhabitant of the garret, whose livid face and evil look showed his quality: he was vicious terror personified.

Shephard was crestfallen:

"It is not the one," he murmured.

If Shephard was disappointed, Number 416 uttered an exclamation of satisfaction.

"What's your name?" questioned Shephard, shaking his prisoner, who articulated:

"Beaumôme."

"Who is your room companion?"

"The Beadle."

"Where is he?"

"Can't say."

Beaumôme gathered courage when he realized Shephard meant him no harm. Also he would make himself agreeable, hoping they would leave him in peace:

"The Beadle," he declared with effrontery, "left for France a dozen days ago, and has not come back. I am annoyed, for he has not left me his share of the rent, and I am asking myself how I shall pay the lodging at the end of the week."

Beaumôme lied.

His interrogation took place exactly half an hour after he had tried to console Nini for the disappearance of little Daniel.

Beaumôme knew the Beadle was there then. What had become of the Beadle?

Much Beaumôme cared, so that he was left free to go his own way!

Beaumôme gave a sigh of satisfaction.

The detective had loosed his hold.

Shephard whispered to Number 416:

"The individual I am after is probably not far off! We must make a thorough search. Will you be good enough to search the rooms on the left? I will see to the others. The Beadle is a big man, bald, not a hair on his face. Arrest all individuals corresponding more or less with this description."

"As to you," he said, addressing Beaumôme, "you are forbidden to leave your lodging until further notice."

Beaumôme muttered some unintelligible words. Adopting the demeanor of one whose conscience is at ease, he stretched himself on his squalid bed.

The policemen separated on the landing.

Each quietly set about his search.

Those forced entries into the tenements with their ragged, emaciated crowd of foul-smelling humanity was a disconcerting experience, even for such case hardened policemen.

Number 416 was now knocking at a door at the end of a passage. It was ajar. He saw a huge negro rise up staggering with terror:

"Good policeman, I not bad. I done nothing. I not go in prison—no one here!"

Number 416 did not answer the negro. He entered the apartment. It consisted of two fair-sized rooms and a little kitchen—a luxurious lodging compared with the others, but ill furnished and badly kept.

A woman certainly shared the rooms. Skirts were suspended

from the wall. Three immense hats with draggled plumes were stuck on hooks. Muddy boots, from which most of the buttons were missing, lay close to a dressing table on which were scattered combs with broken teeth, wet soap, powder, hairpins and false hair.

Number 416 was now interested beyond the usual. He murmured:

"Nini Guinon! Miserable woman! What a comedown!"

Number 416 opened cupboards, rummaged drawers, searching every hole and corner.

When he put his hand on a small box, the negro, who was holding on to the door in trembling silence, let out a yell of terror, and stuttered:

"Not me! Job has not stolen them! He left the photographer without taking one thing. It's not Job! No!"

The negro ran onto the landing and raced down the gloomy staircase. His steps could be heard on the bare stairway. A loud cry echoed through the house, followed by the noise of a fall, succeeded by dead silence.

Number 416 did not disturb himself. He had opened the box. He took out two films, examined them, slipped them into his pocketbook, hid them inside his uniform.

He beamed. "What a stroke of luck!"

Number 416 heard a slight noise. A door opposite was being cautiously opened.

The policeman was out of the room in a bound.

He faced Beaumôme, come out of his garret. He had heard the negro's fall.

Number 416 put his hand on the loathsome hooligan's shoulder.

A strange policeman this! Familiar and brutal:

"Nini Guinon? Taken to her heels, hasn't she? Spit it out now! You must know where she's run off to!"

Speechless, Beaumôme gaped at this policeman. Was he one of the gutter tribe masquerading or a real bobby who knew too much?"

The piercing eye of Number 416 was fixed on him. Subjugated, Beaumôme obeyed:

"The Nini," he said reluctantly, "got back here close on the twelve strokes last night, and not steady on her pins either. Then just on two by the clock, she was squawking the place down . . ."

"Why?"

Beaumôme shrugged, squinted at Number 416, and snarled: "How should I know!"

"Come now! None of that nonsense. Better lay it on the table, and quick! Best way to keep out of the police box!"

Beaumôme knew he must speak out:

"As for that, I think the Nini squawked because they'd made off with her kid."

"Stolen her kid?" echoed the astonished policeman.

"You've hit it, bobby! Nip for the kid. It's not hopped it on its own in the night, you bet! It's somebody wanted a kid without the bother of putting one into the world."

"What has become of Nini since?"

"Probable she's hopped it after the kid," said Beaumôme.

The conversation was interrupted. Shephard called from the floor below:

"Policeman?"

Number 416 left the hooligan at a run. He rejoined Inspector Shephard, leaving a Beaumôme, gratified at such condescension.

"A glass of hot grog, policeman?"

"By Jove, Shephard, I won't say no. I didn't do a bad stroke of business just now. I was hard at it with you!"

The two policemen had left the Belmont Street tenement house, and had entered a bar just opened. The bartender welcomed them with a smile—policemen were a guarantee of "all's well here," when they dropped in for a glass.

Shephard and Number 416 were standing at the end of the bar counter chatting in low tones.

Shephard looked annoyed.

His Belmont Street night raid had not produced any interesting result. He had not discovered the Beadle after several hours' search. Nevertheless, Shephard was convinced the Beadle was in London.

Number 416 nodded agreement with this conclusion:

"But why are you searching for the Beadle?" he asked.

Shephard eyed Number 416. His expression said: "What a stupid question!"

What he answered was:

"Why, because I have my reasons for thinking that individual is guilty of causing the disappearance of one of our colleagues—Detective French—who went on a mission to France to discover . . . But, in fact, that does not concern you, policeman."

"You are right," agreed Number 416, "it is no concern of mine that French, member of the Supreme Council, went to Paris to find Mrs. Garrick, if she was still in existence."

Shephard's eyes were wide with amazement. This man was no fool! He was also in the know further than he had suspected. The whiskey had loosed his tongue. He would confide in this informed and sympathetic Number 416.

He told him of the extraordinary disappearance of French, the theft of the photographs discovered by Mrs. Davis in the Sigissimons Studios.

Said Number 416:

"With reference to all these adventures, Inspector Shephard, it does not seem to me that you have had any sort of communication with the French detective your colleague went to consult in Paris. This Monsieur Juve, this 'famous Juve,' as they call him, has he not put himself in touch with you over this affair?"

"My faith, no!" declared Shephard. "And now I think of it, I am surprised he has not!"

Number 416 smiled at his discontented companion. He also winked:

"Do you know Juve personally?"

"No. But what does that matter? What annoys me greatly is that tonight's investigation is so barren of results. I missed the Beadle by perhaps a few hours, or possibly minutes. I wasted time with unimportant people, this young hooligan, this Beaumôme, who does not inspire me with much confidence, but I have no fault to find with him. Then that drunken fool of a negro who fell downstairs and has broken three or four teeth, and that disreputable French creature, Nini Guinon!"

"Nini!" exclaimed Number 416. "Have you seen her recently?"

"Yes, she had taken refuge with a neighbor."

"She did not complain of anything?"

"No."

Number 416 was silent, turning something over in his mind:

"What would you say, Inspector Shephard, if a woman, a mother, whose child had been stolen, and who, after the theft, had the unexpected opportunity of meeting the representative of authority in the form of a policeman, and did not seize the chance to inform him of her cruel loss? If, on the contrary, she prudently held her tongue regarding this theft, concealing her emotion, and her grief?"

"What are you driving at?" demanded Shephard.

"I only ask you what you would think of a woman who adopted such an attitude?"

"My faith!" declared Shephard. "I should ask myself if this woman were not to be suspected herself, not to be trusted because she hesitated to beg for the help of justice."

"That is what I wanted you to say," concluded Number 416. "Will you accept another whiskey hot, Inspector Shephard?"

An hour later the detective and the policeman left the bar, after regaling themselves with more whiskey and substantial ham sandwiches.

Shephard had a very friendly feeling for this policeman, so intelligent, so sympathetic, so quick to act, and so well informed regarding the inhabitants of the house in Belmont Street, and that though the street was not in his division.

As to Number 416, he had been immensely amused by Shephard's conversation.

It was broad daylight. Whitechapel was once more a commercial and industrial quarter of London's human hive.

When Shephard and Number 416 were about to part, the detective said:

"You have rendered me signal service tonight, policeman. I should be glad if you would do me a further one. Are you disposed to lend me your support to save an innocent man, who is also a colleague?"

Shephard looked careworn, anxious, and spoke with deep feeling.

Number 416 replied:

"I shall always be at your service, Inspector."

"Ah, it must be more than that! You must be almost my partner! I warn you it is a ticklish business. Naturally, I shall secure permission from the proper quarter to make use of your services. But when obtaining the authorization I shall not say why I want you."

Number 416 scrutinized Shephard's face for an indication of what was in his mind:

"Do you want me to agree to join with you in some illegal action?"

"Perhaps."

Number 416 lowered his eyes, considering attentively the points of his shoes. Then looking fixedly at Shephard he said:

"I am ambitious. I want to get on, rise in rank as quickly as possible. Your protection will be very useful to me. If I promise my devoted zeal, will you promise me your support?"

Shephard smiled and signified his agreement. The bargain was made.

"When will you have need of me, Inspector?" asked Number 416 in businesslike tones.

Shephard replied:

"A week hence, and for forty-eight hours, particularly the fourteenth and fifteenth of June."

As the two men were going their separate ways, Number 416 remarked:

"The night of June fourteen-fifteen? That is the date of Garrick's execution, is it not?"

Shephard started: "Really this policeman was so intelligent that a word or two sufficed. He guessed before a thing was explained!" thought the detective. What he said was: "Yes, it is for Garrick's execution I have need of you."

Shephard walked quickly away.

Number 416 stood motionless on the pavement, smiling.

20. The Supreme Council's Devotion

Garrick was pacing up and down his narrow cell waiting for death.

Up and down, up and down he paced, hands clasped behind his bent back, gloomy-browed, anxious. So might a tiger pace restlessly, ever seeking escape through the bars of his cage.

Alas! Easier to escape from a cage of iron than from an English prison.

Garrick would inevitably hang.

Each minute, each second that passed, was lived through by Garrick in the immediate anguish of death.

Tireless as his tiger-pacing, he repeated over and over: "I am going to die! I am going to die!"

The condemned man interrupted his monotonous pacing up and down.

Was he the victim of one of those hallucinations which attack men suffering tortures such as his?

No. His senses were not bewitched. His brain was clear. He recognized his jailer's step echoing in the corridor. This warder of his would enter the cell.

A key was turning in the lock.

The door opened. The warder announced:

"The chaplain to see you."

Garrick stood quiet, with arms crossed:

"Ah," he said quietly. "The chaplain pays me his last visit but one! Is it the usual one—Mr. Hope?"

"It is the Reverend William Hope."

"Admit him, warder."

Garrick smiled. Little suspected the warders that this cleric was a detective, a comrade, almost a friend!

The warder admitted the chaplain:

"You are authorized to pass an hour with the condemned

prisoner, sir. I will return for you in an hour's time. If you wish to leave earlier, you have only to knock on the door three times."

The warder locked the door.

The two men were left together.

"Courage, my friend!" cried Hope, clasping Garrick's hand.

"I have enough courage, and to spare," retorted Garrick-Tom Bob. "But it is horrible."

William Hope was deeply moved.

He withdrew his hand from Garrick's prolonged clasp, pushed him towards the bed, and seated himself on the stool, close to the condemned man:

"Tom Bob," said he, in a voice trembling with emotion, "I come in the Name of the Supreme Council. Tom Bob, you must not die."

Garrick paled.

He jumped up:

"William Hope, you come to me with that message from the Supreme Council?"

"Yes, in the name of the Supreme Council."

"Swear to me, on your honor, Hope, that not one of our colleagues suspects me? That not one of them refuses to admit my innocence?"

William Hope had risen:

"Such an oath is unnecessary! On my honor, it is! It is unnecessary because I am here to ask you how we can save you, Tom Bob?"

"You ask me that?"

"Yes, I ask you."

"I do not understand you."

"Listen, Tom Bob! The Council met this morning. Alas, only three were present, for French is missing, and you are here. Mrs. Davis, Inspector Shephard, and I composed the Council.

"Listen! Seeing that you are to be executed, that we have no legal means by which to extricate you, we have decided to save you, in spite of all."

Tom Bob-Garrick grasped Hope's hand:

"You have done more for me than anybody!" he cried. "But

you cannot save me!"

"Do not say that, Tom Bob!"

"You have a plan of escape, then?"

Hope shook his head:

"No, Tom. We discussed plans of escape for three hours, this morning, and could not devise a sound one. I am here owing to Mrs. Davis, who said: 'There is only one man who can make a plan of escape and carry it through successfully—Tom Bob, and no other.'

"That is why I am here. What you decide on, we will do. We wish to save your life, but you must guide us. Speak then, Tom! I have come to take your orders."

Garrick was overcome. His colleagues, convinced of his innocence, meant to save him!

Tears gathered in Garrick's eyes. He wept.

He mastered his emotion. Minutes were precious. William Hope smiled encouragement:

"Forget that you are the condemned Garrick! Remember that you are Tom Bob, detective!"

"You are right. But first I must say that if I decide to accept your combined aid, it is not because you are my colleagues, it is because I am innocent of the charge brought against me. The charge is false, the jury's finding mistaken, the condemnation a miscarriage of justice. I am not guilty. I have not murdered my wife!"

"For mercy's sake, Tom, speak to some purpose!" cried Hope. "Time is racing by, and we are no further forward!"

"True! The 'further forward,' I can see, is my walk to the gallows!"

"Tom! Exert yourself! You *must* find a way to cheat the hangman!"

Tom Bob resumed his feverish pacing.

Hope waited.

"I can only count on you three," announced Tom Bob.

"You can count on us to the death," said Hope firmly.

Tom Bob smiled:

"It is from the jaws of death you would snatch me, dear

friend. I only hope you will not suffer for it!"

"Ah! You have a plan, Tom?"

"Yes."

"Realizable?"

"Quite. Who will be present at my execution?"

"But you must not be hanged!"

"No, Hope. I must be hanged. The only way out from the condemned cell is the gallows way."

"You see no other way, Tom? You mean it's too late?"

"Not at all."

"Some desperate attempt? Impossible, Tom."

"I do not suggest anything of the kind!"

"Some ruse then? Tom, you frighten me. You cannot count on the hangman to make a fifth in our plot!"

"No. I count the hangman out," said Tom Bob.

"Speak! Explain, for Heaven's sake!" Hope was exasperated with anxiety.

"Hope, they will lead me to the gallows tree, and hang me they certainly will. But what I do not intend to die of is hanging! I laugh at the hangman and his gallows tree!"

"I don't understand you!" cried Hope. He feared Tom Bob had gone out of his mind.

Tom Bob, under immediate sentence of death, stood in his cell shaking with laughter!

Hope looked desperate.

"Reassure yourself! I am in my sober senses, my dear Hope. I resign myself to the successor of Jack Ketch. He will hang me by the neck, but he will not hang me by the neck till I am dead!"

"But how escape death?" asked the puzzled chaplain detective.

"I will give the hangman's noose the slip, Hope."

The enigmatic assurance of Tom Bob was too much for the chaplain-detective's overwrought nerves. He danced a dance of exasperation round the smiling Tom Bob.

"Easy as a slipknot, Hope. Now cease that teetotum performance I beg, and lend me your ear—the two of them!"

"Ah, the plan at last!"

"Yes, my dear chaplain. You know the procedure? The hangman and his crew come to fetch me. They lead me to the gallows. They slip the knot round my neck, the trapdoor tips down, I fall into empty space. As I fall from a height the rope jerks me violently, and I dislocate my back—death is instantaneous. So far good.

"Once my backbone is dislocated, the hangman draws up his rope, and I am left hanging a good hour, the time prescribed by law, so that if my back is not dislocated I shall certainly be strangled.

"Hope, that means I shall have to cheat Death twice."

Hope nodded:

"I seem to see a nightmare," he said.

"My dear Hope, to prevent my back being dislocated, what you have to do—and it's child's play to detectives like you—is to manage that the hangman does not see you substitute a longer rope, so that when the trap door opens I shall not be violently jerked into space, but will drop on my feet. I risk breaking my legs, but my backbone will be saved. You follow me?"

"Very well, Tom. The hangman will come presently to have a look at you and calculate the length of rope required. That rope can be changed, but how can you escape being strangled? Even if the hangman does not notice that you have struck solid earth, he will pull up your body and leave it hanging for an hour!"

Tom Bob smiled:

"It is the more difficult. Not that the difficulty is to avoid strangulation—that again is child's play. But the trick must not be perceived. Bluntly, there must be complicity."

"Alas!"

"Hope, cost what it may, the policeman who watches my body during my hanging, and the hour of suspension after, must be an accomplice—the members of the Supreme Council appoint this man . . ."

"Heaven be praised!" cried Hope. "This policeman has already been chosen by Shephard. Shephard will get him on our side. But, Tom, how will you avoid being strangled?"

"When they come for me, bring me a slender tube of india-rubber. I shall swallow it. It will reinforce my windpipe, and prevent its being fatally compressed by the slip-rope. I shall certainly be able to breathe. It will save me. If . . ."

"If?" repeated Hope anxiously.

"If the watching policeman is deaf to my panting. I shall probably pant and gasp."

Tom Bob was going into explanatory details. The warder's key was turning in the lock. He had come for the chaplain.

Hope had barely time to whisper:

"The rope shall be changed, I swear. We shall save you!"

The warder was entering.

Hope played his part:

"Repent and hope, my son! Heaven's help is sure!"

Garrick replied:

"Yes, yes, I trust in Heaven's help."

The pseudo-chaplain was about to retire when the warder drew back to allow the entrance of two strangers standing in the corridor. They had come to interview the condemned man.

His back to the door, ,William Hope had not seen them:

"I commend you to Heaven's mercy, my son," he said, raising his hands in blessing.

He moved away too full of anxious thought to perceive the figure standing aside.

But Garrick had seen the inquisitive pair. While the warder locked them into the cell and went off, Garrick-Tom Bob collapsed in a heap on his bed!

"This time I am lost!"

Two hours had passed since William Hope had left Garrick. The condemned man sat up. He was trembling like a leaf:

"It is he! It is he! I recognized him!" he muttered.

Whom had he recognized?

One of the two strangers was that sinister personage, the hangman. But his companion was an ordinary policeman!

This must be the policeman who was to help Shephard. The hangman left Tom Bob-Garrick cold. But that policeman. . . .

"I am lost! I am lost!" he repeated.

Then he jumped up, leapt to the cell door and banged it violently. A warder came running.

The peephole half opened:

"What's the matter?"

"Tell the chaplain I must see him at once! It is urgent!"

The warder shook his head:

"It's impossible. Besides, you have just seen him!"

Garrick insisted:

"I have a most urgent message for him. For pity's sake tell him. It is the last wish of a dying man! I must see him! I must!"

The warder was accustomed to the heartrending appeals and fits of despair of condemned men:

"Garrick, what you ask is impossible!"

Pitilessly the warder closed the spy-hole.

Garrick fell fainting on the floor of his cell.

21. The Game of Cards

Next morning, ten o'clock had just struck when a warder un-locked the cell of Garrick-Tom Bob-Fantômas. Behind the warder stood a policeman.

Garrick leapt to his feet.

"Here is a companion for you, Garrick. The authorities allow him to spend some hours with you to help you pass the time. They authorize you to play cards. Your visitor is a great card player."

Fantômas stood stiff as a ramrod.

The policeman had slowly stepped into the cell. The small amount of daylight filtering through the dusty window fell full on his face.

"Good morning," said Garrick calmly.

"Good morning," replied the policeman.

The warder exclaimed:

"I have forgotten the cards! I will be back in a moment."

He went out, re-locking the door.

The two men looked each other up and down. Fantômas started speaking:

"I am Garrick. Who are you, policeman?"

The newcomer slightly smiled:

"I am policeman Number 416."

Fantômas smiled.

The smile vanished. His face was impassive. The warder entered with a pack of cards. He placed it on a small table: that, the bed and the wooden stool was the furniture of this dismal cell.

The warder withdrew.

The two men were pale.

Garrick pointed to the stool:

"Please be seated," he said to Number 416.

Fantômas sat on the edge of his bed.

Number 416 placed his cap on the floor, loosened his belt, and sat down on the stool.

"We have nothing to say to each other, have we?" remarked Fantômas. "Therefore let us start our game."

With firm hand, he spread the cards. Silently the two men cut for the deal.

Fate favored the policeman.

Intent, silent, the policeman played the game.

"We are quits!" cried Fantômas after some rounds.

"The struggle but commences," said Number 416. "Who can foretell its end?"

The policeman shuffled the cards.

Fantômas glanced at the spy-hole. The warder was not there.

Fantômas returned to his seat on the bed.

He pushed away the cards:

"We will stop—Juve," said he.

The policeman retorted:

"Fantômas!"

"Call me Garrick."

The policeman frowned.

"I am known here as Garrick. Why call me anything else?"

Juve's eyes gleamed. He controlled himself. It was difficult to keep calm in presence of this monster.

Juve nodded.

"So be it. Continue."

Juve was disagreeable, gruff.

Fantômas made his voice amiable:

"Juve, all my congratulations! It's not at all badly managed! For my part, I must confess I am quite charmed to receive a visit from you here, to meet you in the getup of a policeman, even when I am in the position of a condemned man! Again, my congratulations!"

Juve was exasperated by this banter. He exploded:

"I have no use for your congratulations! One thing I know. I hold you in the hollow of my hand, and you shall not escape me!"

Fantômas stared unblinkingly at Juve. His look was wicked.

Was Fantômas meditating some atrocious stroke or plan by means of which he could escape his redoubtable adversary?

Juve was on guard. There were too many watching eyes, too many bolts and bars between Fantômas and liberty. Any attempt at evasion was foredoomed. The only way from this prison tomb led to the gallows!

Fantômas was perplexed. What was Juve's game? What strings of high authority had he pulled that he had been able to reach this cell in the guise of an ordinary policeman? Why this subterfuge? Not dictatorial violence but shrewd cunning must be his game, the bandit decided:

"I shall not escape you, Juve. It is true, I am at your mercy. Garrick is imprisoned in a cell, and the policeman charged with his surveillance is policeman 416, who is none other than an Inspector of the French Sûreté, the celebrated Juve, the adversary of Fantômas. Decidedly not so bad!"

"Not so bad," admitted Juve, who was keeping pace with the irony of his adversary.

"It is curious," continued Fantômas, "that a man like you, when he finds himself in the presence of a man like me, should be reduced to suggesting a game of cards, with for stake—Good Heavens! I don't know what—but something quite insignificant, no doubt?"

Juve maintained silence.

Fantômas continued:

"Juve, we prefer to face each other, weapon in hand. You must be set on revenge—revenge to the uttermost?"

Juve's answer was given gravely:

"I take no vengeance. I have duties to fulfill. I have to make justice triumph, right and truth conquer. I shall employ all means to that end!"

"Juve, I know that you have been strictly forbidden to touch a hair of my head. I am a prisoner. You, my guardian, are responsible for my person. . . . Will you allow yourself to forget that, Juve, even for one instant?"

"I shall not forget it."

Fantômas nodded. He continued in an admonitory tone:

"When warders of any kind are entrusted with the honor and responsibility of entertaining those condemned to death, up to their supreme hour, it is the custom to show a little comradely feeling—I do not say friendly regard—towards those whose last moments they are there to enliven. Are you willing that a good understanding should exist between us?"

Juve pretended to fall in with the conciliatory attitude demanded by the bandit:

"So be it."

He added after a pregnant pause:

"Let us play with our cards on the table! Policeman 416 is Juve; the condemned Garrick is Fantômas. Are we agreed?"

Fantômas seemed in despair. He shook his head: "Alas, Juve, you well know it is impossible that the Doctor Garrick here present, the Garrick incarnated by me, is Fantômas! Juve, I beg you not to be so stubbornly obsessed! What is Fantômas? A multiple being composed of divers personalities—a being without a precise personality, without a fixed character! Who can prove to us that the Fantômas of yesterday will be the same as the Fantômas of tomorrow? And that the Fantômas of today is not another Fantômas? These are mysteries which make precise knowledge impossible."

Juve was furious. Fantômas was treating him as though he were an idiot. Banging his fist on the table, Juve cried:

"Enough! I know better than anyone, Fantômas, your ability to disguise your body, as you disguise your thoughts. Yes, Fantômas, is a marvelous actor, and excels in assuming the form of a variety of people, and this extraordinary faculty he has turned to account in many circumstances. But there is one thing, Fantômas does not know how to alter, and by which I shall always recognize him, and that is his look, his eyes! I should recognize them among a thousand. That is why I do not believe in Garrick, and have not believed in many others, as soon as I recognized that these other personages, Garrick included, had the Fantômas look—the eyes of Fantômas."

Mechanically Fantômas lowered his eyes:

"Juve, leave my eyes alone, do not trouble yourself about them. Listen to this:

"Two opposite versions regarding me have been bruited abroad while I have vegetated in this prison, where I vegetate innocent. One is that I am simply Doctor Garrick, guilty of wife murder that I might fly with my mistress. This is what the public and the magistrates think. The other opinion, held by the police, the detectives, the members of the Supreme Council, is that Garrick is the detective, Tom Bob; that Mrs. Garrick has vanished of her own free will owing to jealousy; consequently Tom Bob is innocent, that there is no murder of his wife. . . . Juve, believe me, the detective's version is the true one! It is Tom Bob who is in prison, the Tom Bob you have known, Tom Bob you find here, the victim of a miscarriage of justice."

Juve had to confess to himself that for once the sinister bandit had a show of right on his side.

True it is, that two years before, Fantômas had assumed the personality of Tom Bob owing to an odious assassination, one more in his long career of murder; but apart from that, all he said was strictly true.[*]

Fantômas, under the label of Tom Bob, had been for two years an English detective, and member of Scotland Yard Supreme Council.

Fantômas as Garrick had not killed his wife, and had been wrongfully condemned.

Fantômas was a prisoner, but, strange to say, he was not guilty.

Garrick-Fantômas did not leave Juve to his reflections long:

"Juve, do you remember that some weeks ago I showed how great my confidence in you was?"

"What do you mean?"

"I sent you the collaborator of Tom Bob, Detective French, to ask you what had become of Mrs. Garrick?"

"Mrs. Garrick? Lady Beltham, you mean to say!" cried Juve. Juve stood up.

---

[*]   See *The Long Arm of Fantômas* (Fantômas Series, Vol. 6)

Fantômas stood up.

Juve and Fantômas faced each other.

Juve spoke:

"It is my turn to question. Fantômas, what have you done with Jerome Fandor?"

Fantômas hesitated. Things had not turned out as he had planned. What had become of Fandor? Fantômas did not know. He dare not deceive Juve.

Juve continued:

"I found Lady Beltham, and I lost her. She had but one thing to do, to save you. I got her to promise she would do it. She has refused to do it. What conclusion is to be drawn from that?"

Fantômas grew deathly pale.

He knew Juve was speaking the truth.

The heart of Lady Beltham was closed against him forever!

But, cost what it might, Lady Beltham must be caught. She must free him. Only one man could help him. Juve, Juve, to whom he would give up Fandor in exchange.

Fantômas was livid. Drops of sweat bedewed his forehead. What sinister struggle was racking the soul of this horrible monster?

Juve wondered and watched in silence.

Would Fantômas, driven beyond endurance, make some statement, confession? He would speak the truth, Juve was sure of that.

Fantômas spoke:

"Juve," he said slowly, "if you have lost track of Lady Beltham, I ought to confess to you that after having seized Fandor, after promising myself to preserve him alive as a hostage to use in my dealings with you, I have lost sight of him. I do not know what has become of him!"

"Fantômas! Fantômas!" shouted Juve. "Are you telling the truth?"

"I swear it is the truth!"

"What have you done to Fandor?"

"I have chained him up."

"Where?"

Fantômas stopped short.

He had said enough.

Juve was drinking in the words of the bandit.

"Ah," thought Fantômas, "Juve will agree to all I ask if I tell him how to find his unfortunate, beloved Fandor!"

Fantômas announced:

"Each day, each hour that passes augments the tortures of Jerome Fandor."

Juve clenched his fists. He was powerless! Foaming with rage against this monster he had to entreat, Juve cried:

"Fantômas! Tell me where Fandor is! For mercy's sake!"

"No question of generosity between us!" cried Fantômas. "It's tit for tat, give and take! That's my motto, Juve! If I see Lady Beltham again, you shall find Jerome Fandor."

Juve replied on the instant:

"Faith of an honest man, you shall see her again, Fantômas!"

The bandit coolly replied:

"You have for that five days at the most! Five days. Do you understand, Juve?"

"Why five days only?" asked Juve, as in a nightmare Fantômas emitted a sneering chuckle:

"Where are your wits, Juve? Why because in five days Garrick will hang!"

A sudden silence. Steps approached. A key turned in the lock. The warder entered:

"Two hours up. Garrick goes to the yard. You can come again this afternoon, Number 416, from two to four, and again this evening from eight to ten. Those are my instructions."

While Garrick prepared to follow the warder for his daily exercise, Juve, almost beside himself, betook himself to the clerk's office, and out by the prison gates.

"Tit for tat!" repeated Juve. "Lady Beltham as a set off for Fandor! So be it. I accept the conditions of Fantômas. After? We shall see!"

22. The Compact

Françoise Lemercier was living in retirement. She mourned continually her lost lover, her lost child. She was tortured by the memory of happy days gone forever, days when she was Garrick's adored mistress, days divided between a career in which she was successful, and the joys of her little home, where she joined a cherished son and an adored lover! Exquisite hours never to return!

She was tormented by the ever-present conviction that little Daniel was alive and ill-treated. Had he forgotten her? Was he irrevocably gone out of her life?

Françoise no longer saw her theatrical comrades, her friends of the French colony.

One friend she now had, a friend whose acquaintance she had made in Hyde Park, shortly after her return from America under the surveillance of Detective Shephard.

There she chanced to meet a young woman, quietly dressed, who burst into heartrending sobs as she looked at a little child toddling by with its nurse.

The sight distressed Françoise also. Her sympathy was aroused. Doubtless this stranger wept the loss of a child as did she.

The two young women began to talk. They drifted into confidences. The stranger soon told Françoise that she was a French woman, was called Nini, declared she was a working woman, had had a child by her lover, and had lost it.

Françoise confessed her own grief and loss.

The two agreed to meet again.

If the infamous Nini congratulated herself on having won the confidence of little Daniel's mother, Françoise was thankful that Fate had led to her meeting with so truly sympathetic a friend.

Nini was an excellent comedian and a superb liar. She was the touching heroine who had borne privations with courage, whose unselfish devotion had been cruelly repaid by a false lover, whose adored child, the one consolation left her, had been taken to Heaven by the angels, to leave her desolate.

At last the tenderhearted, trusting Françoise proposed:

"Why not come and live with me? I am sad and desolate. My house is too large now for my needs. I should be glad to have you with me, and of course you would be free to go to your work."

Nini, though flattered, refused at first. She had no mind to curtail the liberty she made such bad use of, keep up the difficult comedy of respectable hardworking, grieving mother, above all to drop her low companions, went against the grain.

Nini changed her mind one day. She must get Daniel back. Lord Duncan might wish to see "his little Jack" again, and on Lord Duncan's allowance Nini depended.

"The deuce if I know who has stolen the kid," she said to herself. "Whoever did will probably have done it to bring it back to its mother. Living with Françoise I shall be on the spot and in the know. And my name is not Nini if I don't lay my hand on the brat again, and not that simpleton of a mother. She may well whistle for her little Daniel then!"

Nini joined forces with Françoise, and bided her time. The time came one day when Nini returned from a stroll with some pals, while Françoise believed her to be hard at work.

Nini found Françoise in tears.

"My dear, why are you in such a taking?" said the lying Nini.

Françoise tried to smother her sobs.

"Read that!" she said, holding out a letter. "I do not know whether I am crying for joy or grief!"

Nini seized the letter.

It was handwritten, plainly disguised, and without signature. Nini read aloud:

> Mademoiselle,
>   Someone who wishes good to you offers you this compro-

mise which will calm at least one of your sorrows.

You are known to be an honest woman, incapable of lying. Give, then, your word of honor that you will never try again to see your lover, Dr. Garrick, that under no circumstances will you renew your connection with him, that never for anything in the world will you again become his mistress, and you shall find your child, your little Daniel shall be restored to you!

If you agree to what is proposed, simply hang red curtains at your window. This signal will be understood, and a meeting shall be arranged.

Nini read, reread this anonymous communication. She was terrified.

Someone offered to return Daniel to his mother! Someone knew where the child was!

Who knew? Who was this mysterious "someone"? What enigmatic personage had stolen from Nini the false little Jack, and knowing who Françoise was, and where she lived, had been able to offer to restore the child to his real mother?

What did the condition of this restoration signify? *"Promise never to see your lover again."*

The miserable Nini felt frantic.

This letter spelled danger for her.

What must she do?

Suddenly Nini recovered self-control.

She saw clear.

Yes, she knew to whose interest it was that Françoise should never see Garrick again! She knew who it was who knew Françoise, who could offer to restore Daniel to her! In a compassionate voice Nini asked:

"And what have you answered, Françoise?"

The sobbing Françoise answered:

"Garrick is done for! Up to now I have had hopes. Now I can have none. Even after his condemnation I thought they would find his wife—but now it is too late. He will die in a few days. I can do nothing more for him. I have every right to save my son."

"You accept, then?"

"Yes, I accept. I accept for Daniel."

Two hours after this scene, Nini left the friend who firmly believed in her affection, and joined Beaumôme in a side street.

The hooligan looked worried.

Nini was in a bad temper.

"Well, what has happened?" asked Beaumôme. "I'm getting jolly well fed up with your business! What's the latest?"

Nini shrugged:

"I don't say my mass in the street. If you want to talk, let's go inside!"

Beaumôme thought the heavens were opening.

"Why, I ask nothing better, Nini! It's up to you, now, my woman! We will talk business, and after that—why, I'm sure you're going to be a bit kind to your man, Nini?"

Nini was furious, but she spoke caressingly:

"Beaumôme, I think I am going to ask you to do something more for me! But there, you know it will be the last. After . . ."

Beaumôme frowned.

"Oh, bless my soul!" said Beaumôme to himself, "I bet she is going to ask me to carry out another little execution for her! Devil take the woman!"

A few days later in Françoise Lemercier's little parlor, three men were sitting in consultation. Grave, elderly, the three spoke in turn:

"Serious symptoms," remarked the first.

"Morbid developments," announced the second.

The third coughed, spread out his hands. He was resigned to the worst.

The three sat silent.

"Nothing must be left untried," remarked one.

"We must decide on something," said another.

"Yes, it is urgent," announced the third.

The door was abruptly opened. Nini entered, red eyed, her cheeks swollen, as though she had wept long and copiously. Her hands were clasped. She ran up to the three consultants:

"Well, doctors?" she gasped.

The doctors eyed one another.

What could and should they say?

The oldest consultant took upon himself to speak: "Your friend is very dangerously ill."

Nini seemed to stifle a sob:

"This is dreadful! What is the matter with her?"

"It is a difficult case. My colleagues hold the same opinion as I do, I believe."

The two other consultants bowed gravely.

"It is this difficulty which has delayed the announcement of our conclusions. Your nurse was well advised to suggest this consultation."

Nini stood, a human note of interrogation.

"First of all, we should like to know how this illness began?"

Nini looked at each doctor in turn. She tried to read their thoughts.

"Why suddenly, gentlemen. A week ago, Françoise was quite well. Then all at once she complained of violent pains in her legs and terrible headaches."

"And she became feverish?" added a consultant. "Yes, very feverish."

"You then called in a neighboring medical man, did you not?"

"Yes, doctor."

"She became delirious, and your medical man advised you to have a nurse?"

"Yes, doctor."

"This same nurse, frightened at her patient's condition, made the strange statement I hold in my hand," and the doctor waved a sheet of paper. "She made it at the nearest police station. The police have therefore charged us to examine Mademoiselle Françoise Lemercier, and find out the cause of her illness?"

"That is so, gentlemen. And you have found out nothing?" Nini was all anxiety.

"We find strange and contradictory symptoms. Your nurse has repeated to us the statement she wrote at the police station,

176 SLIPPERY AS SIN

that it is a case of poisoning. After examining the patient, I must tell you, that my colleagues and I have arrived at the same conclusion. But we do not yet know the kind of poison taken or administered: consequently we have not yet found the remedy."

Nini clasped her hands:

"Oh! this is horrible, frightful! Françoise poisoned! I cannot believe it! Who would poison that sweet creature. An evil fate pursues us! It is enough to drive one mad!"

"Calm yourself, please!" cried the oldest consultant. "While there is life there is hope!

"The patient's condition is stationary.

"We understand from the nurse that Mademoiselle Lemercier takes only pure milk, sent direct from a farm in sealed bottles, milk into which poison could not be put, even by those about you, since you have taken the precaution of opening the bottles only in the presence of the nurse and yourself. Consequently . . ."

"Consequently?" gasped Nini. "What's to be done? Françoise takes nothing else—only this pure milk which nurse and I have drunk again and again without ill results!"

The doctors were touched by this parade of emotion.

"Consequently, my dear young lady," resumed the consultant, "we are going to make a fresh report to the police to the effect that Mademoiselle Françoise Lemercier is suffering from some poison, so far unknown, that energetic measures must at once be taken to discover the poison, and that the police are the proper persons to make the inquiry through the members of our profession in their employ!"

A few minutes later the consultants left the house.

No sooner had the door closed on the doctors, after Nini had implored them, with clasped hands and streaming tears, to save her beloved Françoise, to leave no stone unturned, to spare no effort, than this vile creature smiled an evil smile, cracked her fingers joyously, murmuring:

"Be off with you! You set of fools!"

Quickly she assumed her mask of gravity: a woman was

coming downstairs from the room where Françoise was suffering agonies. She called:

"Miss Nini?"

"What do you want, Nurse Kate?"

"I must go out for a couple of hours. I shall return punctually."

"I am agreeable, nurse. I shall expect you at the end of the two hours."

Nurse Kate, elderly, neat, obliging, put on her bonnet and cloak and left the house.

Garrick was pacing his cell as a tiger paces his cage.

He heard the warder unlocking the door. It opened and a woman walked in.

Garrick wrung her hand:

"You, Mrs. Davis! What fortunate wind blows you in here?"

Shaking hands with the man who was Tom Bob to her, a colleague to be consulted, also a friend in distress and imminent danger, Mrs. Davis said:

"Alas, my poor friend, it is not a piece of good fortune, it is a grave affair."

"A police matter, Davis?"

"Yes, and that is why I refer it to you, Tom Bob."

"Alas, how can I be of use to you in the sad situation in which I find myself?"

"By your advice."

"In that case, speak."

"Swear then, Tom Bob, not to let yourself be upset!"

"What do you mean, Davis? Does the matter concern me nearly? Speak ! Who is it you wish to talk to me about?"

"A woman—a woman you love!"

"Good Heavens! Not Françoise?"

"Yes. Be brave, Tom Bob! Françoise is being poisoned."

At this dreadful statement Tom Bob's features contracted with anguish.

"What is this you say?"

Mrs. Davis was leaning on the back of a chair. Tom Bob had pulled himself together.

"Let me explain, Tom Bob. Some days ago Françoise Lemercier, as I told you before, took a certain Nini into her house. Françoise was quite well, only saddened by your condemnation. Suddenly she falls ill. A doctor, living near, was called in. He examines her, makes no comment, but on leaving the house goes straight to the nearest police station, where he makes a declaration that, according to his opinion, his patient, Françoise Lemercier, has been poisoned. Thereupon, Nini, acting on this doctor's advice, asks the police to send a nurse. My dear Tom Bob, when heard of this while checking the daily police reports, I decided to be that nurse. I make myself up as an elderly woman, present myself at your poor friend's house, am accepted by Nini, who only sees in me Nurse Kate sent from a hospital by the police to take charge of Françoise."

Tom Bob was on tenterhooks:

"Well? What then?"

"Well, I install myself at the bedside of Françoise, note her symptoms, and am forced to conclude the doctor's diagnosis is correct: Françoise Lemercier is dying of poison. How? She takes nothing but pure milk. The bottles are sealed, and come direct from a reliable company. I open them myself. I have taken some of the milk myself, and have suffered no harm. Yet each day she is wasting away more and more. The three consultants agree with the doctor—that it is a poisoning case. Yet Françoise takes no poison. She is now being closely watched."

"You do not think some poisonous gas would account for it, Mrs. Davis?"

"No. I never leave Françoise. If she were being poisoned by the air she breathes, so would I be, so would Nini be, and the one or two neighbors who come to see the poor thing. To sum up: Françoise is in bed, never leaves it now, she only drinks pure milk, she breathes the common air, nevertheless some mysterious criminal is killing her with poison!"

"Impossible," shouted Tom Bob, "what you say is mad!"

"It is as I say, Tom Bob."

"No, no! There is something you cannot have noticed!"

"I spend my time on the watch."

"Without finding anything?"

"Without finding anything."

"Ah, you don't know how to investigate!"

"Neither do the doctors, then," replied the distressed detective.

"The doctors are imbeciles! Asses!" shouted Tom Bob. "Davis, you must not let Françoise die! You must, must save her!"

"I would give my life to save her, Tom Bob!"

"You are sure that Nini—?"

"Nini only comes near her in my presence. I push precaution so far as to make Françoise's bed with her."

Great tears were rolling down Tom Bob's thin cheeks:

"And to think I am a prisoner! That they are killing her for me, and I can do nothing!" he cried in a fit of despairing rage.

"Everything is against me! I who have never known fear until this hour am sweating with anguish! I ought to cry for mercy! It is Fate! He, he only can save her!"

The grief of the condemned man was painful to see!

"'He!'" echoed Mrs. Davis, "Only 'he' can save her? Of whom do you speak, Tom Bob?"

Tom Bob hesitated:

"He? Oh, you ought to understand, Davis! I speak of—God!"

Mrs. Davis stared at Tom Bob. Never had this colleague shown the slightest religious feeling. And now he invoked God!

"What is to be done?" cried Mrs. Davis.

Tom Bob pulled himself together:

"Before everything return at once to Françoise. Your surveillance, even if it cannot save her from their machinations, may at least embarrass the assassins enough to make it difficult for them to carry out their horrible work. Go! Go! I am going to take council with myself."

Mrs. Davis was about to leave when Tom Bob said in a self-controlled manner:

"Davis, ask the warders as you go out, to send me the policeman told off to play cards with me every day."

23. Avenge Me!

Preceded by the turnkey, Juve entered Garrick's cell a few minutes after Mrs. Davis had left it. In his hoarse voice the turnkey announced:

"Garrick, here is your partner. My word you are mad on cards!"

"I like a game well enough," replied the prisoner with his back to the door.

"Play away, then, and good luck!"

So saying, the turnkey left Number 416 in the cell, locked the door, his heavy steps dying away in the distance.

Number 416 said quietly:

"You asked to see me?"

"I did."

The condemned man turned abruptly and faced Juve. Juve drew back, startled:

"Fantômas! What is the matter with you?"

"A horrible grief."

Two big tears rolled down the pallid face of the bandit, his eyes shone with a feverish light. Juve wondered what could have happened to Fantômas. He seemed in the depths of despair:

"You are in great trouble, Fantômas, and you have asked to see me. Please explain."

The bandit did not seem to hear Juve's question. He was thinking hard, his head bent.

Presently he looked up, facing Juve with an impassive countenance:

"Juve, you recall our conversation of the other day?"

"I remember it, Fantômas."

"You remember that it was a case of tit for tat, and also give and take?"

"I do."

"That you confessed Lady Beltham had escaped you; and I confessed I had lost track of Fandor's whereabouts; that you promised to find Lady Beltham again, and I promised to provide you with the means to save Jerome Fandor. Do you remember that?"

Juve had grown pale. He feared bad news of his dear Fandor, had feared some bad trick on the part of that elusive monster, Fantômas, since he had been given the message from Mrs. Davis.

"I remember all that. I promised to bring Lady Beltham to you and I shall do so."

"Good! Juve, will you trust me for one hour? Will you lend me your aid for an hour?"

"Trust you for an hour, Fantômas? Possibly. Help you for an hour? No. Fantômas, you are the incarnate spirit of Evil. Everything you do has terrible consequences. Not even in exchange for my dear Fandor's life will I let myself be the instrument of your abominable deeds!"

"Juve! You deceive yourself grossly, stupidly! Between men such as we are, there should be no misunderstandings of this sort. It is a compromise I offer you—but an acceptable compromise. I have no intention of asking you to do anything repugnant to your conscience, for I know you would refuse to do it. But I think it proper to ask you to help me, to help me in a good work, a necessary work! I implore you to spare me the most terrible grief—mourning for a death!"

"A death? What! You are threatened with a loss through death? Lady Beltham?"

"No, Juve. It is not Lady Beltham I am troubling about!"

"Who then?"

"About . . ."

Fantômas could not finish. He dreaded having to beg Juve's help. He hated to put himself at his adversary's mercy. How determined, how relentless an adversary, Fantômas knew only too well!

"Listen, Juve," said Fantômas, "you are persuaded that I am a despicable being, incapable of noble feelings, even the slightest! Well, before making my request, it pleases me to put myself entirely in your hands. After that, it seems to me you will be obliged to help me, you will feel that you owe me your aid!"

"Fantômas," retorted Juve, "do not make me the confidant of your secrets, if you think that by so doing you can drag me into wrongdoing. Not even to have the victory of holding you at my mercy will I agree to such conditions!"

"No, no! Don't talk to me in that fashion, Juve! Every minute is of serious importance. Listen to me without mental reservation! You have my word for it that I am going to tell you the truth, and it is of Fandor I wish to speak. But I shall not ask you to do anything you cannot do!"

Fandor! Each time he heard Fantômas mention the name of one dearer to Juve than any, he felt as though he had been dealt a blow on the heart:

"Speak!" he cried. "Speak!"

"Juve, Fandor is of all on earth most loved by you! You do not know what has become of your friend, and you would do anything to find him. If it were in my power at this moment to point out to you the exact means of saving Jerome Fandor I would do so—but things are not like that!"

"You cannot tell me where Jerome Fandor is?"

"No."

"But what have you done with him?"

"Listen!"

Fantômas told Juve how he had got hold of Fandor, how he had imprisoned the journalist in a hidden room he had arranged for the purpose, and how he meant to hold Fandor as a hostage in order to frighten Juve and paralyze his police investigations:

"Fandor could not have escaped from this carefully planned room, and no cries of his could be heard."

"But where is this room?" shouted Juve.

"I do not know!"

"Not know?"

"That is so, Juve. It is the true truth. I do not know. The room I had made is really an enormous case or box. When I imprisoned Fandor in it, I was arranging to have it exported to a far off country. You know how events were precipitated! I meant to travel with the case. Destiny willed otherwise. The day after Fandor's incarceration I went off to join Françoise on *The Victoria*. Since then I am a prisoner!"

"But this case?" cried Juve. "This prison-box, what has become of it?"

"As soon as I had closed the door sealing Fandor's prison, I made all arrangements for the forwarding of the case. Unfortunately, part of these arrangements was to notify Lady Beltham!"

"You lie!" protested Juve. "At that time Lady Beltham was no longer with you!"

"I do not lie. I tell you the truth, Juve. Lady Beltham had left me, but she knew my plan regarding Fandor. I knew she still loved me, and I did not doubt she would do all she had agreed to do, and at the time fixed on.

"Alas, Juve, what makes me fear the worst is that I now realize that Lady Beltham, who refused to appear at my trial and so prove my innocence, hates me with the diabolical tigerish hatred of a jealous woman—and I fear she has changed the destination of Fandor's case!"

Juve wrung his hands in despair:

"If that is so, Fandor must be dead of hunger!"

"No, no, Juve. Fandor was amply provisioned. Be sure he lives. I have no doubt we can still save him if Lady Beltham will tell us—rather tell me, for she will never tell you—where Fandor is."

Juve was seated on the prison bed, elbows on knees, head buried in his hands: all grief and indignation.

"Horrible! Horrible!" he burst out. "Fantômas, you are about to die, but your death, even death by the hangman's rope, will never sufficiently expiate your crimes!"

"Juve!" replied Fantômas, "I am going to confide in you! Are you going to repay my trust by hatred? Do you forget I have a favor to ask of you?"

Juve realized Fantômas had told him the truth:

"Fantômas," said he, "you have asked me to procure for you an interview with Lady Beltham, why I do not know, nor do I wish to know. You now declare that Lady Beltham alone can, on your order, permit me to find Fandor. I renew my promise—I will do anything in the world to procure you an interview with Lady Beltham, if that is what you now ask of me?"

While speaking, Juve shivered. Secret anguish clutched him. Only three days, and Garrick would be hanged! Could he find Lady Beltham within that short time?

Fantômas meanwhile had been pacing the cell with tireless step. He stopped. He put his hand on Juve's shoulder:

"Juve, I trust you to fulfill your promise regarding Lady Beltham. It is a fresh favor I would obtain from you. If I do not see Lady Beltham before my death, I will pay for this fresh favor by giving you the means by which you can force her to reveal to you the place where Fandor is suffering cruelly."

Juve jumped up: "You will do that? Fantômas, I have sworn to do all in my power to bring Lady Beltham to you, but, for pity's sake, if I do not succeed, provide me with the means to force her to save Fandor."

"I shall do it, Juve, if you will consent to hasten to Françoise Lemercier, and drag her out of deadly danger!"

"What do you mean, Fantômas?"

"Juve, someone is poisoning Françoise! Who! I do not know who the assassin is!"

Fantômas, in a voice of anguish, told Juve what Mrs. Davis had stated in that very cell but a short while ago:

"If I were free I should know how to safeguard Françoise from those slowly murdering her. Only one man can take my place, is capable of it—you, Juve. I implore you to save Françoise!"

"I wish to save her," replied Juve. "But, Fantômas, Fandor will be freed?"

"You shall save Fandor, if Françoise lives."

Juve asked no more than that. He crossed the cell, prepared to knock on the door as a signal to the warder that he wished to leave.

Fantômas recalled him:

"Juve, I give you a valuable piece of information, that is if you have not already guessed it: Jack, Nini's son, you know he is dead?"

Juve shrugged. His tone was contemptuous:

"No, I am not ignorant of that! Oh, I understand your wiles and tricks, Fantômas! He whom Lord Duncan believes to be his son, is little Daniel, son of Françoise Lemercier, the child you stole from your mistress to give to Nini, in order to extort money from the rich English peer."

Fantômas lowered his head. In a dull voice he replied:

"Yes. The living Jack is Daniel, whom I stole from Françoise—a crime I feel the deepest remorse for, because all my present troubles spring from that mistaken crime."

Fantômas was overcome with such grief that Juve pitied him. Again Juve was about to call the warder, when the cell door was unlocked. The door opened. The warder announced: "Mrs. Davis."

Fantômas had fallen on his bed. He was weeping. Policeman 416 stood near him, frowning.

Mrs. Davis came with dreadful news.

Françoise Lemercier was dead.

Fantômas wept, heart-stricken.

Juve was torn with anxiety.

Françoise dead, Juve feared Fantômas might take refuge in disdainful silence, might refuse point-blank to help Juve to rescue Fandor. And Juve had only three days in which to produce Lady Beltham, whose whereabouts he had not the slightest idea of!

The hoarse voice of Fantômas broke the painful silence:

"Go, go! Avenge me in avenging Françoise! Go there! If you require a fresh promise, I give it you! Arrest the murderers of my poor Françoise: do all you can to secure my interview with Lady Beltham! Trust me as I trust you. I swear to you that on my side I will so arrange things that you shall find your friend again!"

24. The Capture of Beaumôme

There were two exits to Françoise Lemercier's house. The front
door opened on to Jewin Street. The door at the back opened
into a small courtyard, which led into a narrow passage.

Françoise Lemercier died at four in the afternoon. At eight
o'clock that evening the rooms of the poor dead woman were
humming with gossip and talk.

Curious neighbors had invaded the premises: they stared
about them, gazed with inquisitive eyes, with shudders and
conventional grief, at the corpse scarcely cold. They condoled
with the dead woman's only friend, who had been at her bedside
up to the last.

Nini was controlling herself with difficulty. The neighbors
loudly praised her resignation, her self-possession, her quiet
grief.

"This French girl can keep her head like an Englishwoman,"
said some.

"You see she feels her friend's death so much she can't shed
a tear," said another.

Of what had Françoise Lemercier died? It was believed a
wasting sickness had carried her off.

A man in black came on the scene. A neighboring undertaker to whom Nini gave charge of the funeral arrangements. A
doctor appeared, talked to Nini apart, granted a death certifi-
cate, recommended that certain sanitary precautions should be
taken as the dead woman had died of a species of fever.

His recommendations were given in a voice loud enough to
be heard all over the house.

That was not the doctor who had attended the dead woman,
some neighbors declared.

Nini preserved a stony silence.

Women brought flowers, offering to lay out the corpse. Nini

retired to the next room. Here a jumble of clothes, and linen used by the dead woman latterly, were scattered about.

Nini picked them over with meticulous care, placing them in various bundles.

So absorbed was she in this work that the women departed long before she had finished.

Night having fallen, Nini lit a lamp.

She was alone in the house with her victim sleeping the last long sleep!

Nini was superstitious.

She avoided the death chamber like the plague. The undertaker's men had placed the bier, and the coffin on it, in the little parlor. Nini would not go near this great oblong box, open, gaping, so threateningly sinister.

Nini took refuge in the kitchen. She meant to pass the night there.

She heard a slight scratching on the door leading into the courtyard and narrow passage.

She shivered, rose, opened the door.

A seedy looking individual faced her.

Nini stifled a cry of joy.

It was Beaumôme!

"Ah!" cried Nini, when they were safe in the kitchen, "I have been expecting you since the morning. You know what has happened?"

"Yes, I heard of it hereabouts. So that's that!"

"Yes. That's that!" repeated Nini.

The pair looked at each other. They grew pale.

"Nothing to drink here?" asked Beaumôme. "I ran to get here. I'm thirsty."

Nini went to a cupboard in the wall, took out a gin bottle, half full, poured out a bumper for her hooligan lover, and took a large mouthful of it:

"That puts new life into you," she murmured.

Beaumôme wanted another glass of this fiery liquid. His thirst quenched, he turned his attention to practical details:

"The linen! Got to get rid of it! Don't want those about here

SLIPPERY AS SIN

poking curious noses into it!"

"That's so," replied Nini. "I thought of it. I've made up a bundle of sheets."

"Best destroy them as quick as we can," advised Beaumôme.

The hooligan and the woman he hoped to make his mistress, shut themselves up in the kitchen, and stuffed the cooking range with a vast quantity of linen they intended to burn to tinder.

But they were clumsy and in too great a hurry. Despite their efforts, the linen would not burn well. A thick, acrid smoke poured out, suffocating, suspicious.

"Good Heavens!" cried Nini, alarmed. "The neighbors will want to know what we are up to!"

Nini stopped trying to draw up the fire. Beaumôme tore the bundle of linen from the range, threw it on the stone floor, caught up some sacking from a corner and made a big package of the lot.

"What do you mean to do with it?" asked Nini.

Beaumôme explained:

"I am going to plant it somewhere . . . in a sewer . . . on some wasteland . . . throw it into the Thames!"

"When?"

Beaumôme had shouldered the package:

"Immediately," he replied gloomily. "Got, to get rid of compromising articles of this sort."

Nini knew he was right, but she could not bear the idea that Beaumôme was going to leave her alone:

"Shall you come back soon?"

The hooligan looked her up and down:

"That depends. In ten minutes or tomorrow morning."

He saw that Nini was afraid of remaining in this sinister abode by herself, with the coffin on one hand and the corpse on the other.

Maliciously, he held his peace. It was his turn to make her fume with unsatisfied desire for his company.

Nini realized the spiteful feelings Beaumôme was indulging in. She was furious with him, would have willingly strangled him, but she dissimulated her feelings. She began wheedling and coaxing:

"Beaumôme!" she begged in a voice sweet as poisoned honey. "It is not kind of you to leave me alone like this, not to promise you will come back to me immediately, and that when I am frightened, when I am so sorrowful, so troubled!"

Beaumôme burst out laughing:

"Sorrow! Oh no! But how many times have you made me sorry, given me trouble? As to being frightened, I don't say no. But that can be soon set to rights. If madam wants someone to guard her, she can have him, only for things like that there is a price to pay!"

Nini understood that the moment had come when Beaumôme would no longer be put off with promises. She would have to give in to him.

So be it!

"It's agreed, Beaumôme. Return, and you shall have your reward."

The hooligan smiled:

"An installment, then!" he said imperatively.

Nini's answer was to go up to Beaumôme, and press her lips to his in a long kiss!

Beaumôme slipped noiselessly down the stairs, intoxicated by Nini's tender caress.

The hooligan, convinced that his dearest dream was about to come true, hummed a joyous tune as he hurried across the little courtyard.

He slipped into the narrow passage.

He kept close to the wall, moving cautiously. He came into a street somewhat wider. Before going further he looked up and down it.

It was deserted.

Beaumôme settled his big bundle well forward on his shoulder, his eyes searching about for a suitable dumping place. He must rid himself of this cumbersome burden.

But Beaumôme had gone but a few yards when he heard three shrill whistles.

He knew that signal!

Beaumôme swore viciously.

He was not mistaken.

A colossus of a police sergeant appeared before him. Then to Beaumôme it seemed to rain policemen! They were closing in from all sides.

The police sergeant signed to the trapped hooligan to stop:

"Where are you off to?" he demanded.

"Home," replied Beaumôme.

"Where do you live?"

Beaumôme gave his Whitechapel address, and prepared to resume his interrupted walk, but the policeman wanted further information:

"What are you carrying in that bundle?" he demanded.

"Linen . . . old dirty linen."

"Where does this linen come from?"

"From one of my friends whose woman pal is dead. She lives close by."

Beaumôme's replies were so definite and given so naturally that the sergeant hesitated to pursue his interrogation, and to prevent this individual from continuing his journey. After all he had the right to carry linen through the streets of London, even at this late hour:

"Go your ways, then," said the sergeant. Beaumôme did not wait to be told twice. He moved off between the group of policemen, and was congratulating himself on getting off so easily when, a man in civilian clothes stepped in front of him.

At sight of him Beaumôme was so overcome that he let fall his bundle of linen.

Beaumôme had recognized this man.

It was Juve!

Juve, who was looking him up and down. Juve, who had so planted himself in front of Beaumôme that the wretched hooligan could not pass him.

Beaumôme's conscience was so laden with crimes that he was ever on the alert, anxiously expectant of trouble.

What could Juve want with him?

Beaumôme soon found out!

Juve signed to the police sergeant, and a rapid dialogue ensued:

"Sergeant, I beg of you, secure this individual. He is a criminal. It is absolutely necessary to arrest him, interrogate him!"

"Excuse me, sir, but I don't know you. By what right do you intervene?"

Juve mentioned Shephard, he named the individual he wanted the sergeant to arrest:

"The fellow calls himself Beaumôme. He has committed a crime. He has assassinated Detective French!"

Juve spoke with such assurance that the sergeant wavered. At this precise moment Beaumôme, who had not lost a word of this disquieting conversation, attempted to make off, leaving his bundle on the pavement.

Relying on his agility, he made a dash for safety and freedom. It was a fatal blunder.

Three herculean policemen threw themselves on Beaumôme like a flash of lightning, rendering him powerless.

This attempted evasion, following directly on Juve's declaration, greatly impressed the sergeant of police:

"If this individual is trying to make off he must have an uneasy conscience," said the police sergeant to Juve. "Nevertheless, sir, I do not see on what grounds I can carry out his arrest. He has not been caught in the act. How can you prove the truth of your accusation?"

Juve stared concentratedly at the bundle Beaumôme had dropped:

"I am not so sure about not being caught in the act," he remarked.

He turned to the police sergeant:

"Look here, sergeant, will you have this fellow taken to the police station, and keep him there a couple of hours? If within that time I bring you undeniable proofs, I presume you will definitely detain him?"

Beaumôme was storming and blustering, calling on his gods that he was innocent, that he had nothing to reproach himself with, and could not understand what they wanted with him!

The police sergeant paid no heed to these assertions. He had noted Juve's assured tone and felt convinced he had not spoken at random.

"I will certainly do as you suggest, sir," said the sergeant. "This man appears to me to have been acting suspicious—but I do not know you. You ask for two hours in which to bring me proofs—you are going to make an investigation then? If I accept your offer, I warn you that I insist on one of my men accompanying you, for if you are playing a trick on the police, you will be severely punished."

Juve could not agree to this. He needed to be alone if he was to carry through the project he had in mind. How was he to get rid of the sergeant, and especially the policeman who was to be told off to dog his steps, without arousing their suspicions, without encouraging them in their belief that he was having a joke at their expense, and consequently causing them to release Beaumôme?

Juve could no longer hesitate. He must produce his credentials, though much against the grain. He showed the astounded sergeant his identity card.

"You are one of us, Number 416!" he cried. "It's all right, then! I will meet you two hours hence at the police station. We will then settle the arrest question of this individual one way or the other."

25. The Triumph of Juve

Two hours!

Juve had two hours in front of him!

He left the group with Beaumôme in charge, found a taxi, and was driven to the prison.

A little room had been put at his disposal adjoining the clerk's office. Here he changed into uniform, and appeared to the warder in Garrick's corridor as Policeman 416.

The warder unlocked Garrick's cell, and in his presence the two men adopted a friendly official attitude:

"Good evening, Garrick."

"Good evening, 416."

No sooner had the warder locked them in and withdrawn from the cell door than Juve declared:

"Fantômas, I have just been investigating at your unfortunate friend's house."

"Well?"

"Well, I cannot for the life of me see how Nini has been able to poison your mistress. But I had a queer encounter which may contain a clue. I ran across Beaumôme, the hooligan, leaving Françoise's house, and I secured his provisional arrest."

Fantômas seemed profoundly troubled:

"Why have you had Beaumôme arrested, Juve?"

"He was making off with a bundle of linen."

In a strained voice Fantômas repeated:

"A bundle of linen!"

Fantômas, ghastly, his face distorted with anguish, seemed incapable of speech.

Tense silence held the two men spellbound. Suddenly Fantômas asked brutally:

"Well, what do you expect of me, Juve?"

"An explanation, Fantômas! You have asked me to avenge

you, to avenge Françoise. I am convinced now you have the
means to help me. I have managed to have Beaumôme detained
at the police station. I want you to collaborate with me in this.
Look here! Answer me straight, Fantômas. Can you imagine
how Nini and Beaumôme, for they are surely accomplices, have
been able to poison Françoise?"

Fantômas hesitated. The bandit was reluctant to help Juve,
but he was driven to do it:

"Juve, if it was not a question of avenging Françoise you
would get no help from me! But they have murdered my innocent, my adored mistress. In attacking my mistress they have
attacked me. I am not to be defied with impunity! It is war to
the knife!

"You want my explanation of this atrocious crime? You shall
have it. I know what Fantômas has done! In the past, when he
has had occasion to rid himself by poison of someone obnox-
ious to him, he has repeatedly sprinkled that person's sheets
with arsenic. Through the pores of the skin this arsenic powder
is introduced into the system, and that person dies of slow poisoning, a death that cannot be accounted for! Other poisons
can be so used also. Something assures me that Françoise has
been the innocent victim of this method of poisoning. Juve!
I beg you to get analyzed the sheets of the bed in which my
unfortunate Françoise died!"

Horror made Juve mute.

The veil was torn from his eyes. Yes, the atrocious plot of
which Françoise Lemercier had been the victim, must have
been concocted and carried out just as Fantômas said. Fantômas
better than anyone knew all the ways of murder. Ah, he was an
amazing adversary! He was not only Fantômas the elusive, he
was now and ever the essential genius of crime!

Juve thanked his implacable adversary quietly:

"I understand, Fantômas. Thanks. I shall now keep
Beaumôme in prison. You shall be avenged."

And as though he felt it painful to owe the arrest of
Beaumôme to Fantômas only, Juve hastened to add:

"Beaumôme is also the murderer of Detective French. I am

sure of it! I have proof of it!"

"The proof? Are you sure of what you say, Juve?"

"Yes. Certain."

Juve drew from his pocketbook the documents he had carried away from Nini Guinon's, the photographs taken by French which Job, the negro, accomplice of the band, had stolen from Sigissimons' studio.

On these photographs, at Lady Beltham's elbow, could be distinctly seen the characteristic figure of Beaumôme. This proximity, coupled with a hundred other details, made Juve sure that Beaumôme was the murderer of French.

Juve's deductions were confirmed by Fantômas, who was anxiously examining the photographs.

"You are right, Juve! You are very strong, almost as strong as I am! I congratulate you on the intelligent way you have conducted this investigation and succeeded in unmasking the murderer of French! Again my congratulations!"

Juve would not put up with this sarcastic banter:

"Enough of that!" he cut in. "I am now armed to take definite proceedings against Beaumôme. I leave you!"

Juve was about to signal the warder. The key would be inserted in the lock the minute after.

Fantômas stopped him:

"You forget our solemn leagues and covenants, Juve! Tit for tat, you know! I have just made it easy for you to keep under lock and key a cowardly murderer, whom I am not sorry to see caught by the heel. You must render me a service in exchange. You promised to find Lady Beltham. You have not found her?"

"Not yet," replied Juve. "But soon . . ."

"I want something better than that," retorted Fantômas. "When you have unearthed Lady Beltham, you must bring her here—here! Don't bother about authorizations; I will obtain them from my colleagues. When Lady Beltham is here, she and I will decide whether or not she should declare she is Mrs. Garrick."

Juve dared not promise.

Though he counted on finding Lady Beltham very shortly,

could he agree to bring her to her lover, Fantômas? Ought he to reunite the two bandits? It was to favor the evasion of one, the impunity of the other. If Fantômas wished to see Lady Beltham, it was because he had some formidable aim in view.

Juve hesitated.

Fantômas applied the screw:

"Juve, bring Lady Beltham into my presence, make it easy for us to have a talk together! It is your one and only chance of finding Jerome Fandor again. Make up your mind!"

Juve accepted the situation:

"Agreed. I will bring Lady Beltham."

Juve thus acknowledged that he was going to be the instrument by whose means Fantômas would prove his innocence and obtain his freedom. Fantômas would not fail to make Lady Beltham declare she was Mrs. Garrick.

The accusation would fall to the ground. By producing his so-called wife, Garrick-Fantômas, an innocent prisoner, for once, would be set at liberty.

"So be it," thought Juve. "It is much better that Fantômas should not be executed under the name of Garrick. I accept the challenge! Garrick liberated, acquitted, Tom Bob will be more important than ever. I shall be on his track from that moment, and shall certainly unmask him!"

Juve hurried away to doff policeman's uniform. When in civilian attire, he hailed a prowling cab and had himself driven at top speed to the police station, where the sergeant who had detained Beaumôme awaited him.

The hooligan had been prostrate for a while, grinding his teeth in a dull fury. Then his reckless law-hating temperament asserted itself, and he kicked up a shindy fit for Bedlam. Seized by the collar, he had been jerked into a cell, raising Cain the while.

Flung on the floor, he saw an individual half asleep in a corner, by his side a bottle of gin.

Beaumôme's uproar aroused the drowsy individual. Soon the two fraternized over the bottle of gin. Beaumôme grew gay. He chuckled at thought of Nini Guinon. Why she must be at her wits end by now! She must be racked with anxiety because he had not returned, must be fearing he had got into an awkward scrape, and must be terrified to distraction at the idea of having to pass the night alone between a gaping black coffin and the corpse of Françoise Lemercier!

Nini was up to the neck in trouble too! Beaumôme laughed and sniggered. He swallowed copious bumpers of delicious gin.

His boon companion shammed drinking. He kept a watchful eye on Beaumôme. As the hooligan gradually became more and more intoxicated, the individual took the lead in their conversation. He presently began to talk of thieving, of crimes, of assassinations. He boasted of his doings.

"As for me," declared Beaumôme, puffed up with vanity and gin, "I've done better than that! I've . . ."

At this moment the warders introduced a third individual into the cell of the two drinkers: an individual with curly black hair, and a thick beard covering three parts of his face.

It was Juve.

Juve played the part of a beggar taken up as a vagabond, made himself agreeable to Beaumôme and exchanged signs of understanding with the hooligan's boon companion, who was really a policeman:

"Don't stop talking because I've joined the merry party," said Juve-vagabond.

He pretended to settle himself to sleep.

Beaumôme's boon companion remarked:

"They say you settled Detective French's hash for him, but I doubt that! You don't look enough of man for such a job!"

Beaumôme's gorge rose at such an insult:

"Not man enough! What do you know about it? I tell you I'm brave right through. I'm no jumper at my shadow, especially when I've an eye on a cove. I'd got a down on this French. He'd run me in a time or two for some tomfoolery or other, nothing at all! Then when Nini Guinon said to me: 'You've got to let the life out of that pig of a cop,' I didn't hesitate to tumble him overboard to feed the fishes. A quick journey, I bet! What a dive the bloke made for sure! A plunge from the boat above into the big cup below!"

Beaumôme's companion seemed incredulous:

"Claptrap, my lad! Bit of brag!"

Beaumôme shouted between mouthfuls of gin:

"Not on your life! Haven't I the look of a fellow who could pay off old scores with a bit to me? Pitch a man into the water? Why it's nothing! A newborn infant could do it easy as easy! Besides, the Nini and I have done better than that—we two!"

Juve pretended to wake up. He cried:

"Done better jobs than that? What are you stuffing us with? Why you're not capable of it!"

This spurred Beaumôme's on.

Garrulously drunk, this braggart cast prudence to the winds with both hands. He first drained the last drop of gin from the bottle, then in a thick voice, twisting his tongue round long sentences, muddling French and English, slurring difficult words, the hooligan gave an account of the slow poisoning of Françoise Lemercier down to the minutest details. He boasted that the crime must be chiefly laid at his door, though Nini Guinon was the principle author of it.

Juve listened with closest attention. He asked another question:

"But why ever did you make cold meat of Françoise Lemercier? Did she get in your way, or did the Nini want to be rid of her?"

Beaumôme put on an air of mystery:

"Ah, those are things you can't understand—they're complicated affairs. But I can tell you that if the Nini has demolished the Françoise it's to do with the brat. A woman of the tip-tops had written to the Lemercier that she was going to return her brat to her. But Lemercier's brat, Daniel, was as you might say the substitute of the Nini's brat that died, little Jack. But it's not worthwhile explaining—you can't understand—nor that cove in the corner either!"

Juve saw all clearly. He felt that he would soon grasp the key of the mystery.

"That Willesden woman has tricked Nini all right, and that's what makes me laugh!" said Beaumôme.

Juve took a chance, it might draw the hooligan:

"The woman who hangs out in Wilbur Street—isn't it?"

Beaumôme shrugged and fell into Juve's trap:

"Not a bit of it! I see you know not a peppercorn about it! The Willesden woman doesn't live in Wilbur Street. Her shanty's in Rosendale Avenue. If you know your way about that part it's the last house before the railroad bridge."

Juve noted this important address with immovable countenance.

He was filled with joy. Not only had he got Beaumôme arrested, discovered the horrible crime of Nini Guinon, but he was convinced the "woman of Willesden," who had held back Françoise Lemercier's child, could be none other than Lady Beltham!

Day was now dawning. Beaumôme was holding forth still, but the fumes of his gin drinking dulled his mind more and more, till at last, heavy eyed, with burning throat and limekiln mouth, the abominable hooligan slid sideways, sank huddled on the floor, snoring.

His companions rose softly, slipped from the cell which a turnkey had quietly opened for them.

While Juve had a long talk with the sergeant, the Inspector, who had passed the whole night in the company of Beaumôme in order to induce him to condemn himself out of his own mouth, commenced his official report, a report which would be the hooligan's irremediable condemnation.

26. Judge and Accomplice

Willesden is a middle class residential suburb in the northwest district of London, whose inhabitants, for the most part, lead regular respectable lives. Lights are seldom seen in the houses after midnight, and save for a few belated cabs and a sprinkling of pedestrians, the roads are deserted at that hour.

On this particular evening, a woman, muffled in a black cloak, was hastening along one of the avenues, stopping from time to time under the electric lamps at the crossroad corners to study the white plaques with the road names on them in black lettering.

It was the night following the arrest of Beaumôme, a night of horror passed by Nini Guinon in Françoise Lemercier's tragic abode.

The pedestrian turned into Rosendale Avenue. She knew her way now, for she marched straight ahead until she reached the end of the Avenue. She paused before the extensive garden of the last house. With a trembling hand she pressed the button of the bell placed at the side of the garden entrance. After ringing twice she saw the gate open automatically. She entered the grounds. She perceived a dark mass in the distance—the house.

Along graveled paths that crunched under her hasty irregular steps, she approached the building. The garden was empty of other human life. Except for the night wind rustling the trees, the only sound was the crunching march of the woman.

She reached the porch. A glimmer of moonlight shone on a sheet of copper covering the top step of a flight leading to the front door.

With delicately gloved hand she knocked thrice. Long minutes passed. The door opened, showing a slit of darkness.

A voice came from the gloom:

"Daniel."

The visitor replied:

"Françoise."

The door opened wide. The voice said:

"Come in."

The visitor obeyed. The door closed.

The newcomer felt her hand taken by someone who groped a way forward.

Another door creaked. The visitor had the impression that they passed from a vestibule with a tessellated pavement, into a room with a carpeted floor. This darkness and mystery worried the visitor. She murmured:

"How dark it is! Why is there not a light?"

The next moment a click was heard, and the room was illuminated with electric light.

In an elegant drawing room two women faced each other.

She who had admitted the other uttered a cry:

"Nini Guinon!"

"Who are you?" asked Nini.

She found herself facing a tall, slender, fair woman—a beautiful lady with masses of red gold hair, regular features, and a distinguished air. A queenlike creature.

Nini seemed to know this figure, this face. Ah, she knew! It was Mrs. Garrick!

"You are Mrs. Garrick!" cried Nini.

The tall, fair woman trembled slightly. She did not deny it. She questioned Nini:

"Why are you here? How is it you have come to my house when I expected Françoise Lemercier?"

Nini put on a sorrowful look:

"Françoise Lemercier is no longer of this world. She died yesterday, alas! She made me promise to come instead of her."

The tall, fair woman laughed ironically. In a voice trembling with indignation she addressed Nini Guinon:

"Nini Guinon, you are a monster! If Françoise Lemercier is dead, it is because you have murdered her! Oh, I was warned too late! I should have acted sooner!"

Nini set her lips. She clenched her hands. She would brazen

it out! She said in a determined tone:

"I have come to take away Françoise Lemercier's child, and I mean to have him!"

So declaring, she made a quick movement towards the open door of an adjoining room. She had caught sight of a child sleeping on a Chesterfield couch. It was little Daniel.

The tall fair lady stepped in front of Nini:

"Nini Guinon, you have stolen Françoise Lemercier's little Daniel once. You shall not commit such an abominable theft twice!"

Nini shook with rage and fear. This woman must know all! Who was she really? Nini had a flash of enlightenment. She was the woman who had come through the window of Nini's room and had carried off little Daniel while Nini was lying on her trundle bed helplessly drunk! That mysterious shape was identical with the form of this tall, fair woman!

Flinging caution to the winds, the murderess of Françoise Lemercier threatened the woman blocking the way to little Daniel:

"Ah!" she shrieked. "It was you stole my Jack! What have you done with my child, abductress?"

The tall, fair lady stood her ground:

"Oh, yes. I took little Daniel away from your house, Nini Guinon. I happen to know that your child, Jack, is dead, and that, to deceive your husband for your advantage, you passed off little Daniel as your own child, you abominable creature!"

"Wretch!" yelled Nini, rushing at the tall, fair woman. "You would ruin me?"

The lady Nini Guinon believed to be Mrs. Garrick glanced disdainfully at this threatening virago:

"It is possible. I may be ruining you. It is what you richly deserve!"

"The child! I will have the child!" screamed Nini.

"Useless," replied her adversary. "You shall not have it. If you did get little Daniel, he would not serve your purpose. Lord Duncan has been warned. He knows how basely you have deceived him!"

"Informed?" shrieked Nini. "By whom?"

"By me!"

The words were a knell.

There was dead silence.

The tall, fair woman uttered a cry of terror. With lightning rapidity Nini had rushed up to the sleeping boy.

In her hand was a hooligan's knife.

Beside herself with rage, she darted at little Daniel and buried her dagger in the child's breast.

Daniel did not utter a sound. Blood gushed from the wound. He was stabbed to the heart. He was dead.

"There!" screamed the frantic Nini. "You would not give him up to me! You shall not have him either!"

Nini Guinon uttered no further word.

A loud report, and the miserable creature sank on the floor with a cry.

The fair woman had shot Nini Guinon.

On the rich carpet, the blood of Nini Guinon mingled with that of her innocent victim. At sight of the two dead bodies the fair woman nearly fainted.

She leaned against the wall to prevent herself from falling:

"Oh, what has that wretch done?" she murmured. "And what have I done?"

"You have executed justice, madam!" declared a grave voice. The fair woman turned. At sight of the personage who had appeared before her she was dumbfounded. The new arrival stood with folded arms quietly considering her.

The fair woman collapsed. She fell on her knees, blood all about her:

"Juve! It is you, Juve!" she wailed in a thin high voice. "How is it you are here?"

Juve stared fixedly at this woman, overwhelmed with torturing emotion.

He said slowly:

"Yes. I am Juve. You recognize me, Lady Beltham?"

Then Juve rushed forward and grasped the upraised elbow of the tragic woman. She had seized the revolver with which she had shot down Nini Guinon like a dog, and with shaking hand was pointing it at her own forehead.

"That is forbidden!" cried Juve, sternly.

"I wish to end it all!" stammered this crushed being.

Juve disarmed her, compelled her to rise, to leave the dreadful room, and made her sit down in a low easy chair in the drawing room adjoining.

Bending over her, Juve said:

"Calm yourself, Lady Beltham. What you have just done is well done. Make yourself easy also; I do not come to you as an enemy."

Lady Beltham passed her hand over her forehead. She closed her beautiful eyes, opened and closed them again. She had been faced with such frightful alternatives in the space of a few minutes that she could not coordinate her thoughts.

As though Juve's last words had brought a ray of hope to her crushed soul, she roused herself with a supreme effort. Looking up at Juve, she asked:

"You do not come as an enemy? In what capacity, then, are you here tonight?"

Juve hesitated, then confessed:

"I come, madam, as a messenger bearing a flag of truce."

"A messenger? From whom, pray?"

Awaiting his reply, Lady Beltham looked distracted with terror and anxiety.

Juve's voice was calm, his tone even:

"I come, madam, bearing a flag of truce from Fantômas."

This reply was plainly unexpected.

"From Fantômas?" Lady Beltham repeated. Her air was bewildered. "How? Why?" she questioned. "And it is you, Juve, who come to me on behalf of Fantômas?"

Juve lowered his eyes:

"Yes, madam, and if I spare you it is because I wish to save someone whom Fantômas has caused to disappear—someone whom he has promised to find for me if I, on my side, find you!"

"This someone is?" asked Lady Beltham.

"The being dearest to me in all the world, the noblest of friends, a being as dear to me as though he were my own son—Jerome Fandor."

Lady Beltham had risen. She was staring at Juve, her fine eyes blazing with feverish brilliancy:

"Is it possible?" she cried. "Fantômas has caused Fandor to disappear? He has promised to restore him to you, if you succeed in finding me?"

"Just that, madam."

"Heavens above!" ejaculated Lady Beltham. "Has the supreme hour struck? Has Fantômas attained his goal? Is it the consummation of his crimes?"

This outburst surprised Juve:

"What do you mean, madam?"

Lady Beltham slipped down into the armchair:

"I am at the end of my forces," she murmured faintly.

Juve saw a glass of water on a small table. He held it to the exhausted woman's trembling lips:

"Compose yourself, I beg, and explain your words, Lady Beltham," commanded Juve, sternly.

She drank the water at a draft. Revived, she spoke in a clear voice:

"I will tell you this: Fantômas has a tremendous secret in his life, a fact, or rather a being, whose intervention someday will alter his whole existence entirely. When will the hour of vindication strike? I know not; but now that you tell me of Fandor's capture, of Fandor living, of Fandor preserved as a hostage, I know that the awaited hour when the secret of Fantômas will be revealed, is an hour close at hand, imminent!"

"But, madam, if you know where Fandor is, I beg you to tell me! Where is he?"

Lady Beltham shook her head. She wrung her hands in desperation:

"I do not know! I do not know!" she wailed. "Yet to save him, to save us, it is necessary that I should know!"

Juve drew close to Lady Beltham:

"Fantômas will tell you, madam."

"Fantômas!" groaned Lady Beltham. "But I cannot see him! I cannot meet him again!"

"But you will see him," asserted Juve.

Lady Beltham revolted:

"See Fantômas again? See again the man who has so infamously deceived me? The man who has wounded me to the depths of my heart? Who has tortured my soul? See again Fantômas, the lover of Françoise Lemercier? Never!"

"You will see him, madam. You must," insisted Juve.

Lady Beltham's splendid eyes flashed. Her beautiful body trembled with indignation at the idea that she must return to her false lover, humiliate herself, bend in supplication before him, take his orders, the orders of him whom she had loved so much, who in her eyes was nothing but a perjured traitor. She also knew she was caught on the horns of a dreadful dilemma, that if she refused to obey Juve he would wreak his vengeance on her.

Then her lovely eyes were dimmed by tears. Ah, in spite of everything, she loved Fantômas, she would always love him!

Juve urged her:

"Madam, you must act without delay. Otherwise by this time tomorrow Garrick will be hanged!"

Lady Beltham was shocked to quick decision. Her passion triumphed over jealousy. Françoise Lemercier was out of her path—dead. She looked Juve in the eyes:

"No second thoughts, no mental reservations, no equivocations!" she declared. "You have my word, sir! I will follow you, obey you! But you know the consequences that will follow from my visit to Fantômas! You know what will happen when I stand face to face with the condemned Garrick, and they recognize me as Mrs. Garrick?"

"I know it, madam. When you show yourself, that fact will prove Garrick innocent of the crime for which he has been condemned."

"Garrick will then be set free, Juve. Fantômas will be released from prison."

"At that price I buy the liberty of Fandor, madam."

"But, Garrick once at liberty, what happens to Fantômas?" demanded Lady Beltham.

"Madam, the struggle will be renewed more fiercely than before," declared Juve firmly. "It is a truce and a compromise we have agreed to. Be assured I shall see that Fantômas keeps his word!"

"He accepts these conditions?"

"He accepts them, madam."

Lady Beltham rose, the image of cold resolve: "You believe the word of Fantômas," she said. "Do you, Juve, believe that of Lady Beltham?"

"I accept your word, madam."

"Good. Now tell me what I must do? When do we leave here?"

Pale dawn light shone through an opening between the curtains.

Juve looked at his watch:

"We have three hours yet. At the end of that time you will come with me to Garrick's prison, and you will declare that you are Mrs. Garrick."

Towards seven in the morning a wan and weary Juve presented himself at the prison clerk's office.

A head warder noticed him:

"You already, 416! Plague take you but you are an early bird! I thought you did not go on duty till nine o'clock! It's your last day on guard anyhow, for Garrick hangs tomorrow!"

"That remains to be seen," answered Policeman 416.

"What do you mean?" asked the warder.

"Suppose a fresh fact supervenes? For instance, suppose Mrs. Garrick thinks of coming forward to prove her husband did not murder her?"

"Well, that would be something out of the ordinary, but I fancy that will not happen. The truth is something fresh has come to light these last two days."

"Really? What?" Number 416 was intensely interested.

"There's something new in the sense that Mrs. Garrick is not

Mrs. Garrick!"

"What can you mean?" Policeman 416 looked puzzled. Juve shivered with apprehension.

Someone who had heard his voice opened the door of a small office adjoining and called:

"Number 416, as you are here, come with us!"

It was Inspector Shephard.

Puzzled, Juve entered Shephard's office and saw Mr. Tipling, the magistrate and coroner, who had had to do with the Garrick trial.

Juve saluted and waited to be interrogated.

The magistrate took no notice of Juve. He continued his conversation with Shephard. He held in his hand several photographs. Juve recognized them. They were the portraits of Lady Beltham.

Said the magistrate:

"Shephard, she must be arrested at the earliest possible moment. They assure us this woman is hiding in England. It is our duty to effect her capture."

Shephard nodded assent:

"You may be certain, sir, that we shall do the impossible to arrest Lady Beltham. We shall then learn why the mistress of Fantômas had French assassinated, and why she wished to pass herself off as the dead wife of the condemned Garrick."

Juve did not move a muscle, but he understood that Lady Beltham's identity had been discovered.

What had happened? If they had found out that Mrs. Garrick and Lady Beltham were one and the same, had they realized that the formidable bandit under sentence of death as Garrick was none other than Fantômas?

Juve said to himself:

"Fantômas unmasked, Lady Beltham arrested means the two guilty ones will assuredly be punished, but it also means the certain loss of Fandor, for the bandits, convinced that I have betrayed them, will refuse to keep their promises: they will not tell me what has become of my poor Fandor."

Standing at attention, stiff as a ramrod, Juve burned with

impatience. What did Shephard and Tipling know about this complicated affair?

His curiosity was to be satisfied. Shephard called him nearer:

"Number 416, we must tell you the latest development touching the Garrick case, for we shall require your help. Here is the photograph of a woman. Look at it well."

Shephard handed Juve the portrait of Lady Beltham.

"We thought for a moment that it was Mrs. Garrick, but we have learned through communications from Paris, by the admissions of the Beadle, arrested in Paris yesterday, by fresh statements of Beaumôme, now under lock and key thanks to you, and by other means, that this woman who pretends to be Mrs. Garrick, no doubt to conceal her real personality, is Lady Beltham, mistress of the sinister Fantômas. No one knows who Fantômas really is, nor where he is, and it is not our business for the moment to search for him. But we know Lady Beltham is in England. She was seen in London quite recently. Several of our men are hunting for her. I know your qualities, Number 416, and Mr. Tipling and I have decided to put you in charge of the hunt for the mistress of Fantômas."

Shephard handed Juve the warrant for Lady Beltham's arrest, whispering in his ear:

"This arrest, 416, will win you your sergeant's stripes."

"What a situation!" thought Juve. At the precise moment he had managed to bring Lady Beltham to see Garrick-Fantômas, he learned that the English police had discovered her identity, had decided not to acknowledge her as Garrick's wife, and were making ready to arrest her!

And he, Juve, was charged to effect that arrest! And they had told him they did not know where Fantômas was, and he, Juve, well knew that Fantômas was in a cell close by!

Juve had both criminals under his hand. Lady Beltham was waiting in a cab outside the prison gate, and Fantômas was safely locked up inside the prison. Never had the bandits been so completely in his power together, yet Juve dare not take advantage of the situation!

Juve's conscience ordered him to tell the truth. He had but

to say the word, bring the bandits face to face in the presence of Shephard, Mr. Tipling, and other police officials.

But Juve could not say that word.

To bring about the downfall of these monsters was to sign Fandor's death sentence. Fantômas would show no mercy!

It was a frightful dilemma. Juve must commit one sin to prevent another.

To save Fandor he must make himself the accomplice of Fantômas and Lady Beltham. This interior struggle lasted but a few seconds. Juve's exterior was tranquil.

He turned to Shephard:

"Inspector, I deeply regret that I cannot accept this charge. For purely personal reasons I wish to resign from the force. But I will finish what I agreed to do: in accordance with your wishes I will be present at Garrick's execution. Tomorrow, after his death, Number 416 will again ask you for his release."

A combat of wills ensued.

At last Shephard cried:

"416, this is not your last word, surely?"

"Inspector, I cannot alter my decision. It is irrevocable. Someday, possibly, I may be able to explain to you my reasons for making such a decision."

"Very good," replied Shephard coldly, "after ten o'clock to-morrow morning you will no longer belong to the English police force."

Juve saluted and withdrew. He left the prison at once.

He hurried to the cab in which Lady Beltham was seated heavily veiled.

"Well?" she queried anxiously.

Juve shouted an address to the driver, then seating himself next the mistress of Fantômas, he said:

"It has been a narrow escape! We must fly!"

27. The Hangman's Prerequisites

Dame Betty was a diligent housekeeper and a constant grumbler. This morning her temper was on edge. She was a few minutes behind her usual time, judging by her alarm clock. She was late for her Bible reading.

She took down the shop shutters with angry hands. It was a toy and sweetmeat shop belonging to her master, Mr. Joe Lamp. Her master was exacting and avaricious: to lose a pennyworth's sale of sweets to a passing schoolboy was a calamity.

Betty was making a loud noise. Mr. Joe Lamp had sharp ears:

"Betty!" called an angry imperious voice. It continued to call.

The owner of the voice came downstairs: a little man, fair, thin, with rounded shoulders and bow legs. He abused Betty in shrill tones. She protested. He ordered her to hold her tongue and get on with her work.

Joe Lamp, mean looking and excitable, had been official hangman for three years.

On certain mornings this seller of sweetmeats and toys would don a black jacket and correct official garments. While he hastened to Pentonville to do his duty, Betty would remain at home offering up prayers against the hauntings of the hanged, while picturing her master at his dreadful work. Betty knew from her daily paper that the date of Garrick's hanging was close. On this particular morning Joe Lamp was walking up and down his shop:

"Betty?"

"Sir?"

"I am going to give you two shillings more wages a month!"

"Well I never! It's the first rise I've had since I entered your service! All the same, I don't want the money—not that money."

"What money, you fool?"

"Hangman's money."

"You old idiot! The money I earn with my rope is for me, not for you! What I get for my trouble, I keep. But now and again I get an extra few shillings for special services rendered. And as I shall need your help . . ."

"What do you mean, sir?"

"Betty, you must let me have a large sheet."

"What are you going to do with it, sir?"

"Inquisitive woman! That's not your business! I want to take it away."

Joe Lamp knew his housekeeper well enough to be sure she would not give up the keys of her linen cupboard without a struggle. Let him rummage among her treasured store of sheets, embroidered pillowcases, damask tablecloths and napkins? Never!

Joe Lamp resigned himself:

"Betty, I want to take a sheet to Pentonville."

"What do you want to take a good linen sheet to that dreadful place, for?" Betty's voice was aggressive, her face crimson with fury.

Joe Lamp was being cornered.

A shabby old man entered the shop. He looked like a rag and bone merchant.

Betty came forward. He might be a good buyer. Appearances were deceitful:

"What can I get you, sir?"

"I do not want to buy anything of you, madam. I am Professor John Smith, M.D., F.R.C.S., and I wish to speak to Mr. Joe Lamp, the hangman, I believe!"

Dame Betty looked scared:

"The hangman? I'll leave you then. There is Mr. Lamp!"

Betty pointed to her master, turned on her heel and marched out of the shop.

Joe Lamp came forward:

"What can I do for you, Professor?"

"You are the hangman?"

"Yes, Professor."

"It is you who will hang Garrick tomorrow?"

"Yes, Professor."

"Well, Mr. Hangman," said professor John Smith in sharp tones, "I am here to purchase from you the body of this wretch, and to arrange with you for the immediate delivery of it after the execution."

Joe Lamp was agitated:

"It's—I don't know, Professor! To tell you the truth . . ."

"What's the matter?" demanded the doctor. "I do not think my request is extraordinary?"

"Certainly not, sir ,but . . ."

"But what?"

"I have already sold the body. I have promised to deliver it up."

Professor John Smith looked annoyed:

"It's the truth you are telling me, I suppose? To whom have you sold it?"

"It's so much the truth, sir, that when you entered my shop I was asking my housekeeper for a large sheet to wrap the body in, so as to deliver it in a shroud at least!"

"And you have already been paid?"

"No, sir, but . . ."

"Ah, good! Nothing is lost then!"

"How? Nothing is lost?"

"A contract is not valid if no earnest money is paid. What price had you agreed on? I will double it!"

Joe Lamp considered. He had not lied. He had sold Garrick's body. Still, the doctor was right! He had only accepted in the first instance. He was legally free to make another arrangement. He said tentatively:

"Would ten pounds be too much for you, sir?"

"I will give you that sum now, and ten pounds more when you bring me Garrick's body. I expect to carry out some exceedingly interesting experiments on it. As I do not wish any mistake on your part, I must ask for a written promise from you, Mr. Lamp. Does this bargain suit you?"

"Yes, sir. When should I deliver the body?"

Professor John Smith showed no surprise at the hangman's quick acceptance of his over-generous offer. He did not believe a word of Lamp's statement regarding a sale already concluded. He opened his pocketbook and drew out a sheet of letter paper. He wrote out the statement required, handed his fountain pen to the hangman, pointed to the space left below the statement, saying:

"Sign there, please. Good. Thank you! Here are the ten pounds! Here also is a paper of instructions as to how you are to bring Garrick's corpse to me. It must be brought in the very quickest possible time. Not a moment must be lost when the official requirements are complied with. Rapidity is essential. Do you understand my instructions?"

Joe Lamp ran his eye over the instructions:

"I understand them. You may rest assured, sir, that come what may, you shall dissect Garrick's corpse less than an hour after he is hanged, exactly as you ask me."

Professor John Smith nodded approval.

"Good. I rely on you. Now I must be off to make preparations in my laboratory for tomorrow's experiments."

Professor John Smith bustled away, mighty pleased.

Mr. Joe Lamp stood in his toy and sweets shop rubbing his hands over an excellent bargain.

Dame Betty was raging outside her linen cupboard, calling Heaven to witness that such a wicked waste of linen was no sin of hers!

28. The Execution

Silence reigned in Pentonville.

Muffled steps of warders on their rounds in the deserted corridors beat dully on listening ears.

The great prison slept.

At six in the morning it would awake.

But in the East wing, where the condemned cells were, there was some movement.

Garrick was to be hanged that morning.

In a passage near by the condemned man's cell, two warders were talking in low tones:

"What time is it, Edward?"

His companion stepped under the electric bulb and looked at his watch:

"Ten past four. Only forty minutes more."

"Have you seen an execution, Edward?"

"Not yet, Jacob."

"I saw one at Manchester."

"Is it very horrible?"

"Hmm!" was Jacob's enigmatic answer.

After a pause, he went on:

"That depends very much on the attitude of the condemned. Some go to their death with courage; others are in a fainting state from the moment they come to fetch them; some from the very minute they are awakened; others struggle and shriek."

"How do you think Garrick will take it?" asked Edward.

His companion did not reply. He stepped on tiptoe to the end of the passage opposite Garrick's cell:

"Who goes there?"

"I," replied a suppressed voice.

Jacob could not see his interlocutor:

"I? That's not a name! What is your name?"

"I tell you it is I—Robert."

Edward had come up also. He and Jacob recognized the newcomer:

"Why it's the sacristan from the chapel. What do you want, my friend? It was the chapel keeper and sexton, a fat, bald man, dressed in black like a clergyman. He stammered a "good day":

"I came up here, though I hadn't the least wish to—but I can't find my matches, and I've come to ask you for some."

"Matches? What do you want them for?" asked Jacob.

"For the chapel candles . . . if the . . . condemned wishes to hear Divine service."

Jacob handed him a box of matches:

"There's what you want—till presently then!"

The sacristan went off muttering:

"I don't know about 'presently.' Perhaps Garrick won't want to hear the service. Anyhow I'm not obliged to be present at the . . ." The rest of his mutterings were lost in the distance.

Jacob and Edward looked at each other. Edward observed:

"Poor fellow! This affair will give him some sleepless nights, I'm sure!"

"Bah! You forget everything in time," declared Jacob. "You've got to get accustomed to this sort of thing in jobs like ours!"

"It's about time," he added, "that we went down to receive Sir Ellis, the sheriff, who must be present at the execution."

Garrick in his cell had heard the sounds in the passage. He had not slept.

He had passed the first part of the night a prey to extreme agitation. He was all fevered emotion.

Through the peephole the watching warders had seen him walking nervously about his cell, knocking against the walls of that strait place: a human tiger in a cage.

Little by little his nerves seemed to relax. His face bore its usual expression of power and alert intelligence, decidedly attractive and impressive.

Towards three o'clock the condemned man had stretched himself on his bed. He must relax his limbs even if he could not sleep.

An hour later he rose, arranged his bedding according to prison rules. Then he made a quick toilet. It was evident Garrick meant to die decently.

The watching warders approved.

Was this man resigned to his fate, they wondered?

After an access of despair had a new hope risen in his heart, the hope that he might escape the supreme punishment?

In reality two things only preoccupied this sinister bandit: the first was that he had not had any news of Lady Beltham.

Had Juve not got into personal touch with her? Had she refused to come with Juve to see Garrick? These hypotheses seemed improbable to Fantômas, for Juve could quite easily meet Lady Beltham, after the revelations of Beaumôme, and Fantômas would not admit to himself that Lady Beltham had such a grudge against him on account of his love passages with Françoise Lemercier, that she would carry it so far as to let him die! The fact was, Fantômas did not know that since the evening before, his friends had strictly prohibited anyone whatever from approaching his cell, their object being to prepare more surely for the rescue of him whom they were convinced was Tom Bob, their colleague, and an innocent man.

The second fear of Fantômas was this:

Had Juve betrayed him?

Did Juve now wish him to die?

Had Juve revealed and proved that Garrick, that Tom Bob, was Fantômas?

"A dangerous game," thought Fantômas. "For if Juve has done this, it means he has given up all hope of ever finding Fandor. But I cannot believe he has resigned himself to that, in view of his present attitude. No! It is not possible! Nevertheless! . . ."

Fantômas grew frantic.

Was he afraid of death? No. But he did not wish to die yet. He must not, he could not. What powerful, enormous, formidable thing compelled, obliged him to live? Ah, this secret which was the mystery of Fantômas, the whole explanation! And perhaps

the excuse for his monstrous conduct, his criminal existence!
Fantômas regained courage!

In the pale dawn light the condemned man realized that the
decisive hour was at hand. One more hour must pass—an hour
of sixty minutes like all other hours, but for him, the strangest,
the supreme hour of his life. When that hour had passed into
the abyss of Time, the healthy, strong living body of Fantômas
would be dead . . . or . . . ?

Keys were jingling, clashing.
A key was grating in the lock.
The condemned man shivered. The cell door opened.
Two men appeared.
Fantômas knew one of them. He greeted him with a meaning
smile. It was his colleague, the clergyman, William Hope.
The other man, who flinched under the piercing glance of
the condemned prisoner, introduced himself:
"I am the Sheriff of London, whose duty it is to be present at
your execution, Garrick. May God help you!"
The Sheriff, sensitive, highly strung, overcome with horri-
fied distress at the situation, could only murmur a few words
more. They were unintelligible. Fantômas came to the rescue:
"Mr. Sheriff," said he, "I thank you for your words. I will
endeavor to be courageous."
The prisoner turned to the clergyman:
"Will you ask Mr. Sheriff to seat himself on this stool? I fear
he is not feeling well."
Indeed the Sheriff was half fainting. Garrick's firm attitude
was affecting him strangely. A curious silence fell.
Conforming to custom, William Hope, clergyman, asked
the condemned man if he wished to hear Divine service in the
chapel.
The prisoner replied by a negative shake of the head.
Now twenty awful minutes had to be lived through by the
three men, the dreadful twenty minutes preceding the official
hour of execution. Twenty minutes must steal by in that sad cell

faintly lit by the pallid light of dawning day.

A desperate Fantômas was on the alert.

To the mute interrogation of William Hope, who questioned him with a look, Fantômas had replied by an evasive sign, which signified equally that he was resigned to die, and was convinced that he would cheat the hangman!

Turning to the Sheriff courteously, and without the slightest tremble in his voice, Fantômas asked:

"No doubt, sir, this is the first time you have had to attend an execution in your official capacity?"

A muttered "Yes" was the Sheriff's reply. Fantômas continued:

"You must not allow yourself to be so greatly upset, sir! Owing to life's chances, the strange hazards of existence, I have witnessed several executions. They are not very dramatic. In Germany, the axe is used for capital punishment; in France, the guillotine; in Spain, the garrote. We have in these methods of execution not only the brutality of the act itself, but we have the unhealthy publicity surrounding such executions. Now in England there is quite a homelike privacy. The execution is admirably intimate. The crowd, so avid of unwholesome emotions, cannot sate their curiosity; it is compelled to wait outside a prison wall, and to say that something is happening behind that wall. They used to announce the execution of the condemned by hoisting a black flag above the building in which the punishment had just been inflicted. I think that henceforth officialdom will be content to ring a bell."

The Sheriff shuddered.

At this precise moment the quarter before five sounded from the distant clock of the prison. The sound of it was the sound of a passing bell. The emotion of the Sheriff had not escaped the eye of the man nearing the hangman's rope:

"It is funereal, is it not, sir? A mournful warning sound?"

The Sheriff sat on his stool, moved beyond speech. Fantômas added with a sigh:

"What a horrible prologue to a hanging!"

Despite his formidable will, Fantômas paled. From his eyes

undying ferocity gleamed. He stood in his condemned cell with clenched hands facing his companions, confronting his fate, daring destiny, the unconquerable tiger-man!

Instinctively he glanced about him, searching a loophole of escape. His eyes fixed those of William Hope, who had made a sign that he wished to pass something to him.

The Sheriff was staring at them.

Nothing could be attempted yet.

Fantômas continued his remarks:

"As to hanging," said he, "that is not the correct word to use, for nowadays they no longer hang those condemned to death. Thanks to the arrangement by which the flooring of the scaffold suddenly sinks under the weight of the body, it is the rupture of the vertebral column that determines death—sudden death they say—death beyond question say the specialists."

"Occasionally death does not result," ventured the Sheriff, whose brain seemed to be turning upside down.

Fantômas threw him a glance of astonishment:

"Do you believe that, Mr. Sheriff?" questioned Fantômas skeptically. "Such examples are almost unheard of, surely! They say, I know, that the hanged have been resuscitated in the past. I do know they go through certain medical formalities to make certain the hanged man is not buried alive."

Fantômas now addressed himself specially to the clergyman. His tones were low, his sentences abrupt:

"In such cases frictions, hot water applications, violent revulsives useful . . . bleeding the feet . . . efficacious . . . artificial respiration . . ."

Tom Bob-Fantômas stopped short.

Someone had knocked on the door of the cell. Warder Jacob's voice was heard calling for the Sheriff.

Sir Ellis rose from his stool with difficulty, dragged himself to the door, leaned against the wall, listened through the half-opened door to the words of the warder humming in his ears.

The supreme moment approached. It was five minutes to five o'clock.

Fantômas and William Hope took instant advantage of the

occasion. Fantômas said in a clear voice for all to hear:

"Mr. Hope, will you come quite close to me! It is a dying man who, with you, wishes to ask Heaven's pardon for his sins."

The two men threw themselves in each other's arms. While thus embraced they exchanged a brief dialogue:

"All goes well, Tom Bob, I hope. The rope will be too long. You will drop onto solid earth, so be prepared!"

Hope slipped a hardened india-rubber tube into Tom Bob's hand. With this Tom Bob-Fantômas could keep open his windpipe. By thus dilating his throat air would reach his lungs. In spite of the slip-rope's compression round his neck he could breathe.

"Are you sure of your helpers?" It was Fantômas-Tom Bob's last utterance.

"Yes," nodded Hope.

Thereupon Fantômas swallowed the tube. Now that it was in position, not one word could he articulate. His anxious eyes questioned the clergyman.

Hope reassured him:

"We can count on them absolutely," he whispered. "It is the policeman devoted to Shephard who has seen to everything. It is this 416 who has replaced the short rope by the long one which will save your life. It is he who will keep watch over the duration of the hanging."

Fantômas staggered and would have fallen had not Hope supported him.

Juve held Fantômas at his mercy! Those fools of detectives had let themselves be completely taken in by him! What was Juve going to do?

He had not appeared since last evening. Juve had sworn to bring Lady Beltham to the cell. He had not brought her. What to think? What conclusion to draw? Had Juve refused to bring her? Had she refused to come?

One thing was certain:

Juve had Fantômas at his mercy. The fate of Fantômas was in his hands.

And Fantômas was dumb!

Fantômas could give no sign of his anguish. The warders, Edward and Jacob, had entered. As though eager to get this dreadful business done with, they hurriedly bound the condemned man's hands behind his back. They loosely shackled his legs with rope as though he were a horse being led to the slaughter.

Fantômas! Fantômas the elusive, the uncatchable, was naught but a rag of humanity to be cast on the dust heap of dead and useless things.

Incapable of moving without the aid of his two warders, Fantômas had some fifty yards to cover between his cell and the gibbet awaiting him.

Would he meet Juve at the gallows' foot? Juve the implacable lover of justice? Would Juve allow Garrick to die without first proving to all the world that Garrick was Fantômas?

Slowly the little group moved along the corridor. William Hope walked in front.

Fantômas, between his warders, held himself erect, facing his doom.

The Sheriff, pallid, trembling with nervous emotion, followed in the wake of the condemned man.

A door at the end of the corridor opened. Beyond was an inner courtyard. Fantômas had to cross it before he could reach the fatal spot.

When he found himself on the threshold of this door where daylight fell full upon him, he blinked his dazzled eyes. He was facing the east and the crimson rays of the rising sun.

A lean little man showed himself.

Tom Bob's eyes were fixed on him. No need to tell him who this puny creature was.

It was Joe Lamp, the hangman.

Lamp approached the prisoner, who henceforth became his property. He held in his hand a kind of black gauze veil, and prepared to cover the face of the condemned man.

Fantômas, who, two minutes before, had uttered his last word, now looked about him for the last time.

Keenly, intensely, looked.

He saw in front of him, through an open door, a sort of shed, empty. He saw in it a rope hanging from the roof, a long white rope ending in a noose.

On the right, in the turf, he saw a hole new dug. It was an open grave, the grave that awaited the corpse of Garrick, if the hangman, who was its owner, should decide to bury it there, at the side of the other executed criminals, resting under the earth, nameless.

On the left, at the end of the little yard, rose the figure, enigmatic, somber, dreadful, of a policeman—Policeman 416.

Juve!

The glances of the two men met.

They looked each other up and down.

Did the glance of the condemned man threaten or supplicate?

None could say.

Darkness fell!

The hangman had covered the face of the condemned man. The dumb was blinded.

He was drawn rapidly forward.

Steps sounded on the gravel of the yard, then the noise of thick shoes on hollow planks.

The abrupt stop told Fantômas that the supreme moment was imminent.

He was under the fatal shed.

Something cold, rough, touched the chin of the condemned man. His neck was lightly struck: he felt a slight contraction of the throat.

The noose was around his neck!

The two supporting warders withdrew.

The condemned man was alone, facing eternity. Vaguely he took note of a tremulous monotonous voice reading. It was Garrick's death warrant. At the end of it he would be precipitated into the gulf which would open beneath his feet.

Fantômas did not listen to the words. He drew himself together, stretched his muscles, ready for the moment when the rope would drop him to the ground below the opened trap.

He drew a great deep breath, testing the apparatus he believed would save him from strangulation.

During those poignant moments speeding by with inconceivable rapidity, Fantômas felt himself so brimming with life, health, vigor, that death seemed powerless to touch him. Life, the fullness of life rioted in him.

He would be saved. All care of that had been taken! Then before his mental vision rose the figure of Juve, enigmatic, grave, solemn. No! All hope was lost! Juve had come to see Fantômas die!

Fantômas ceased to think.

The ground beneath his feet gave way.

The condemned man was precipitated into space. A cry broke from the Sheriff's lips. He fell fainting at the moment the body of the executed criminal disappeared in the trap-hole!

29. Is Fantômas Dead?

In a drawing room on the ground floor of a house in the thickly populated Waterloo district stood a woman, rigid with terror.

With an anguished cry, she broke the leaden silence:

"What are you going to do? What are we going to see?"

The woman faced an iron bedstead prepared for an invalid, a coffin on the floor, and a man bending over it.

He was hurriedly unscrewing the coffin lid.

The woman involuntarily drew nearer, then recoiled, repeating:

"Oh, what are we going to see?"

The man answered:

"Him, madam! Him only!"

"What are we going to do?"

"We are going to attempt the impossible!"

It was a humble coffin of varnished deal. The screwdriver was doing its work on the cracking boards. A last turn of the screw, a wrench of the lid. It fell on the bare floor with a resounding clatter.

The woman buried her face in her hands.

The man unfolded a winding sheet of fine linen, revealing a congested face.

It showed no sign of life.

Exerting all his strength, the coffin-violator lifted the inert figure from its shroud, placed it on the bed, called for help:

"Come, madam! I need you!"

The woman dragged herself to the bed.

She stared shuddering at the empurpled face on the snow-white pillow.

Intent on his object, the man was working on the body, puncturing the muscles with a Pravaz syringe, placing a strange apparatus on the uncovered chest. With the woman's help he opened the mouth, inserted forceps, and extracted an india-rubber tube about twenty-five centimeters in length. He massaged the tongue with rhythmical movements, did all in his power to induce artificial respiration. From time to time he put his ear to the heart of this inert body. He uttered a cry of triumph:

"He lives!"

"Heaven be praised!" cried the woman. Both watching closely, they marked the subtle signs of returning life.

Gradually the face grew less congested. The turned-up eyes became normal.

Eyelids, lips, fluttered.

Thanks to unremitting efforts, thanks to oxygen absorbed from an iron cylinder, the inert being began to breathe.

Active, silent, absorbed, the man and woman took drops of cordials, administering them to the resuscitated human creature.

An hour of unceasing effort stole by, the man giving brief orders, the woman making succinct replies, or asking terse questions.

Finally the resuscitated man moved, his lips grown insensibly redder, emitted inarticulate sounds. His eyes, wide open, stared at the man and the woman. He articulated two names:

"Juve! Lady Beltham!"

They drew back, crying as with one voice:

"Fantômas!"

Yes. The arch-brigand had once more shown himself to be Fantômas the Elusive, thanks to the misguided efforts of his credulous colleagues, firmly convinced of the innocence of Tom Bob, thanks above all to the hideous dilemma forced on Juve by the diabolic astuteness of this bandit without scruples.

Fantômas was fast recovering from the frightful shock. He would shortly be on his feet again. This bandit was endowed with the resiliency of Incarnate Evil.

Juve considered him with a ferocious eye. His piercing gaze sought the bandit's. His voice threatened:

"Fantômas, the final hour has struck. I have kept my promise.

Here is Lady Beltham! Where is Fandor?"

The bandit made a painful effort to rise, murmuring: "Alas! I do not know! I do not know!"

Juve's lips curled. His voice was harsh:

"No more delay, Fantômas! I give you five minutes to tell me where Fandor is to be found, and to prove the truth of your statement. If you do not obey . . ."

"If I do not obey?" demanded Fantômas.

"Then I will unmask the pair of you! You are both at my mercy. I shall have no pity."

"Juve! Juve!" implored Lady Beltham. "Spare us!"

"I have already waited too long, madam! I have already compounded with my conscience too much! Let Fantômas speak! Only four minutes remain."

The two bandits regarded each other, overwhelmed. Lady Beltham fell to the floor.

Fantômas, by an intense effort of will, forced himself to a sitting posture. He fell back exhausted.

"Fandor," he stammered, "I do not know where Fandor is!"

Juve, his face pale and drawn, was looking at his watch, counting the passing seconds.

A bell rang loudly.

Lady Beltham rose.

"Who is it?" She looked at Juve.

"Justice, madam. Go, open the door to Justice!"

"Juve!" Lady Beltham implored.

The policeman had given his orders. They must be carried out. She staggered to the door, and left the room.

"For the last time, Fantômas, will you tell me where Fandor is to be found?" insisted Juve.

The elusive bandit's answer was to lift his left hand to his lips, press with his teeth the spring in a jeweled ring on his third finger, and swallow some drops of liquid contained in a hollow beneath the jewel.

Juve was too late to intervene.

The body of Fantômas quivered convulsively, strange fire glowed in his eyes:

"Juve," he articulated. "You would not believe me! You were wrong. It is finished."

The face of the bandit was livid.

Juve watched the last agony commencing. He was horror stricken.

He turned at a bitter cry.

Lady Beltham had returned. She was on the threshold when she saw the gesture of Fantômas. She understood that Juve had been inflexible, that her lover had taken the supreme step rather than fall alive into the hands of Justice.

Lady Beltham rushed to her lover. She pressed desperate kisses on his lips.

A newcomer presented himself:

"Michel!" cried Juve, staring.

It was indeed Inspector Michel of La Sûreté, Paris, who had arrived breathless at this house, the address of which he had learned from a sealed letter left for him by Juve at his domicile.

"Juve!" gasped Michel, "I bring a great piece of news for you—a wire from Fandor!"

Michel handed Juve a crumpled telegram with Juve's Paris address on it.

Michel had opened the telegram. Juve read:

> Juve, save me, I am in the hands of Fantômas, and each day that passes I sink lower. I must kill myself. Come. You must.
> FANDOR.

Juve read this aloud. Fantômas heard the words. Reacting against the moribund torpor invading his body, tearing himself from the passionate embraces of Lady Beltham, the bandit shouted:

"Juve! Where does that telegram come from?"

"From Pretoria—from South Africa," replied Juve.

Fantômas laughed wildly:

"Victory!" he cried. "I understand everything! Juve. Come here in three days' time. Do not forget. Have confidence and we will save him. Fantômas gives you his word. Juve. *Till three days' hence!"*

Juve, bewildered by these words of the dying bandit, bent over him, watching his last breath, his last look.

Was Fantômas conscious? Were his words the wanderings of delirium?

The elusive bandit had sunk into a comatose condition. His face had the pallor of death, his limbs were stiffening, his heart had ceased to beat.

"He is dead," gasped Juve, staring at Lady Beltham.

This remarkable woman was fully mistress of herself. She faced Juve without a tremor, and replied: "Juve, he said to you: *'Till three days hence!'"*

The sinister drama of Garrick's hanging was barely ended when Shephard and William Hope rushed into the small yard where the executioner would proceed to bury the body.

The detective had not been authorized to attend the execution, even the Rev. William Hope had been obliged to leave his penitent at the moment the hangman slipped the fatal noose round his victim's neck.

Shephard and Hope were deeply moved when they entered the tragic place. Anxious expectation gave way to horror:

Hangman and corpse had vanished!

They interrogated the warders:

"Garrick?" said they.

"Hanged high and sure," replied Edward. Shephard pointed to the open, empty grave:

"The burial?"

"It has not taken place. The hangman has carried the body away—it belongs to him."

Shephard looked at Hope.

Certainly the hangman was within his rights, but why had he not told them what he meant to do?

A dreadful doubt seized the detectives. Had the horrible and final act taken place in spite of their efforts and precautions? Had their innocent colleague, Tom Bob, died an ignominious death after all?

They must take action without delay.

The two detectives left the prison. They raced to Joe Lamp's house.

They found the hangman comfortably seated in his back parlor, partaking of the plentiful tea spread for him by Dame Betty.

"Joe Lamp, what have you done with Garrick?" demanded Shephard. "Where is the body?"

The hangman, amazed at the expression on the faces of the distracted detectives, answered quietly, exhibiting four bank notes:

"The body? Why I've sold it, as I have the right to do."

"To whom? To whom?" questioned Shephard and Hope.

"I have sold it . . ." The hangman stopped short. "What does it matter to you?" demanded Lamp defiantly. "The bodies of those I hang are my property, aren't they? And I'm free to . . ."

Beside himself, Shephard gripped the hangman's shoulders: "Speak! If you do not I will strangle you!"

So formidable was Shephard's wrath that the hangman was scared:

"Now! Now! Quietly now, Inspector! Quietly!" Lamp gave the detectives Professor John Smith's address, the doctor to whom he had sold the body of Garrick and the coffin containing it, for twenty pounds.

Lamp would have questioned the detectives, but they having the information they sought, had actually run from the house helter-skelter! They had jumped into their taxi and vanished.

Joe Lamp was upset. He returned to his tea and toast, but the toast stuck in his throat. What had happened? What was happening? Why the detective's sudden invasion and rapid flight? Had he committed some unfortunate blunder? Were the detectives hotfoot on some wild goose chase?

"My faith, I'm not easy about it!" exclaimed the perturbed hangman. "I shall go and talk it over with Mr. Tipling. Safest way!"

Fantômas had scarcely closed his eyes. Juve had not had

time to talk to Michel, when steps heavy and hurried could be heard in the passage of the quiet house.

Shephard and William Hope burst into the room. They drew back at the sight of the body of their colleague, Tom Bob, on the bed.

Shephard walked up to Juve:

"Policeman 416! You here? Why? What does this mean?"

Juve simply pointed to the dead body of the sinister bandit.

Was he about to reveal the truth? Identify Lady Beltham? Divulge the secret of Garrick-Tom Bob-Fantômas?

Lady Beltham, learning from Juve the night before that the police were searching for her, had altered her face with cosmetics and deft touches of the pencil brush, and had covered her red-gold hair with a dark wig. But she knew Juve could make her show herself in her natural colors.

Juve was perplexed. He recalled the supernatural rendezvous Fantômas had given him with his last breath.

Meanwhile Shephard, believing he understood everything, rushed up to Juve, pressed his hands affectionately, thanking him with sincere feeling:

"Ah, Number 416—my friend—you knew as did we that Tom Bob, called Garrick, was innocent! That in order to save him you passed yourself off as à doctor—that you have bought his remains from the hangman! Inexpressible thanks, my friend! What you have done is well done! Alas, circumstances have conspired in the most lamentable fashion to prevent us from proving to human justice, the innocence of our colleague. But his innocence was made clear to us! And the Duty Heaven dictated to us was to save him!"

"Save him?" queried William Hope, casting an anxious glance at the motionless body on the bed.

The two members of the Supreme Council now noticed the corpselike rigidity of him they took for their colleague:

"Tom Bob does not move! Is it by evil chance . . . ?"

Juve nodded solemnly.

Shephard understood.

William Hope fell on his knees by the bed, murmuring

prayers.

Shephard uncovered:

"Poor Tom Bob! He is dead!" murmured the distressed Shephard.

Michel, who could make neither head nor tail of the extraordinary happenings which had followed one another uninterruptedly since he had entered this tragic room, now moved mechanically to the door. He had heard noises in the passage outside.

He drew back to let two men pass.

Their sudden irruption made a sensation.

One was Joe Lamp, looking scared, twisting his cap between nervous fingers.

The other was Mr. Tipling.

What had they come for?

The two detectives were terrified. They were in a dreadful position.

Shephard was aquiver with anxiety.

Juve spoke:

"Whom have I the privilege of addressing?"

The Magistrate-Coroner gave his name.

Juve bowed. Said he:

"Mr. Tipling, to what do I owe the honor of this visit?"

Mr. Tipling explained:

"I have been positively driven to call on Professor John Smith, purchaser of Garrick's body, owing to the hangman's protests and entreaties. He fears something out of the ordinary, something abnormal, has occurred."

Juve's answer was given calmly:

"I am Professor John Smith, Mr. Tipling. Nothing abnormal, nothing out of the way has occurred with reference to my action. I acquired this corpse, as I have a right to do, in order to make some anatomical experiments. That is all!"

Mr. Tipling was nonplussed. He realized that things had been done in order, that his intervention was irregular, and he was annoyed, embarrassed.

He looked searchingly at the two detectives. He demanded

in a supercilious tone:

"Tell me, doctor, what are these detectives doing here? The executioner informed me that they seemed very anxious to know what had become of the corpse of the condemned Garrick, hanged this morning. Their presence here seems incorrect. How do you justify it and them?"

It was Juve's turn to hesitate. To what motives ought he to attribute their presence here?

Shephard spoke up:

"Mr. Tipling, you knew, did you not, that Garrick was really Tom Bob, our colleague and a member of our Supreme Council? When we learned that his body was in the hands of a man of science for dissection purposes, it gave us a sad shock, as you can easily understand. We sought out the Professor without loss of time, to beg him to give up his acquisition untouched, so that we might bury him decently in a Christian cemetery."

Mr. Tipling showed his approval of Shephard's sentiments by repeated nods:

"I approve your sentiments, Inspector Shephard. They do you credit. What reply to your humane request did the Professor give you?"

Shephard turned to Juve.

Juve nodded in the affirmative:

"I grant your request, gentlemen. The body of Tom Bob is at your disposal, if you wish to bury him according to the rites of the religion to which he belonged."

"Heaven be praised!" ejaculated the Rev. William Hope.

Mr. Tipling, convinced that the Professor's decision was due to his intervention, retired well pleased.

Joe Lamp had slipped away as soon as he knew he had properly carried out his duty as hangman, and had not overstepped his functions.

Directly Mr. Tipling's back was turned, Shephard went up to the pseudo-doctor whom he had only known as Policeman 416:

"A thousand thanks! I thank you from the bottom of my heart!" he declared.

Shephard was curious as well as grateful:

"Pardon me!" he said. "Besides, you need not answer me unless you wish—but while you have been a member of our English police force you have made some sensational discoveries, you have effected some remarkable arrests! Without being a member of our Supreme Council, without being in our confidence, you have divined our feelings, our wishes. You have understood that Tom Bob was innocent of the crimes for which, under the name of Garrick, he was condemned by a cocksure ignorant judge, backed up by a jury of crass idiots. All this is remarkable! Tell me then, Policeman 416, who you really are?"

Shephard saw a bitter smile curve the lips of the man he had questioned.

The two men gazed at each other consideringly. Then the pseudo-doctor, the ex-policeman 416, said simply:

"I am Inspector Juve of La Sûreté, Paris."

"Juve!" cried Shephard. "Do you know, I suspected it! Bravo, Juve!"

Shephard held out his big hand in cordial greeting to his celebrated French colleague.

Lady Beltham remained motionless in a corner, as far away as possible from Juve and the detectives. She was breathlessly anxious as to the issue of these events, these extraordinary events succeeding one another with a rapidity which seemed to her tormented soul so slow-moving that she was reduced to a state of despair.

30. Three Days Hence

Modestly, decently, anonymously, Tom Bob, detective, member of the Supreme Council of Scotland Yard, was buried. Some hours after the departure of the detectives, the grave-diggers had appeared on the scene. They had put Fantômas in a coffin. At nightfall the bearers had come for the coffin, had placed it on a hearse, taken it to a cemetery, and lowered it into a vault.

Juve and Lady Beltham watched each other, lynx-eyed. If Lady Beltham was anxious, Juve was perplexed. He could not doubt the burial of Fantômas. He had seen with his own eyes the successive operations of the funeral ceremony.

Nevertheless Juve doubted the elusive bandit's death. He had noticed that Lady Beltham's grief had suddenly calmed down; from that Juve feared some new mystery. Had not Fantômas said: "Juve, till three days hence?"

As a rule the last words of a dying man could not be taken as the exact expression of his meaning, but when this dying man was Fantômas, one might be prepared for anything!

Juve believed in the death of Fantômas when he left the cemetery, and, for an instant, as he walked at Shephard's side, he even thought of telling him everything, especially when he saw Lady Beltham step abruptly away from them, Lady Beltham whom, up to then, he had passed off and introduced to the witnesses of the funeral as a paid nurse merely.

Determined not to lose sight of the mysterious woman, Juve had followed hot on her heels.

Lady Beltham understood this spontaneous movement. She grew pale, she glanced defiantly at Juve. In a clear, firm voice, she said:

"Juve, you have waited so far, you have had confidence, you have been right—Fantômas had only one thing to say: *'Till three days hence.'*"

Juve, paralyzed by these words, remained motionless. Lady Beltham moved away, and vanished.

Juve did not return to the house he had hired in the Waterloo district. It had served its purpose.

He betook himself to the rooms he generally occupied when in London. They were in the West Central district, the neighborhood of the French Colony. For two days and two nights he had not left his rooms. Ceaselessly he reflected on the last words of Fantômas, repeatedly he read and reread the strange telegram he had received from Fandor.

He gave no address. The telegram was known to have come from Pretoria.

What did the declaration mean: *I am in the hands of Fantômas,* since, in reality, Juve had had Fantômas under his eye for several weeks past!

Why had Fantômas shown such satisfaction when he heard Fandor's appeal?

What was going to happen at the expiration of the time fixed by the bandit?

Juve thought over the strange words of Lady Beltham. She had spoken of an event which might alter her lover's mode of existence and perhaps turn him to a better way of living.

Fantômas had declared that if Fandor's life was in danger, it was not because his abductor willed it; the danger was due to circumstances over which he had no control. What did all these hints imply? . . .

On the morning of the third day Juve rose with the dawn, feeling alert and ready for anything.

When he opened his window to let in the early morning sun, he said to himself:

"I am convinced it was not for nothing Fantômas said *'Three days hence!'* Time is up! What is going to happen?"

At that moment a bell rang! . . .

THE END

THE FANTÔMAS SERIES #1–7
NOW AVAILABLE FROM ANTIPODES PRESS

#1 Fantômas
Originally published as *Fantômas* in 1911.
Paperback: 310 pages. ISBN 978-0-9882026-1-0.

#2 The Exploits of Juve
Originally published as *Juve contre Fantômas* in 1911.
Paperback: 196 pages. ISBN 978-0-9882026-2-7.

#3 Messengers of Evil
Originally published as *Le Mort qui Tue* in 1911.
Paperback: 298 pages. ISBN 978-0-9882026-3-4.

#4 A Nest of Spies
Originally published as *L'Agent Secret* in 1911.
Paperback: 336 pages. ISBN 978-0-9882026-4-1.

#5 A Royal Prisoner
Originally published as *Un Roi Prisonnier de Fantômas* in 1911.
Paperback: 184 pages. ISBN 978-0-9882026-5-8.

#6 The Long Arm of Fantômas
Originally published as *Le Policier Apache* in 1911.
Paperback: 336 pages. ISBN 978-0-9966599-1-8.

#7 Slippery As Sin
Originally published as *Le Pendu de Londres* in 1911.
Paperback: 238 pages. ISBN 978-0-9966599-2-5.

www.ingramcontent.com/pod-product-compliance
Lightning Source LLC
Chambersburg PA
CBHW061033120726
47910CB00006B/2222